THE
PROMISE

a novel by
Jon Mills

Published by Direct Response Publishing

For those who have struggled with addiction
and lost the battle and to those who take
it one day at a time.

Stay strong.

PROLOGUE

I *never imagined my life would end here. Someone once said that when you hit rock bottom, the only way to go is up. I guess the same can be said for love. Problem is, whoever said that probably never had the whole world watching.*

CHAPTER ONE

July 12th, 2011 New York

S am Reid downed the remaining bourbon from the glass. He took a deep breath and stepped out of the black SUV into the blinding glare of cameras flashing. The publicity circuit was insane. An onslaught of fans and paparazzi screamed his name like a rowdy mob. *You have to do them; it's part of the contract,* his manager would remind him. And he was right—unless, of course, you wanted to leave yourself wide open to lawsuits, you did as they told you. Yeah, even A-list actors weren't off-limits to the legal hoops they made you jump through. It wasn't personal, just business, they would say. Interviews, premieres, junkets, photo shoots, public appearances, and international press tours were things he still hadn't gotten used to despite them having been a large part of his life for the past five years. And what a crazy five years it had been. Going from being an unknown actor to having your face plastered on anything they could sell felt odd.

Sam made his way over to the throngs of fans pushing themselves against the steel barriers. They flapped photos of him in the air and jabbed their pens at him like knives. "Relax, calm down," one of the bodyguards yelled repeatedly as he and two others hedged Sam in. The plan was always the same—move fast, sign a few, and get inside.

Of course it all seemed glamorous at first; who wouldn't be taken aback by all the attention? He'd gone from someone who'd barely gotten a second glance on the street to a household name almost overnight. Plastered on magazines, fast food cups, posters, T-shirts, and trinkets. Heck, they even had a Sam Reid doll. Creepy as hell, but it was all just part of the machine. Feed them the dream and sell them the fantasy. But sure enough, like any fad, eventually the excitement waned—for him, not the public—and what once was a thrill soon became overwhelming, when the simple pleasures like taking a stroll to get a newspaper or loaf of bread felt more like an undercover sting operation. Sure, he could have had his personal assistant do it, but in all the years he'd been a celebrity he just couldn't bring himself to let go of that freedom. But it came with a price, and no amount of hats, scarves, or oversized sunglasses seemed to work. Now, of course, there were some days he slipped through crowds like a ghost—*oh, what bliss*—but more often than not, someone spotted him.

"Can you make that out to my daughter, and this one out to my cousin, and oh, and this one out to my aunt Agatha."

Sam politely smiled and scribbled black ink furiously across one photo to the next. Sometimes he would sign a different actor's name, just for kicks. Last week it was Morgan Freeman, the week before that it was Steve Martin.

Most didn't care, as long as they got something, and usually he only did it to those who seemed pushy or overly greedy. Anyway, the bodyguards always kept him moving at such a pace, he was lucky if he could scribble two letters out before he was ushered down the line.

The crowds, well, they were always the same. He'd become quite acute at distinguishing those who showed up. For instance, you had your die-hard fans who would follow you from event to event—those you could do no wrong by; then there were your scalpers, the ones who stockpiled and copied autographed photos for sale on eBay; following closely behind them and usually sneering in the background would be the creeps who for whatever reason or no reason at all would slit you from ear to ear if they could get close enough. Finally, you had your bug-eyed crazies who would donate their left kidney for a lock of your hair, name their baby after you, and more than likely had your face tattooed on a part of their body that they were all too willing to show you in public. It was a whirlwind, a complete circus, but he couldn't imagine doing anything else. He loved it.

"Sam, where's Kate tonight?" someone shouted as he posed for a photo.

"Filming."

Kate Evans was his other half; in his mind, his better half. To the rest of the world they were Hollywood's sweethearts. They had been living together since they met on set five years ago. It had been his first serious relationship in years. They'd both been in relationships before, but this had lasted longer than the typical celebrity hookups that went sour within a matter of weeks. Most of Sam's relationships were short-lived and consisted of not much more than bedroom antics. His mother would often ask if he'd considered dating someone not in the business. It had crossed his mind, yet in this line of work, you could go months without seeing each other and well, seeing someone who wasn't ... his thoughts drifted ... well, you could never know if they were really in it for you.

So it was no surprise that he and Kate had warmed up to each other quickly while on set. Some might have said it was their interest in films or their similar love for music and art that attracted them to each other. But those close to them knew better. On or off screen, their chemistry and attraction for one another was what really made it work. It was true; they couldn't keep their hands off each other. She was from LA and he was from England, and though at times they felt like worlds apart in their views on life, somehow they made it work.

For the most part they were inseparable.

The only times they were away from each other were when either of them was off filming, and even then they made every effort to fly out on alternating weekends to see each other. And it worked well when they filmed stateside, but now she was in Europe working on some remake of an old 80s movie.

Oh, how Hollywood loves their remakes, he thought, faking another smile just in time for the camera.

He inwardly groaned, hoping they could wrap it up soon as his jaw was beginning to ache and he was tired of answering the same questions umpteen times.

As he continued pressing toward the doors of the TV studio, out of the corner of his eye Sam caught a glimpse of a shadow moving in fast. Before he could figure out if it was an assailant or an overly enthusiastic fan that'd broken through the barrier, one of his bodyguards had taken them down. The rest was a blur as he was rushed into the building by the other two. It didn't matter how many times he did these events, there was always someone who wouldn't take no for an answer. Luckily, he'd never been hurt but there had been a few close calls, and that had only intensified since the roaring success of his previous hit movie.

Inside, Sam ran his hand through his hair and straightened out his Armani suit, catching his breath for a second while they waited for Kris to join them.

"Kris, I thought we agreed that the next time I would take them down."

"Very funny, Mr. Reid," Kris said.

They kept talking as he moved through the lobby to the elevators.

"Kris, how long have I known you?"

"Four years, Mr. Reid."

Sam came to an abrupt halt, turned, and cocked his head.

There was a brief pause before Kris clued in. He gave a half nod. "Understood, Mr.—I mean, Sam."

The bodyguards were in the habit of referring to him as sir or Mr. Reid, but Sam couldn't stand it. He knew they were trying to keep things professional but it felt so impersonal; he found himself reminding them constantly that he was no different from them, and well, if they were going to live in each other's shadow day and night, they might as well be on a first-name basis.

Jenny, Sam's personal assistant, fell in step with her boss.

Sam was surprised. "Jenny, I thought you were staying home tonight."

"My mother's looking after him."

He shook his head. "Jenny."

"I already have everything you requested in the green

room. Jack Daniel's, pack of Marlboro Lights, two bags of Doritos, PG Tips, and a dozen roses."

"Jenny."

"You'll be picked up at eleven fifteen and —"

"Jenny." This time he purposefully placed a hand on her shoulder and stopped her in mid-sentence. "Go home."

She bit the side of her lip and smiled. "Okay. Thanks, Sam."

"No, thank *you*."

Sam smiled as he stepped inside the elevator and the doors closed behind him.

* * * * *

Around the same time and over a hundred miles away in the small town of Walton, New York, a loud echo of keys hitting the floor broke the silence inside the beautiful late-nineteenth-century farmhouse.

"Sounds like you had another fun evening?" Charlie called out from the kitchen as he wiped soapsuds from a plate.

Hailey Welland didn't reply; she entered the kitchen and just shot him the look. One she knew her father was all too familiar with, as she had inherited it from her mother. She opened the fridge and pulled out a carton of milk, grabbed a glass from the cabinet, and began to pour. Charlie wasn't her biological father, but he was all she had ever known. He'd been there since she was an infant. Her mother had given birth to Hailey when she was only eighteen. In her teens she was curious about her real father, but her mother had no idea where he was, and unlike other kids who may have let curiosity get the better of them, Hailey had no desire to pursue someone who could have walked out so easily on her mother. No, Charlie was her father and that was it.

"C'mon, Hailey," a voice yelled outside.

Charlie flipped the dishcloth over his shoulder and pushed aside one of the curtains to see Tommy Farlan making his way back to his truck.

"You want to talk about it?"

She looked up, holding back anger or tears while grinding her teeth, a habit that she had picked up as a child.

She shook her head. "Not really."

A light shone briefly from outside and then it was gone.

Sliding out a chair at the head of the large oak table in the center of the kitchen, she took a seat. Gazing intently at her glass, she circled the top with her finger, pretending not to care. There was a moment of silence before she couldn't contain the anger any longer.

"Men." She shook her head. "They're all the same."

Charlie leaned back against the granite counter.

"Okay, what was it this time?"

She tapped the table in perfect rhythm with her fingertips. "Well, let me see, last week I was taken into town on a tractor, the week before a romantic dinner was a corn dog at Maggie's Diner, and this week it was cow tipping, and the rest, well, I don't even want to say. Oh, and the smell, well, it seems their idea of deodorant is pig manure."

"What do you expect from farmers?"

"Obviously too much."

Over the past few years, several of the guys in the area had taken a liking to Hailey. She had fallen hook, line, and sinker into the dating game. What a mistake. First there was Dalton. Dalton was unlike any man she had ever met; he was good-looking but he talked nonstop. That might not have been so bad if the topic of the conversation all night hadn't been about him and his pig farm. He even smelled like one of them. Hailey could have sworn the couple one table over moved to a different booth on account of the stench that drifted over. Even the waitress taking their order looked as if she was turning a slight shade of green. He'd spent weeks pestering her for a second date and Hailey just didn't have the heart to break it to him. Her best friend did though—wow, that was a mistake. Cassie reassured her that she'd let him down gently, though that wasn't what Dianne, one of her coworkers, had said. She informed her in no uncertain terms that Cassie had told him that he smelled like a working horse and to take a shower. That was the last she heard from Dalton. And it was the last time she'd tell Cassie about the intricate details of her dates.

Then there was Wyatt, the next guy she dated. He wasn't as good-looking, but at least he took the initiative to take a bath and throw on some clean clothes. Problem was his idea of a good night was TV dinners or a corn dog with some late-night fishing. Oh, and who could forget his slick mode of transportation—a John Deere tractor.

Finally there was Tommy Farlan, on the surface an ordinary hard-working guy at the local garage in town. Now he was persistent, she gave him that. She'd known Tommy since high school. Back then, he barely ever paid attention to her. Tommy was your typical high school jock, going through women like he went through jockstraps. After many of the girls left for college and with few other options left or women to become another notch on his belt, he'd turned his attention towards her. Now perhaps she was lonely, or maybe it was mud in the eye at the time, but for whatever reason she'd decided to give him a chance. *Big mistake!*

Oh, he could lay the charm on thick until he got several beers in him—and then he became Jekyll and Hyde.

Truth was, it didn't matter how many dates she went on, it just never felt right. Then again, there was the glaring fact that she'd never intended to stick around long in the town. And it's not as though she wasn't flattered by their interest. Hell, there had been a few she'd actually pursued hard but for one reason or another it never quite worked out. Now maybe it was fantasy she'd held on to since she was young, but Hailey always felt that she'd know when it was the right one.

Some folks in town might have called her picky. But it wasn't that, heck, it wasn't even security she was looking for, or good looks, though those would have been nice.

In all honesty, she wasn't quite sure what she wanted.

She just knew that when she felt it, her world would stop spinning. It would feel grounding and yet freeing all at the same time.

"If you keep this up, you'll be old and alone," Charlie quipped.

"Thanks, you make it sound like I have one foot in the grave."

"They're good lads, Hailey, of course, a little rough around the edges for sure, but honest and hard working. Any one of them would take good care of you."

"I hope you're not referring to Tommy," she said, with a clear disdain in her voice. "And anyway, I can take care of myself, thank you very much."

There was nothing like a good bit of stubborn tradition. It was good enough for her mother, and it was good enough for her.

Charlie chuckled. "Just saying prospects around here are

slim. Now, you know the pickings wouldn't be slim if you lived in the city."

Hailey breathed an exasperated sigh. "Here we go again, Dad, you know I can't go."

"Hailey, c'mon, I've got Albert to work the gardens and Maggie said she could chip in throughout the day. You'll only be two and a half hours away and if you're that adamant, you can help out on weekends."

She gazed into her glass, shaking her head. "There's too much to be done."

He shrugged. "Like what?"

"Like …"

"It's been two years, Hailey, and no one new has walked through those doors. I think she would have understood," he said.

There was a moment of contemplative silence.

"Okay, I'm going to turn in."

He kissed her on the top of her head and with that he walked out.

"Oh, by the way, I need to get the truck fixed, it keeps stalling," she hollered over her shoulder, hoping he heard.

Hailey breathed out another long, exasperated sigh, and then opened the fridge to put away the milk. She could hear the sound of her tabby cat purring behind her. Misty had entered the kitchen through the cat flap and was now pushing the side of her head against Hailey's leg.

She bent down and cupped her tiny furry face in her hands. "Men trouble too?" She smiled with pouted lips before pulling the carton back out and pouring some milk into Misty's bowl.

Making her way out, she shut off the lights and went upstairs.

Inside her bedroom it was simple—a double-sized bed with piled-up colorful pillows, a rocking chair that once belonged to her mother, a flat-screen TV, and handcrafted oak cupboards for her clothes. Drapes covered her windows and a few mementos and local dancing certificates lined her walls.

At the foot of her bed, she closed her eyes and fell backwards into the softness of her white duvet. A few minutes later, Misty leapt onto her bed, startling her. Reaching over to her bedside table, she snatched up her cell phone and called her best friend.

CHAPTER TWO

Hailey switched the phone to her other ear and pulled Misty close, scratching her under the chin.

"I told you. Now that's twenty bucks you owe me," Cassie said.

Cassie and Hailey had been friends forever. They grew up together, attended the same school, worked at the same summer jobs, and on occasion had even dated the same guy, though not at the same time, of course. Cassie now worked at a local beauty salon in town. She had hooked up with Matt Liming, an accountant and probably the only decent catch in the entire town. She was always a hub of insight into the dating world and what men wanted; at least that's what she liked to make you think.

"You know you can always try one of those dating sites online, I had a customer telling me about it. It's what they all do nowadays. I mean, who's got the time to find anyone? Throw up a picture. Tell them what you will and won't put up with and get ready for the dates to roll in."

"No thanks, no doubt most of them fake their profiles. Knowing my luck I would end up with a psycho who's still living with his dead mother."

Hailey flipped on the TV and began channel surfing while listening to more of Cassie's bright ideas. Cassie could talk the ear off a donkey; it was the reason she got such good tips from her clients. She was like the local town therapist, except she cut hair at the same time.

Hailey eventually settled on the late-night show with Ted Carson. He was interviewing Sam Reid.

Hailey had seen him before; there probably wasn't anyone who didn't know who he was. His face was plastered all over magazines in stores and outside the local theater. She couldn't figure out what all the hype was about. Sure, he was a handsome man but women lined up for hours just to catch a glimpse of him entering and leaving venues? *Please*, she thought.

"Are you listening to me?" Cassie asked.

Hailey responded by hemming and hawing. Really she hadn't taken in a word, too busy trying to pick up on what the interview was about. Eventually Cassie clued in. They often watched the same shows while on the phone. It drove Cassie's husband mad but she didn't care. They had done it ever since they were kids and they swore they would continue doing it long into their old age.

"Okay, what channel you watching?"

"Nine."

Hailey could hear her rustling around while on the phone and then the sound of the same channel on the other end of the line.

"Sam Reid. No wonder. Isn't he scrummy?"

"Ah. I'm sure all the fame has gone to his head."

"Oh, who cares, I wouldn't kick him out of bed."

"Cassie."

"What? C'mon, and you would?"

Hailey said nothing, but simply smiled in amusement.

They spent the next few minutes in silence, watching the show.

Hailey turned up the sound.

"...so Sam, your new movie *Screamers* is coming out. As we all know, *Raging Hearts* was one of the top-grossing franchises ever and it made you an international star. But now that is over, so what can we expect to see with *Screamers*?"

"Well, it's definitely a darker movie, that's for sure."

"It's kind of a change of pace for you. Did you plan on doing this after the huge success of *Raging Hearts*?"

"No, actually, I was planning on taking a break and falling off the radar for a while. But I liked the script; it's different from what I've taken on before. Plus, I've been wanting to work with the director for some time."

"Okay, so now that you are a huge star and you can't seem to go anywhere without drawing massive crowds, what's that like? How are you handling all the women throwing themselves at you?"

Sam laughed. "Well, it's, uh ... I don't know, kind of odd."

"Come on, give us the inside scoop. So you've never gotten sucked into it all? Found yourself waking up at six a.m. with more than one lady?"

Sam gave a wry smile. "You've been reading one too many tabloids."

Hailey hit the off button.

"Urgh. Had my fill of trash for one night."

"Hailey, it was just getting good."

"Well, you keep watching, I need to turn in for the night."

On the other end of the line she could hear the faint sound of Matt grumbling about Cassie being on the phone, and Cassie telling him to put a sock in it or go sleep in the other room. Hailey stifled a chuckle.

"Hailey, darling, your Prince Charming, he's out there. Trust me. Just he might own a few cows."

"Thanks. You're starting to sound like my father." They both broke into laughter.

* * * * *

Sam yanked his tie loose and threw the jacket into the back of the car. Sinking into the leather seat, he felt his muscles relax. It was always a relief to get interviews out of the way; they felt awkward and staged, with questions decided on before he went on the air. They were nothing more than a list of do's and don'ts—all your typical PR nonsense. Oh, no, you couldn't rock the boat. No, you had to be seen in the best light; everything had to come across well polished.

Afterward, the same routine was religiously followed; slip out unnoticed in a separate car through one of the building's other exits. If they were lucky it worked, but honestly, who did they think they were kidding? The paps had wised up to that unoriginal plan a long time ago.

As they made their way through the lit-up streets of Manhattan, he poured himself a drink. Sandwiched between the bodyguards, he had to continue to remind himself why he needed them. He briefly reflected on the run-in he'd had with an overly enthusiastic group of females who had spot-

ted him out shopping on Fifth Avenue. Crazy and determined to take home a piece of him, they had pushed him
out into oncoming traffic. He was lucky that time, but it was
a little too close for comfort. While it hadn't happened
since, giving up that freedom had come with a price, but it
was for his safety, his manager would say. No doubt, in time
it would change, but for now his manager had taken matters
into his own hands. Sam didn't like it one bit and despite
what his manager wanted, he wouldn't let it stop him from
sneaking out once in a while without them.

As he took a swig from the glass full of ice and bourbon
a call came in.

Sam looked down at the screen, and tapped Accept.

"Hey, Eric."

"How's my favorite client doing?"

"Eric, I swear you tell all your clients that."

"Only the best. By the way, great show tonight. I wanted
to let you know that you have two more left to do in a couple of days and then we need to discuss some other opportunities that have come up."

"Yeah, about that ... I was thinking of taking a break
and heading out to see Kate."

There was a hesitation in his reply. "Sure. Um. Let's get
these next few out of the way and then maybe we can chat
again about that."

"You okay, Eric? You sound a little off."

"Yeah. Yeah. Never been better. In fact, uh ... look,
how about we get together for brunch tomorrow? I've got
you staying at the Mandarin Oriental Hotel tonight, so ...
meet you downstairs at eleven?"

"All right. Sounds good."

After working together with Eric for years, Sam had become accustomed to Eric's peculiar behavior, but he couldn't help note the edge in his voice. He was a great manager but a terrible liar.

CHAPTER THREE

Faint rays from the morning sun shone through the gaps between the planks of shabby wood, lighting up the inside of the barn. As Hailey opened wide the creaking red doors and made her way in, dust particles from the straw above fell. She'd always loved the way it reminded her of fairy dust. The whole place carried a scent that was both comforting and nostalgic. As if being transported back in time, she could almost hear the sound of her mother's voice.

Rising early was a habit she'd become accustomed to since an early age. Her mother had always reminded her that if she wanted something badly enough she'd have to be disciplined and willing to give up comforts. Those words had stuck with her all these years. Back then she needed an alarm clock; now her internal clock did the trick.

Half of the barn was used for her father's business and the other for storage. Stacks of rickety old chairs lined the sides of one wall and old dusty tattered boxes with holes eaten away by mice were on the other. The huge clearing in the center provided more than enough room for her and her mother to practice dance.

Long before Hailey's mother had met her father, she was a dancer with the American Ballet Theatre Company in New York City. Classical ballet had been a passion of hers and one that she had passed on to Hailey as soon as she could walk. She adored it, though Hailey's true love was contemporary—a mixture of classical and modern dance. There was a freedom and fluidity to it that satisfied like nothing else. As of late, it could have easily fallen to the wayside with all the shifts she was pulling at Maggie's. Instead, she squeezed in sessions after her run in the morning or late at night.

Hailey selected a tune on her iPod, tucked it into her armband, and closed her eyes. A series of vivid memories flooded in. She saw herself sitting as a young child on top of the boxes and watching her beautiful mother elegantly glide and spin. She could have sworn her mother was able to float on the air. She was incredible to watch, every movement like a painter striking the canvas with a new color.

Hailey had taken all that her mother had taught her and mixed it with her own love for hip-hop, break dancing, and urban street style.

Suddenly, the sound of rhythmic beats kicked in. Hailey's eyes opened and she leapt, twisted, and performed moves that were smooth, hard, and raw, yet each impeccable. It was the one thing she could get lost in, the one part of her life that would immediately connect her with her mother. Like a movie playing inside her mind, she danced as if her mother was beside her. As she spun in circles, the sound of the driving music blended with each thought.

Lost in the music, she hadn't seen or heard her father come in. Whipping her arm around, she almost smacked him in the face as he approached.

Startled, she tugged the headphones out of her ears. "Oh, Dad. Sorry, did I get you?"

"You really do have your mother's right hook," he said, leaning back against a tower of boxes far out of harm's way. Hailey smirked as she tried to catch her breath. Sweat streaked down her brow and her light blond hair stuck to her skin.

"Breakfast is ready."

She looked down at her wristwatch. "Already?"

She'd completely lost track of time. She grabbed her bottle of water off the ground and turned back to see her father looking around the room. He rarely came inside the barn. For him the years that had passed still felt like yesterday.

"Your mother loved this place."

She nodded in agreement. "Yeah, she did. I love it too."

He turned back to her. "I could have sworn it was your mother dancing when I walked in."

Hailey gave a slight smile.

They both left and made their way up the snaked-shaped path of paving stones that led up to the home. Inside, the smell of bacon, eggs, and toast filled each room. Hailey began to feel a twinge of hunger as her belly groaned.

"I'll grab a shower and be right down."

"It will be cold by then," her dad protested.

"I'll nuke it."

* * * * *

Sam pulled the skin beneath his eyes down and stared at

the bloodshot eyes. His head was throbbing and the pressure was building with every movement. Even at twenty-five, mornings still made him feel as if he was fifty years old. Late nights, drinking, and partying into the early hours of the morning were definitely starting to take a toll on his body. It was hard not to get caught up in the party scene. Being a celebrity had its perks and he took full advantage of them. Free access to VIP rooms in clubs, drinks on the house, and then of course the continual flow of narcotics that came with the package. Despite his obvious faults, Sam had always been careful to avoid the crowd that handed out bags of powder. It wasn't that he wouldn't do it; he just knew if he went down that road there would be a good chance he wouldn't return. Problem was, alcohol wasn't much better.

He rubbed the sides of his prickly face and then ran a scoop of water over his head, soaking his dark hair. A quick shower, shave, and a splash of cologne and he would be ready to join the land of the living again. When he came out he poured himself a cup of fresh coffee and took a long swig. Fresh coffee and waking up late was a beautiful combination. Another perk that he took full advantage of when he wasn't on set.

Now the only thing better was waking up with Kate beside him. He loved the way she slept and the way her long hair would fall across her face. He loved to tuck it behind her ear and wonder how he had gotten so lucky. She was beautiful in every way.

Sam gazed out the window and took in the breathtaking view of Central Park and the New York skyline. From the Mandarin's fifty-third floor you could see everything. Whenever they were in New York they stayed there, as the presidential suite had it all; handcrafted rugs, exquisite art-work, silk walls, a king-size bed that felt like you were sleep-ing on a fluffy cloud, televisions in the bathroom, hot tub, and more. It was the best that money could buy.

Standing close to the window, wearing a casual pair of jeans and T-shirt, Sam checked his phone for text messages. He hadn't heard from Kate for the past forty-eight hours. It wasn't like they needed to hear from each other all the time. But texting, phone calls, short, spontaneous trips to see each other in different countries while filming was normal. He figured she must have gotten busy or lost her phone, though it did strike him as a little peculiar.

His thoughts were rattled as a sharp knock at the door caught his attention. Opening it, he was greeted by the fa-miliar face of his bodyguard, Kris.

"Morning, Sam, Eric has been downstairs for the past ten minutes, did you want me to send him up?"

"What? It's only eight-ten a.m." Sam shot a glance over his shoulder at the clock beside his bed. It was still showing the same time as when he got in the night before.

"Ah man," he groaned. "Twenty thousand dollars a night, you would think they would give you a working alarm clock."

"So ... what do you want me to tell him?"

Sam raised an eyebrow.

Kris turned. "I got it."

* * * * *

By the time Sam made it to the restaurant, Eric had al-ready ordered and was halfway through a dish of linguini. The restaurant was on the thirty-fifth floor, providing a stunning view of Manhattan, Central Park, and Sixtieth Street. The place was a hive of activity with penguin-style waiters navigating their way around the white-clothed tables and balancing glasses like expert jugglers. The clinking of cutlery and a guy playing a grand piano almost muffled the noise of guests talking.

Eric gestured to him from across the room and Sam nodded.

"Another late night?"

Sam didn't reply right away, motioning to one of the waiters to get his attention and asking for a bottle of beer.

"Is that what Kris said?" Sam asked.

"No, but he tends to sweat when he's lying." Eric wiped his mouth with a napkin and took a drink of water.

Eric scooped at his food. "So the press circuit has gone well. Looks like the film is going to bring in a packet at the box office when it opens," he said, slurping up his pasta like a dog.

Numbers—that's all it was ever about, Sam told himself. Who could bring in the most on opening night. The old days of artistic expression had pretty much gone out the window. Now it was all about going bigger, better, and whenever possible throwing a ton of CGI effects in for good measure. It wasn't like he couldn't take on a role that was challenging or different from the usual scripts that the suits wanted you to read. But if you signed on for that, it was like signing a death sentence. Hollywood wasn't very forgiving; you got one shot and God forbid a movie didn't pull in three times as much as it cost to make. It didn't matter that the script may have been doomed to failure from the moment it was green-lit, or that some suit trying to impress his boss above him had practically destroyed the script with his notes.

All that mattered were the numbers.

A waiter arrived with Sam's drink. There was nothing better for a hangover than another drink. It worked like magic. He placed his order and began chewing on some truffle toast while he waited. A few chews and he was ready to spit it out.

One thing hadn't changed since becoming an A-list celebrity and that was his taste buds. He still couldn't understand why high-priced establishments insisted on serving up fancy specialty food instead of old-fashioned American cuisine. It wasn't even as if it was impressive; most of the time there was more plate than food when it arrived. No, if he had his way he would have outlawed half the junk that was on the menu. The way he saw it, if they were going to serve junk it might as well be America's finest. Hamburgers, fries, or pastrami sandwiches; heck, wasn't that what the city was known for?

Sam took another gulp of beer. "So the opportunities you mentioned?"

"Yes, um. Well, there are a number of great scripts that have come in; I want you to take a look at…" He pulled up a soft brown briefcase, unzipped, and pulled a stack of papers.

He pointed to one of them. "If you want this one, they are ready to take you in. No audition, it's yours."

Sam had flipped through a few pages when Eric slipped another in front of him. Though this one wasn't a script; it was a well-known tabloid.

Sam looked confused.

"What's this?"

Eric flipped it over. The front page featured a large photo of Kate in the arms of her film's director. Above, a smaller photo of himself and Kate and in big bold lettering underneath it read: Kate cheats on Sam.

Sam found himself wordlessly transfixed on the image of Kate; he hadn't seen her in weeks. Blood drained from his face, his pulse quickened, and his breathing became shallow. He couldn't believe what he was seeing. A part of him felt pleased to see her and yet the longer he looked at the photo, the more torn he felt inside.

He let out a slight chuckle, bit the side of his lip, and lifted his eyes to Eric with a look of confusion and then back to the paper.

"This ... this is a joke, right?" He looked backed up again. "I mean they print crap like this all the time, right? Eric?"

Eric wasn't smiling; he looked almost embarrassed by it all. He cleared his throat and took a long drink from his glass, all the while looking away.

Sam quickly thumbed through the paper until he reached the center. Both pages were plastered with zoomed-in snapshots of Kate. Photos taken through a trailer window. Kissing, cuddling, and....

He closed the paper and with it his eyes. His train of thought had become jumbled up in a tornado of confusion, anger, and pain.

"What?"

"Hey, Sam, come on. You didn't do anything wrong. Look, as hard as it is, it happens. You know better than anyone else. Celebrity relationships don't have the happy ending. They never do. Hell, you've been lucky to have had it last as long as it has."

Sam shook his head.

"She stopped answering my voice and text messages.

Last time I saw her, she was acting all weird; she wouldn't let me near her phone." He ran his hand through his hair and breathed in deeply. "God, I'm so stupid —"

"Sam."

"No, I should have seen this coming."

Sam took a long pull on his drink, downing the rest of it all in one go. He stared outside at the traffic, completely lost in thought; it felt as if someone had torn out the rug beneath him, stabbed him in the heart, and suffocated him all at once. He shook his head, watching the yellow cabs zip in and out of traffic and people going about their day. Beneath them was a bustling ocean of faces. How many of them had been cheated on? Sure, he wasn't the first to have this happen, millions had, but to have it aired out in public like this ... without even ...

He turned back to Eric. "When? I didn't ...?"

"Yesterday." His voice lowered almost to a whisper. "I got word from the tabloid that they were going to run this. Look, I tried to stop it but you know—there's no stopping something like this once the media has it. If it wasn't them it would be another."

Sam's chair screeched as he got up. "I need to..." He trailed off

"Yeah, yeah, um, I'll take care of this. Take your time, take as much time as you need." He paused. "And, I'm sorry, Sam."

"No, it's..." His mind was elsewhere now. Barely able to concentrate entering the elevator, he reached his room. He turned to Kris, who hadn't spoken a word all the way up.

"Take the rest of the day off and let the others know."

"Sir, I mean Sam, I think at least one of us should stay."

Sam shot him a look; Kris nodded and stepped back into the elevator.

Inside his room, he stared out across the green trees of Central Park. A flood of memories from when he and Kate were together besieged him. The rest of the day passed in a blur. Sam lay on the bed and flipped through channels mechanically. He slept a while, drank a bit more, and walked Central Park chain-smoking cigarettes. He'd tried giving them up and smoking the new-fangled electronic cigarettes, and for a while he was doing well. But after this, he couldn't care less about his health.

Back at the hotel, he got a text from Liam. He'd known Liam for years; they'd worked on a number of films together. Liam's career had never really taken off. He always struggled to find parts, but he managed to scrape by with the little he did get, plus royalties and the odd handout from Sam. He'd always played the poor card, but Sam didn't buy it. He stayed at the best hotels in the city, drank endlessly, and always seemed to have enough to feed his habit.

The text message read: Heard the news, sorry, man. Let's hit the clubs tonight, my treat.

CHAPTER FOUR

In the years following her mother's death both Hailey and her father had begun the difficult task of picking up the pieces. It had been a slow process. She had never cried as much as she did in that time. The loss of losing her mother was unbearable; she meant everything to Hailey. In that first year it had been emotionally and physically difficult watching her father fall apart. It wasn't as if they weren't prepared for it. They had both watched her health slowly deteriorate as the cancer spread throughout her body. They had been with her as her body tried to purge itself of the disease.

Her mother hated hospitals; she had an abnormal fear of them. Whenever Hailey was sick, she would be forced to endure natural remedies her mother had concocted, some of which Hailey was sure had made her even worse. But that was her way. She would always say that everything we needed could be found in nature; there was no need for unnatural drugs that doctors prescribed.

They'd given her only weeks to live by the time her father finally convinced her to go to the hospital. Though that didn't last. Within days she had requested to be brought home. Dying in a hospital bed wasn't the way she wanted to go; she wanted her family around her. She wanted that which was familiar. In those final days, Hailey recalled her mother's strength. She put up a strong fight and even went far beyond what the doctors had said, lasting three additional months before the disease took her life. In that time they grew closer as a family, and even when her mother's body was weak, she would still put on a smile and say she was beating it. But Hailey knew that she only did it for her.

Hailey was only twenty-four when her mother passed.

The following weeks and months seemed to move in slow motion. Even with Hailey's best efforts, the business that had once flourished had become too much for Hailey to manage by herself. Eventually, it dwindled until there were only a handful of patients remaining. With a heavy heart, Hailey had to let the staff go. That didn't stop the calls from those who came from miles away to their farmhouse. It had a good reputation—more specifically, the Wellands had a reputation—and it wasn't going to go away overnight.

Slowly they began to feel the pinch with the drop in income. Hailey knew her father wasn't going to be in the right state of mind to work any time soon, so taking the burden upon herself she took a job at Maggie's Diner, pouring coffee and waiting on tables to cover some of the basic costs until her father was ready. On her days off she would read to her father on the front porch swing, or simply look out over the lake that was within walking distance. For the most part her father would sit in silence, only exchanging small talk before he would look off into the distance. Days turned into nights in the blink of an eye and before they knew it, two years had passed since they'd laid her to rest.

Hailey drifted back into the present moment, watching her father lay painter's tarp over the floor in the living room. She wasn't quite sure what had changed in him over the past few months.

It was as if a light had switched on again.

She no longer had to remind him to change his clothes, take a shower, or shave. His curtains were open, and some days, he was even up before her. His drive to reopen the treatment center had become the discussion at the table in the evenings. Trips into town for supplies usually were filled with conversations about getting in touch with old contacts and picking up where they left off.

Truly, it made her happy to see the spark in his eyes again, but she knew it wasn't going to be easy. Being closed for so long meant those who usually would have referred people were now in the habit of referring patients elsewhere. But it didn't seem to faze him.

"Got some good news," he said, looking all chipper.

"Yeah?"

"I spoke to Jim Sorensen today in the city. He said he would let the other organizations know that we're back in business again."

She cocked her head. "That's great, Dad. Did he give you any idea when they can send people?"

"Well ... no. He was surprised to hear from me," he mumbled. "It's going take a while."

"And in the meantime?"

"It will give me time to get the place back in shape. I have to fix a number of things around the grounds, and

well, I think the house could use a fresh lick of paint," he
said, holding a can of paint in one hand and a brush in the
other. "What do you think?"

She looked him straight in the eye and smiled.

"I think you should hire a painter."

* * * * *

Inside the Dream Hotel's electric room the music was
belting out. It was the third club they'd visited that night.
The whole room was a fiesta of energetic writhing as people
danced the night away, guys attempted to pick up women,
and couples tucked themselves into darkened corners. It
was smaller than the other places. An unknown DJ did his
best to entertain the crowd, playing dance-friendly hits. For
the average folk walking in, finding a table was like a game
of musical chairs, with more people than seats.

Sam had frequented the place; he knew the owner and
whenever he came they were always good. If a table didn't
exist, they made one available. As he and Liam shouldered
their way through the crowd, Sam tried to hold in his breath
from the overpowering cloud of cologne and sweat. If you
were claustrophobic you didn't stand a chance in this place.

Seated on a leathered couch, Sam immediately ordered in
a line of shots. It had been a while since they'd been out together. With his schedule it was rare to be in New York
longer than a weekend. Sam lit up a cigarette.

Liam took it out of his mouth and stubbed it out.

"You know you can't smoke in here."

Sam rolled his eyes.

On any other night, Sam's bodyguards would have been
scanning the room looking for potential nutcases who were

stocked up on liquid courage. But tonight, without them, he couldn't care less.

He slammed back one shot after another.

"Sam, you got a death wish? Might want to slow down there, bud."

Sam scowled, feeling the effects of the alcohol taking over. It was always the same; the sense of relaxation, the fits of laughter, the final slide to a dark place.

"Really, Liam? You're gonna lecture me?"

Liam raised his hands.

"God, I'm so tired of people telling me what to do. Stand over here, say these lines. Show up for this, can I get a photo with you, sign that." Sam knocked over several glasses, sending liquid pouring off the table.

"Maybe we should call it a night. People are staring."

"That's never stopped you before," Sam said. He threw back a shot and laughed. "Oh, come on, we're just getting warmed up. Let's see how many clubs we can get to by the time the sun comes up."

More and more people were piling into the place. A group of women at the bar were staring at Sam. It didn't matter where he went; he became a spectacle. Fame was a strange thing. It wasn't real, but they didn't know that. People only saw the red carpet, the awards, the characters he played. They had no clue what made him tick, what really pissed him off, or what he was really like. If they did, they probably wouldn't have looked at him so favorably.

"Anyway, mate, you're a fine one to talk." Sam motioned to Liam's nose, with the fine line of white beneath it. "You might want to be a little bit more conspicuous yourself."

Liam wiped it and laughed. "You sure you don't want some? Makes everything right in the world."

For a split second, he was tempted. He'd never taken cocaine. He'd always played it safe. Made a point to avoid it. As far as he was concerned, nothing good ever came from it. He'd seen others spiral down into obscurity, slave to the line. But for once in his life, he could see the appeal. He drank to forget. But this … well, this might be interesting. Before the urge could grow any stronger he caught sight of the girls at the bar for a second time.

"Nah, I think I'm going to chat with the ladies at the bar. Those beauties haven't taken their eyes off us since we walked in," Sam said, whacking back another drink.

"And neither have their boyfriends." Liam grasped Sam's arm. "Let's leave."

But Sam didn't care. He'd heard enough crap for one day and the last thing he wanted now was a lecture from his best friend. Sam shook him off, snatched up the bottle of bourbon in one hand and a couple of shot glasses in the other, and began edging his way through the crowd, keeping the drink above people's heads. His hips swayed to the sound of the music as he approached.

Sam placed the drink on the bar and nodded. "Ladies. Can I get you a drink?"

The women smiled and turned towards him. One of them, a tall redhead with a short skirt and high-heeled boots, moved in close. Her eyes fixed on his.

"I'll take you up on that."

As Sam went to pour one of the shots, she grabbed his wrist and slowly lifted the bottle upwards. Provocatively she opened her mouth, letting the liquid flow in.

Sam laughed. "Ah, now that's a woman after my own heart."

Another woman chimed in, pressing her finger against his chest with slurred speech.

"Sam Reid? You're Sam. Hey, didn't Kate Evans just cheat on you? It's all over the Internet."

He smirked, feeling even more intoxicated. "That would be me."

He took a turn gulping down a mouthful of bourbon directly from the bottle.

"What a bitch, you should dump her ass."

"Kind of late for that now." He pointed at her, his speech beginning to slur. "And I'd appreciate it if you didn't call her that." He slammed the bottle down, then said, "Enough about me, where are you girls from?"

Before they could reply, an overly large Italian guy with a fake tan appeared beside them. Beside him stood several other *Jersey Shore* lookalikes. He spun Sam around.

"What the hell do you think you're doing?"

The redhead piped up. "Oh, Mickey, go back to the others."

"Yeah, Mickey," Sam said, straightening in front of him and patting him on the shoulder. He gestured with his fingers. "Go take a seat ... get another tan or whatever it is you do."

They all started laughing as Sam turned back to the bar.

"What the hell did you say?"

"Settle down," Sam said. "It was a joke. Like the grease in your hair." Sam patted his arm and turned back to the bar with a wide smirk on his face.

The guy pulled him back around and swung his fist into Sam's face. Sam fell against the bar. He turned back with blood coming out the corner of his lip. He wiped it with the side of his hand, looking at it run down his hand. The guy swung again, but Sam kicked him back before his fist made contact. The guy collapsed on top of his friend behind him. At this point all hell let loose. Another one of his friends grabbed hold of Sam and Sam reacted by yanking himself away and punching him twice in the face until he fell back on a table, collapsing it. Drinks spilled over the floor and people began yelling and screaming. Liam and several of the club's bouncers were already in the thick of it but couldn't calm the total chaos, fists flying and glasses being smashed as more and more people joined in. Sam grabbed a fire extinguisher off the closest wall and began spraying several of his attackers with its powder before throwing it down. Out of the powdery cloud, Liam grabbed hold of Sam.

"We need to get out of here now," Liam shouted.

Shielded by the darkness of the club, extinguisher powder, and people pummeling each other, Sam and Liam ducked and squeezed through the crowd until they reached the door. Before slipping out, Sam couldn't resist it; he pulled on the red fire alarm, setting off ringing bells and the sprinkler system.

The fighting had spilled over outside with several of the guests tackling each other. One of them tried to prevent Sam from leaving by grabbing his jacket, to which he reacted in his drunken state by elbowing the guy in the nose and knocking him to the ground. Other bystanders were shouting to the bouncers to stop them. Sam dove into his car, Liam jumped in the passenger seat, and they pulled away. Before they made out of the car park, two police cars responding to the alarm blocked them in.

* * * * *

"You were damn lucky those guys didn't press charges."

Sam sat quietly across from his manager, slowly stirring his coffee. The smell of food being served permeated the air. It had been several days since that embarrassing evening. After he was released from the hospital for multiple injuries, the police had arrested him and filed charges. A court date had been set for next month. No doubt the media would eat that up. To them, nothing made prime TV better than a good celebrity arraignment.

"What the hell were you thinking?" Eric said. "You still face charges of public intoxication, driving under the influence, and vandalism. Now, I'm trying damn hard to see if we can reach a plea bargain, but it's not going to be easy, Sam."

Sam was trying to take it all in but every part of him felt numb and distant as if he were watching himself from afar. Truthfully, he didn't know what to say and it had only gotten worse the morning after he left the hospital. Tabloids and the Internet were running amok with mug shots of his arrest, all of which had him sporting a partial black eye.

If that hadn't been bad enough, since the initial tabloid had hit the stand, Kate had released a public apology, announcing her regret for cheating on Sam. And a film he'd signed on to do, well, they pulled the plug and went with someone else. He was too much of a liability, his manager said.

The film he didn't care about, and the mug shots, sure, they bothered him, but it was Kate's actions that troubled him more. It was so unlike her. She hadn't taken the time to phone, text, or even have one of her friends apologize to him; instead, she made a decision to go public with an apology? Sam didn't know what hurt more, being cheated on or having her apologize publicly. They hadn't spoken since he had seen the magazines; as far as he knew from Eric she was staying with friends or family.

Eric slammed his cup against the saucer. "SAM!" He raised his voice. "Have you heard a single word of what I've said?"

Like snapping out of a dream, Sam looked up at him.

"Yes, court date. Plea bargain. I heard you."

Looking unsatisfied with his answer, Eric scowled and took a large drink from his cup.

"Listen, I'm going to need you to work with me on this one. This is some serious PR damage that I've got to mop up, and quite frankly, if it wasn't for our long-standing business relationship, we wouldn't even be having this conversation."

Other people in the restaurant were beginning to stare, whether because of Eric raising his voice or the public spectacle he'd made of himself Sam wasn't sure. There was no doubt; this one was going to stick with him for a long time. He could already hear Letterman and Leno lapping it up at his expense. If there was anything the public loved more than a rags-to-riches story it was watching a train wreck, and his train had finally derailed. And the media loved it even more. Lifting you up to slap you back down. It sold magazines, it gained web hits, and it made photographers disgustingly wealthy. And yet now he had no one else to blame except himself.

"So here's what you're going to do, and I need you to promise you will do it."

"Yeah, whatever."

"No, not whatever."

A waitress came over to the table.

"How's everything?"

Eric's eyes were locked on Sam's.

"Fine, thanks," Sam casually replied.

She went off to serve others.

Sam lifted his hands. "Okay, I promise," he said.

"You're going to rehab," Eric said.

Sam coughed, nearly choking on the coffee he was swallowing. He dropped the coffee stirrer in his hand and his eyes widened. He raised his fingers to the side of his temples and kneaded them, as if he could feel a headache coming on. Finally he spluttered, "Come again?"

"You want all this to go away, right?"

"Yeah, but—"

"No buts," Eric jumped in. "The only way we're going to wangle out of this is through a plea bargain. You need to put your best foot forward. Having you go off to rehab under the premise of stress is going to go a long way. Everyone knows about you and Kate. You've already got the sympathy of the public. It won't take much to persuade them that this was all the result of stress."

"Under the premise?" he said, looking confused. "It *was* stress and …"

Eric looked at him as if waiting for a truthful admission.

"Let's be honest, Sam, your drinking is out of hand."

Sam frowned.

"And don't tell me you've got a handle on it. I smelled it on you the moment you walked in here."

Sam leaned back against the leather booth, not taking his eyes off Eric for even one second.

"C'mon, Eric?"

Eric narrowed his eyes and shook his head. Sam knew he wasn't getting off lightly. There was nothing that was going to change his manager's mind. He seriously meant it.

Sam exhaled, exasperated. "So where you sending me? Betty Ford? Hazelden?"

"You wish."

Eric reached into his briefcase and pulled out a sheet of paper and a black pen and began scribbling. Sam tilted his head sideways to try to make out what he was writing. Once Eric was done, he turned the paper and slid it across the table to him. Sam picked it up. All that was on it was an address and a name.

"Walton, New York?"

"Yes. You've burned your bridges," Eric said. "Trust me, you'll like it."

"And if I say no?"

Eric didn't answer. He simply snapped the clips on his briefcase, left a fifty-dollar note on the table, and got up to leave, only stopping briefly to look sideways at him.

"Sam, it's your choice. Rehab or jail." And with that he left.

CHAPTER FIVE

M aggie's was the kind of diner that was always filled with locals. It was one of three restaurants that existed in Walton and was by far the oldest. Vinny's Italian had opened up last year and a new Chinese all-you-could-eat buffet had been operating out of the old used-car dealership since May. Needless to say, most of the locals frequented Maggie's. Everything was cooked fresh. It had a home-style feel to the place, serving cheap breakfast all day and some of the best bacon sandwiches in New York state. Word had it she even ran a customer out of her place with the kitchen broom after they demanded streaky bacon. Apparently, there was no way on God's green earth that she was going to serve up that stringy fat masquerading as bacon. Maggie was from Scotland, and she was a straight shooter. It was probably why Hailey liked her. She spoke her mind and didn't have time for gossip. She left the gossip for Carol, one of the other waitresses. Maggie had immigrated to up-state New York when she was only eighteen and got hitched to a local tradesman. Despite her husband passing away thirteen years ago, she was a pillar of strength to others in the community. In all the years Hailey had known her, she couldn't recall a time that she didn't have a smile on her face or a warm word to share. The folks in Walton loved her and so did Hailey. She had been one of her mom's best friends and with her mom gone, Maggie had clearly felt the need to take it upon herself to keep an eye on Hailey.

The heat in the kitchen was intense. Beads of sweat dripped down Hailey's back within minutes of stepping inside. In the summer months everyone would take turns standing in the full-size meat cooler out back, just for a few seconds of relief. It was heaven.

Wafts of fresh toast, bacon, and eggs couldn't mask the smell of the scraps in the garbage as Hailey scraped off the leftovers. She tossed the cutlery into the sink and the water splashed over Danny. Danny was like a one-man show, both cooking and washing. He knew what it meant to work hard and yet he never took it too seriously. Life was about living, he would say.

"Do I really smell that bad? I thought the shower I had this morning was enough but you've given me four since you've started your shift."

She turned towards him and stifled a laugh.

"Sorry, Danny."

She liked Danny; he was probably the only guy in Walton that hadn't hit on her. Hailey knew why; not only was he old enough to be her grandfather, but everyone knew he was sweet on Maggie and he took every opportunity to let her know. He'd been cooking at Maggie's for as long as she had been running the business. Never married, he had an old-school charm about him that reminded Hailey of what guys were probably like back in the 1940s. While working he would listen to classic jazz tunes by Louis Armstrong and Ella Fitzgerald on an old tape recorder that he stashed out back. Maggie pretended she didn't like him, but her eyes revealed the truth. So did the way she would blush when he would take her hand and attempt to slip in a quick dance when she came back for an order. Or the way she smiled when he would pay her a compliment on the way she looked.

Now if only more men were like that, Hailey thought.

Later that afternoon, as the sun hid behind the clouds, Maggie was busy taking a payment from a customer when Hailey returned from out back. There were only a few servers in the place but enough to make sure you weren't run off your feet. Tommy, Luke, and a few others had taken a booth in the far corner of the restaurant.

"Hon, give me a second and I'll get one of the other girls to take their table."

"No, it's fine. I'll do it."

Hailey was wearing cut-off jean shorts and a white T-shirt. She could feel their eyes on her as she approached them.

"What can I get you?"

Tommy shuffled in his seat and put his hand on her leg. "I don't know, maybe we can discuss it over dinner," he said. He was well built, around the same age as Hailey, and had been bugging her for a date ever since the last one.

The others smirked. Hailey swiped his hand away and scowled.

"What, the meatballs weren't enough, you want seconds?"

The others laughed. Tommy still hadn't lived down the embarrassment of having a plate of spaghetti dumped on his head the one time she had reluctantly agreed to let him take her out. She wasn't normally like that but the guy was an asshole. One date with him was enough.

She took their order and walked off, all the while feeling their creepy eyes watching her. She appreciated having the job but there wasn't a day that went by when she didn't think about quitting and pursuing her dream. The dream her mother had instilled in her from a young age. The dream they'd spent years talking about. To become a dancer in New York City, to follow in her mother's footsteps and eventually travel the world. When it wasn't busy, she would clean the tables and daydream about what it would be like to wake up each day in the city, to feel the promise of adventure in the air. To have an apartment, ride the underground subways and buses. And maybe, just maybe, find someone she could fall in love with, a guy whose aspirations went beyond plowing fields. For a moment it all had seemed so close, within her grasp, and yet now it felt more like wishful thinking.

She went back and forth in her mind between believing it was possible to thinking it was just downright selfish. Who was she kidding? She couldn't leave her father alone. It's not that she couldn't—she was twenty-five and certainly old enough to make decisions for herself—but she didn't want to think about what would happen if she left. He had improved so much in the last few months. What if her leaving was the straw that broke the camel's back? She wouldn't be able to live with that. How could she go about her day knowing that he wasn't able to cope? No, it was too risky. Her mind wandered back to the thought of meeting someone local. Maybe a guy who plowed fields was fine, as long as he loved her.

Hailey sighed as she tacked another order ticket to the steely wheel and carried a few more meals over to tables. Afternoons were always manic, with a large influx of locals, couples, and families, but with all the kids on summer vacation, it was nonstop.

She grabbed a steaming pot of coffee and went over to refill the cups of a couple who looked so mesmerized with one another they didn't even acknowledge her. She wondered what it must be like to have someone so into you that it felt as if the world around you ceased to exist. Hailey was always polite with customers unless they were jerks. She never lingered longer than she needed to, feeling that if people wanted to talk they would; otherwise, she'd give them their privacy, only stopping by to refill.

"Hey, Hailey can I get some more ketchup?" Luke said, holding up an empty bottle. She felt like telling him to go get it himself. Or better still, shove the empty bottle where the sun didn't shine. Instead, she gave a quick nod and went in the back to retrieve another.

From the back Hailey heard the shrill of the front entrance bell announcing more people coming into the café. Hailey was grabbing a new bottle of ketchup from the fridge when she heard Maggie call.

"Hailey, guy here wants to know where the Welland residence is."

Hailey shouted, "You know where it is."

"Oh, you know what my memory is like."

Hailey came out, almost banging into Maggie, who had a devilish glint in her eye. She followed Maggie's gaze and then almost lost grip on the bottle of ketchup when she realized who was making the inquiry. It was Sam Reid.

* * * * *

It had taken Sam the better part of the day to drive up from the city to Walton. It should have taken no more than two and a half hours of pleasant scenic driving, yet by the time he had located the small village in the Catskill Mountains, he had been on the road for almost four hours. He'd adamantly insisted to his driver that he would go it alone, but the GPS kept losing satellite signal and the journey had turned into a series of wrong turns and frequent stops in deserted gas stations.

The whole way up he'd mulled over the images of Kate in the arms of that director. A mixture of anger and confusion welled up inside of him. He still hadn't heard from her and he wasn't planning to go out of his way anytime soon to contact her; it pained him too much and honestly, he wasn't sure what there was left to say. Maybe Eric was right— maybe getting away would give him time to think.

It was close to suppertime by the time he found the town. The sun was hanging low in the sky and while he was relieved not to be driving around in circles, he still had no clue where the Welland House was located. And no amount of phone calls to Eric had helped. He was out of the office and inconveniently unavailable.

Sam must have stuck out like a sore thumb as he drove up and down the roads searching for any inclination of the whereabouts of this house. Frustrated, he groaned. Finding a house on those backcountry roads was like searching for a needle in a haystack.

Luckily, he'd been directed to Maggie's Restaurant by one of the local gas attendants, who highly recommended the food and told him that if anyone knew where it was,

Maggie would. From the road, the diner looked like a space-ship decked out in shiny silver plating with strips of bright turquoise wrapped around it. It was one hell of an eyesore, that was for sure. He only hoped the food lived up to the hype. He figured he'd have a bite and then find the place before it got dark.

Inside the restaurant, he noted how unusual the place was compared to those he frequented. There was nothing fancy about the establishment; in fact, it looked as if he had stepped back in time. All the seats were pink leather, includ-ing the round-top stools that lined the front steely counter. The place had a retro feel, like something out of the 1960s. While he felt like a fish out of water, something about the town's pace was relaxing. People he'd met on the way seemed genuinely friendly and so far no one had recognized him, which was oddly comforting.

"I told him you were just finishing up," Maggie said.

"I am?"

"And ... you could take him there."

"You did?"

Sam could just make out what they were saying. The old-er woman was leaning into the younger, prettier one. It was amusing, to say the least. He wondered if all conversations in this town were this odd.

"Uh," he said, interrupting. "If you just give me direc-tions, that'd be fine."

"No, no, Hailey can take you. Can't you, Hailey?" The older women smiled.

"Do you mind me asking why you're heading that way?" Hailey asked.

"I'm going to be staying there," he said, "for a while."

The cook had stopped what he was doing and was looking on with interest through the kitchen hatch. His eyes were wide and he wore an expression of amusement.

Before she could reply, a guy appeared beside them and took the ketchup out of her hand. He turned back, saying, "I don't remember when this place became self-service, Maggie."

"Tommy, you know where the door is, if you don't like it," Maggie replied with her hand on her hips.

Tommy shot Sam a quick sideways sneer and then returned to his seat.

Maggie subtly nudged Hailey with her elbow. "Go on."

Hailey looked down as she untied the khaki apron around her waist. She glanced up at him as she fiddled with the knot behind her looking half embarrassed, and smiled before handing it to Maggie. Sam for a moment felt a spark of attraction. He watched as she unclipped her shiny blond hair and it dropped past her shoulders and across her face. She wore a pair of jean shorts and a white shirt that hugged her body. He casually cast a glance away from her, not wanting to make her feel uncomfortable.

As he was about to follow her out, Maggie piped up, "Forgetting something?"

She was dangling a pair of keys in the air.

"Oh." Hailey gave a half smile at Sam and retrieved them from her. Maggie raised an eyebrow as if she were inwardly finding some form of delight in it all.

CHAPTER SIX

Outside in the parking lot, Hailey walked ahead while Sam tried to keep up. She was trying her best to remain calm and collected. Yet everything about this situation was making her feel self-conscious. She raked her fingers through her hair, hoping it didn't look like a rat's nest. She glanced down, praying that her clothes weren't splattered with any grease spots or mustard stains. She didn't even want to think about how she smelled.

"What the hell I'm I doing?" she murmured to herself.

"What?" he asked

"Nothing." She could feel her neck and face getting warmer by the second.

It wasn't as if it was a big deal. On the other hand, having a celebrity show up in Walton wasn't an everyday occurrence. It was definitely one for the books. *Get a grip. Okay, he's handsome, but he's just another guy and probably a jerk.* Hailey tried to convince herself as if in some way it would alleviate her tenseness.

She gestured to her beat-up Chevy truck. "You can follow me."

Glancing out of the side of her eye, she watched him walk over to what looked like a brand new sports Sedan.

Hailey jumped in on the torn-up leather seat and slammed the door shut several times before it finally closed. She didn't dare glance over at him through the passenger side window.

She turned over the ignition and the engine started; a split second later it stalled. *Oh God no,* she thought, rolling her eyes and then wiggling the steering wheel and trying again. She pumped the gas and the engine roared, smoke pouring out of the back filling up the lot in a dirty spluttering cloud, and then it stalled again.

"C'mon." She beat the steering wheel, forgetting that he was probably watching all this and laughing hysterically.

Attempting for the third time, she didn't hear the knock on the window. The engine ticked over and then died. Another knock and she turned her head slowly. Standing at the driver side was Sam. Hailey attempted to roll down the window but the darn thing had practically given up the ghost as well, only rolling down a quarter of the way. A problem, she might add, that had given the server at the McDonald's drive-thru no end of laughter and now it was likely doing the same for him.

"Did you? Um …" Sam gestured to his vehicle with his thumb. "Do you wanna …?"

"Yes. Good idea," she muttered over the window before stepping out of the truck completely mortified. She slammed the door twice, hard enough to almost take it off its hinges before it finally took.

"Something wrong?" Sam asked, looking at her.

"Oh," she realized. "No, it's the door. It never shuts unless I do that."

"Ah …" He nodded, with a smile.

Hailey walked over to his car, feeling even more uncomfortable. He followed her to the passenger side door and she flashed him a confused look.

"Oh, is this one of those foreign imports, where the wheel is on the other side?"

He opened the door.

"No, I just wanted to open the door for you."

Her eyebrow arched. Then she nodded, secretly hoping the earth would open and swallow her. He closed the door behind her and got in the other side. Inside, she breathed in deeply the smell of brand new leather. The last time she had been in a car this new was when her father's brother had come from out of state for a visit. He had bought a brand new Lexus weeks earlier and gave them the tour. A total show-off, but it was nice.

Out the corner of her eye, while looking over the dashboard she became aware that he was staring at her. She met his gaze and then ran her hand across her face. *Oh God. Do I have ketchup on my face?*

"You going to put your seat belt on?"

She breathed out, relieved.

"Yeah." She pulled it over. She was so used to not wearing hers in the truck—yet another thing that no longer worked—that it had completely slipped her mind.

He smiled, pressed a button next to the steering wheel, and the car roared to life.

He turned to her. "So you always get into cars with strangers?"

"You're not exactly a stranger."

The short journey to her home was filled with awkward silence and small talk about the area. Either he was feeling uncomfortable about being there or he wasn't a big talker. She had a good feeling why he was going to be staying there, though she didn't recall her father saying that anyone was arriving. And she wasn't going to pry.

The Welland residence was located on the outskirts of the town, just off County Highway 23. It only took about ten minutes to get there. You could barely see the house from the road in the summer, as it was tucked away behind oak trees that lined the sides of the entire driveway. When they gave people directions they would tell them to look for the big red barn, as that stood out clearly from the road in all seasons.

As they turned onto the driveway and made their way up to the house, she could see him looking up at the trees, which acted as a canopy. She loved the way they formed an archway above them. When she was a child she would always imagine the tree branches were fingers entwining together.

"So you never told me how you know about this place."

"I work here."

"You hold down two jobs?"

"The restaurant is part time. We haven't exactly been busy here for quite some time. In fact, you're the first person in two years."

"Why so long?"

Hailey didn't respond. Surprisingly, he didn't pry any further. As they came out the other side, Hailey indicated where to park and he pulled into one of the parking slots. Outside, she could see her father up on a ladder clearing out the gutters in the overhanging sloped porch. It was an old-fashioned farmhouse, with white clapboard siding and dark blue shutters. The red barn was off to the right and the entire house overlooked a large spring-fed lake. In the summer they would take a boat out on it and fish. In the winter the entire lake froze over and people from town would come up and skate on it. The place was surrounded by 200 acres of rolling meadows.

Her father and mother had purchased the house back in the 70s after they'd got married. It wasn't long after that they began using it as a recovery place for addicts and alcoholics. Growing up, she had seen all sorts of people come and go. Some came for stress and others for hardcore dependency.

* * * * *

As they stepped out of the car, a man made his way down off the ladder, cleaning his hands off with an old rag.

"Hailey, I see you've met our guest."

Hailey looked genuinely puzzled. Sam made his way over and extended his hand to introduce himself.

"I'm Sam, Sam Reid." He paused as if half expecting Hailey's father to know who he was. Instead he just looked him in the eye as he gave a firm handshake.

"Nice to meet you, Sam. Welcome to the Welland House. I'm Charlie Welland." There was a moment where the handshake extended beyond the usual length of a greeting. Most centers would give you the look, observing you like a diseased monkey in a cage, but this was different.

"Oh, right," Sam piped up, hoping to break the awkwardness of the moment with what he assumed they wanted to hear—the confession.

"I'm an alcoholic."

Charlie immediately shot back, "No you're not."

"What?"

"You're not an alcoholic."

Sam was confused for a second. What was this some kind of mind game? Who cared, he saw the opportunity.

"I know, that's what I told my manager. Well, I guess we're done here. I'll let him know that the treatment was a raging success."

Charlie's lip curled at the corner, amused.

Right then the wind picked up, bringing with it earthy grit that made Sam squint.

"Why don't you come in and we can get you settled in," Charlie said, gesturing toward the house. "I was wondering when you would show up."

"Well, this is not the easiest place to find."

Hailey cleared her throat.

Charlie turned. "I see you've met my daughter."

Sam glanced over at Hailey. "Daughter?"

Hailey said nothing.

"Hailey, could you give him a hand with the luggage?"

"Well, I'm sure he's capable of handling it himself," she replied, her blue eyes darting back and forth between her father and Sam.

"Hailey," her father said, surprised.

There was a moment of silence before Sam said, "I can take it in, no need to —"

She raised an eyebrow. "See?"

Hailey headed towards the house, and Sam noticed her glance back over her shoulder for a brief moment before disappearing inside. Sam returned to the vehicle and took out two pieces of brown luggage from the back while her father gave him a hand.

Once inside, Charlie had him place his bags to one side.

"I guess you want to go through the luggage?"

"Not unless you have something to show me. Do you have something to show me?"

Sam muttered, "No, I guess not."

It didn't make sense. *I'm not an alcoholic? Now they don't want to check my belongings? Every treatment center did it. They didn't know what you could be sneaking in. It was regular protocol, wasn't it?*

Sam shrugged; this place was bizarre for sure. He shoved his hands into his pockets and began looking around. The floor was a worn cherry hardwood and creaked with every step, the rooms had flowered wallpaper and resembled something right out of a 60s-style magazine. Framed oil paintings lined the walls and an artistic modeling of a ballerina was displayed above a cozy stone fireplace. Fresh purple orchids in every room made the place smell like a garden. It wasn't like the centers he was used to; those felt more like cold, crowded institutions. This place reminded Sam of some of the cottages back in England. It had a homey feel to it.

"Nice place you've got here."

Charlie was getting some paperwork out from a desk.

"Yeah, thanks. It's not the Ritz, but it's home."

Sam continued to wander around the room at the front of the home, taking note of the photos on the mantel above the fireplace. They were small frames holding memories of family, visitors, and one that looked like Charlie when he was younger. He was holding a fishing rod and a tiny girl stood beside him, presumably Hailey. In another, Hailey was hugging an older lady who resembled her. The dining room was directly off to the right with a large table that could have sat ten people. It was connected to the kitchen, with a hole in the wall for serving. Through the hole Sam could see Hailey puttering around in the kitchen.

Distracted by her, he didn't notice Charlie come up beside him.

"If you want to come this way, I just need you to sign off on a few papers and then I'll give you a quick medical."

Sam followed him through to a small study in the back. Charlie went around one side of the desk. On the wall was a stuffed deer's head; the rest of the room was taken up with bookshelves.

"Please. Take a seat." Charlie indicated to the leather chair.

"Did you?" Sam motioned with his head towards the deer.

"No, it was a gift."

"Quite the gift."

Charlie pulled out a clipboard and paper. After asking a number of questions, he came around with a blood pressure cuff and slipped it on Sam's arm.

Sam felt it tighten.

"So how long have you been acting?" Charlie said, continuing to pump air into the cuff and then releasing the pressure.

"Too long."

"You say it as if it's a curse."

Sam didn't reply.

"Well, you're one hundred and five resting when it should be around seventy-four. How long have you not been sleeping?"

"Nine months. Maybe twelve. I only get around four or five hours."

Charlie gave him some natural medication to help with the high blood pressure and detox. Sam pretended to swallow but simply rolled the pill under his tongue, something he'd become accustomed to doing with ease. Charlie finished off by taking his temperature and checking his vital signs. As he sat watching Charlie go through a series of tests, he couldn't believe he was back in treatment. It felt like a joke; a pointless endeavor. Never once had he managed to avoid relapsing.

Restless, Sam tapped his fingers against the arm of the chair. "Do you think we can speed this up? I'm kind of feeling tired."

Charlie raised his eyebrow.

"How long has it been since your last drink?"

"Couple of hours ago."

Charlie unwrapped the blood pressure cuff from Sam's arm and put it away. He went to the door and called out to Hailey to come and show Sam to his room. Sam straightened up as Hailey arrived. Charlie leaned against his desk, observing him.

"Sam, we only have one rule here. We work on a trust basis. We trust you want to get well and you trust that we can help you. Now, I can go through your luggage and remove the bottle or you can remove it. But I'm going to leave that decision with you." He studied Sam for a moment. "Now, having said that, if you don't want to get well, then we're wasting our time, in which case ... well, you know ..."

The comment completely caught him off guard. He could decide? Wasn't someone going to strong-arm his or her way in? He'd been so used to the same routine when entering; the luggage searches, the restrictions. Were they really going to make it this easy? He wasn't sure how to reply; instead, he turned to Hailey and indicated he was ready. She led him out. He collected his belongings and followed her up the winding staircase.

"How long is your stay?"

"Long enough."

She looked surprised.

"Well, you should like it here."

Sam exhaled. "Yeah, that's what my manager said."

"What?"

"Doesn't matter."

At the top of the stairs there were three rooms off to the left and three to the right side of the hallway. She led him to the right and opened a door into a quaint bedroom. There were two single beds with bedside tables, and a large patio window that brightly lit up the room and gave a clear view of the lake, barn, and lush green hills surrounding the property. Hailey held the door open as Sam stepped in. The décor wasn't much better than the rest of the house, which appeared to be frozen in time. Flowered-patterned walls, flowered duvet covers, and another vase full of them; someone sure had a thing for orchids. The whole place had a rundown retirement home vibe to it.

Sam glanced around the room, dropped his bags, and then looked at the two singles.

"Guests used to share rooms but things haven't exactly been busy around here as of late."

She opened the patio doors that led out to a beautiful balcony and stepped outside. A moist gust of air blew in, carrying the smell of the country. The sun was beginning to drop behind the trees and the sky was streaked with different shades of fiery red and orange.

"They say we may be in for some rough weather over the next couple of days. You might want to close the shutters just in case; we had to repair a whole bunch that flew off after the last hurricane hit the east coast. There's no telling when it's liable to hit us."

Sam nodded.

Hailey stepped back in and closed the door behind her. She pushed her hands in her back pockets.

"Well, supper is at seven. The TV, Internet, and phone are all working and the washroom and shower is down the hall. You'll be sharing."

Sam furrowed his brow. "Sharing? I thought you said I was the only guest."

"Well, you and Albert, but don't worry, he has his own room down the hall. And he tends to keep to himself."

"Right."

Hailey motioned towards the door. "So, I better go. I'll be your cook tonight. In fact, I'll be your cook while you're here, as well as a million other things."

"Right," he said.

She waited, wondering if he was going to add anything else. There was an awkward moment of silence and then Hailey turned to leave.

Sam went to close the door behind her. For a brief second he noticed the door at the other end of the corridor was slightly ajar. It shut abruptly, as if the occupant didn't want to make it obvious that they were eavesdropping. Albert, he figured. Sam closed his door and began kneading his forehead; he could feel another headache coming on.

He spat the pill he'd rolled under his tongue into his hand and pocketed it. He moved over to the bed and flung his suitcase on top. Pulling out a phone, he speed-dialed a number. As he waited, he unzipped the bag and flipped it open. He began pushing his clothes aside until he found it. Unzipping an inside pocket, he pressed a button on the handle and took it out. A deep sense of relief washed over him as a bottle of Jack Daniel's emerged. In and out of facilities he had always found a way to keep it hidden when they did their searches. The first couple of times they found it, not because it was visible but because they could hear it sloshing around. That only happened once. He found a simple way to keep it out of view and keep it quiet. He'd had a suitcase custom made. Padding, soundproofed. When you had money, getting what you wanted was never an issue. It worked like a charm.

"Hello?" the sound of a women's voice on the other end interrupted.

"Hey, Jules."

"Sam? I told you not to ring."

"I know, I just … I need to talk to him."

"Look, we've already had this conversation. He doesn't want to."

The line went dead. Sam pushed his fingers through his hair and scratched the back of his head. A feeling of sadness swept over him, a pain that he'd become too accustomed to. He sat down and stared at the bottle. He remembered what Charlie said. But Charlie didn't understand. How could he ever understand?

His hands trembled as he twisted the cap off. He grabbed a plastic cup from the nightstand and watched as the golden liquid poured in. His mouth watered. The aroma was invigorating, like taking in a deep breath of fresh air after being stuck inside for weeks. He knew what it meant. The first one was always fresh and sweet. He leaned back

on the bed and knocked it back like water. Making himself
comfortable among the pillows, he relished the warm wave
of relaxation as it washed through him. He looked down
and noticed his hands had stopped trembling.

CHAPTER SEVEN

An hour later, Hailey was finishing preparing supper. Steam spiraled upwards above the stove. The whirring sound of the fan blended with the mellow jazz music that she'd put on. A large gust of wind blew through as Charlie came in from outside. He slammed the door forcefully and scraped his feet on the bristled mat.

Yanking off his coat, he hung it on the hook. "I'm going to need to pick up some extra protection for the windows tomorrow."

Hailey gave him a passing glance and then set three plates on the table and a forth on the side.

"It smells good, Hay."

Charlie had called her that ever since she was little. The only time he referred to her by her full name was if he was serious. In a town where most were farmers, dealing in farm animals and bails of hay, it had given her no end of grief. Children could be so mean. A shiver ran down her spine as she replayed the numerous events in her mind.

She emptied the potatoes into a strainer and shook them. "Dad, why was it that I was the last one to know about our guest?"

Charlie slipped into a pair of slippers.

"You were already gone by the time I got the phone call."

He went to the table and snatched a piece of steaming hot broccoli out of a bowl.

"So what's the deal?"

"Let's just call it a mutual agreement. We scratch their back, they scratch ours."

"Dad."

Charlie took a seat at the table and pretended not to hear. He switched on the TV, but he wasn't going to weasel out of this one that easily. Hailey switched it off and stood in front of it with her one hand on her hip.

"Hay, c'mon, I wanted to see if there's been an update in the weather."

"What's the agreement?"

Charlie hemmed and hawed and looked flustered for a minute. Finally he said, "They promised to give us a tidy sum of money and a bag load of referrals if we promised to take him on for two weeks."

"What? Two weeks?" She looked flabbergasted. "We'll be lucky if we can scratch the surface in thirty days, but two weeks?"

"Hay, you sell yourself short. You've been doing this long enough and I have every bit of confidence you'll do a great job."

She raised her hands. "Hold on, back up the truck. You are planning on making some calls to the team? Aren't you?"

Charlie glanced up at her and began buttering a roll. "Already tried. They're no longer available."

Hailey groaned.

"Hay, you can't expect them to hold on after all this time."

"We paid them in advance."

"Three months, Hay, not a year."

Hailey emitted an exasperated sigh.

"Well, what about the anniversary?"

"I haven't forgotten, Hailey, but we need this. And anyway, we can't just keep putting things off at this time every year."

She shook her head, unsure of what to say next.

"If you knew we'd have to do this alone, why take him in?"

Charlie paused for a moment as he added another pat of butter.

"Have you seen those bills piling up?" He pointed with his butter knife towards the side where stacks of envelopes were stashed. "As much as I appreciate you pulling shifts at Maggie's, we're barely scraping by and anyway ..." he trailed off before mumbling the next few remaining words, "they won't take him in anywhere else."

Hailey gave a confused look. "Come again?"

Charlie scooped a few vegetables onto his plate.

He coughed. "No other facility will touch him."

She laughed. "Oh, c'mon, you're telling me not even one?"

"I'm serious, Hailey, surely you've read the tabloids."

"I don't read that trash."

"Well, good or bad, he's our responsibility now."

She wiped her hand across her forehead. "Oh great, so

we've got a lunatic on our hands and two weeks to make him clean and sober."

Charlie smiled while nodding.

"I'm not interrupting, am I?"

Hailey spun around, startled at the sound of his voice.

Sam was standing at the entranceway to the kitchen. His eyes moved back and forth between them.

"Have you been there long?" she asked.

His eyes met hers. "Long enough." He gave a half smile.

Hailey could feel herself becoming flushed as she wondered how much of their conversation he'd heard, especially the part about being a lunatic.

"Come on in, Sam, take a seat." Charlie gestured towards the chair to the left of him. Sam sat down.

Hailey turned and served up some salmon, hot veggies, and mashed potatoes and then excused herself, taking the full plate with her.

Charlie watched her go, then pointed to the two pitchers on the table.

"So what will it be? Lemonade or water?"

"Lemonade's fine."

Charlie reached for the jug and poured some into Sam's glass. As Sam lifted the glass to take a drink, he noticed Charlie watching him intently.

"I see your jitters have gone."

Sam paused, looked at his hand, and then at Charlie. Then he raised his eyebrows and pretended to act surprised.

"How about that?"

"Yes." Charlie's eyes narrowed as he continued studying him. "Go ahead, help yourself."

Outside, the sound of the wind was beginning to get loud. The jingling of wind chimes and the knocking of the shutters broke the silence as Sam reached for the bowl of potatoes and took a few scoops.

"Sounds like it's getting pretty bad out there."

"Ah, this is mild," Charlie replied.

A couple of minutes passed and Hailey returned without the plate. She took a place at the table across from Sam. She was no longer wearing the apron. Her hair was pinned up with a clip with only a few strands hanging down. He snuck a few glances at her as she slid some fish onto her plate. Her features were gentle and soft. She wore little makeup but it didn't seem to matter.

Sam turned to Charlie. "If you don't mind me asking. When I came in earlier, you said I wasn't an alcoholic. Isn't that kind of counterintuitive to what you do here? I mean, isn't that the first step? Admitting?"

Charlie wiped the corner of his mouth with a napkin and set it down. "Sam, obviously you can tell we do things slightly different here. I know you've been told by other places that you have a disease, you're powerless, and the best you can do is manage it. But we don't ascribe to that way of thinking."

"I'm confused."

"What my father is trying to say is that we don't deal in steps and we don't cure people here. We assist you in curing yourself."

"Cure? I can't cure this. As much as I hate the other places, at least they had that right."

"Right, once an addict always an addict," Charlie said.

"Yeah."

"Relapse is part of recovery."

"You got it," Sam replied.

"Both untrue."

"What?"

"Sam, those beliefs are part of why you continue to relapse. You take another drink and you convince yourself you're on that road to recovery."

"Well, aren't I?"

"You tell me," he said. "How's that working for you?"

There was a moment of silent tension.

"What, so you're better than them?"

"Not better." He shook his head. "Just different."

"If you don't mind me saying, sounds like a lot of woo-woo to me."

Hailey placed her cutlery down abruptly, causing Sam to look up as he was about to take another bite. His gaze was steady on hers.

"Hey, I don't mean any offense, I'm just not used to this," Sam said.

"Few are," Charlie added.

"Listen, I just want to get through this time and get out of here." He nodded.

"No one is holding you here, Sam. Though I'm pretty sure the consequences don't exactly look good if you leave," Hailey added.

Sam stared at them. As much as he wanted to pack his stuff and leave, they were right. He'd only be shooting his own foot off.

All at once the lights went out.

A few seconds passed and then the sound of the generator churned as it kicked in and the lights came back up. They flickered and went out again.

Charlie stood up. "I'm going to check on the generator."

Hailey started to rise. "I'll come help."

Charlie dismissed the offer with a wave as he turned towards the door. "I'll be right back."

The only light came from the moon as she fumbled around in the dark searching for some candles in one of the kitchen drawers.

"Need a hand?"

"I need some matchsticks. They're up in the cupboard behind you."

Sam flipped on his phone, using it like a mini flashlight. He carefully navigated his way over and felt around the cabinet until he retrieved the box of matches. Hailey lit up a few white candles and placed them around the kitchen. Their flickering amber light cast shadows on the walls. Sam took a seat back at the table and watched Hailey push back the curtains and peer out. In the illuminated glow he studied her, until she noticed he was looking.

"Your father. How long has he been doing this?"

Hailey moved back across the room and sat down.

"Ever since I was a child. I grew up here."

"And your mother?"

For a moment Hailey looked away.

"She was a dancer, she passed away a couple of years back."

"I'm sorry."

She took a sip from her glass and set it back on the table. Sam waited to see if she would add anything further but she didn't. They continued to eat in silence until Charlie returned.

CHAPTER EIGHT

A fter supper they joined her father out on the porch, where they drank tea.

"So, how did you get into acting, Sam?"

"Theater mainly. I like to say my sister dragged me into it, but I guess it was just meant to be. I followed her along to a few auditions, mainly to watch her. One thing led to another and I landed a part. I haven't stopped since."

"Must be tough."

"What?"

"Being in the spotlight and whatnot."

"Ah, it has its perks."

"And downfalls?"

Sam met his eyes before turning away. He wasn't an idiot; he knew the moment he stepped on that property it had begun. They loved to size you up. Rehab centers were all the same. They had a knack for getting under your skin, no matter how they tried disguising their method of operation.

In his mind this place was no different. Sure, they were odd. But there was always a loophole, something they would have overlooked. It wouldn't take him long to figure out their game.

He'd been aware of Hailey observing him throughout the evening. She was quiet and only seemed to speak when Charlie asked her what she thought.

"So help me out here. If you don't adhere to a program of steps, what treatment do you follow?" Sam asked.

"You'll see," Charlie said, taking a sip of his tea.

Feeling a little uncomfortable being there, Sam excused himself.

"Well, it's been a long day. If you don't mind, I'm going to turn in."

Sam got up to retreat into the house. Hailey moved her legs so he could pass, and he glanced at her as he walked by her.

"See you bright and early at seven a.m.," she said.

"That early?" This was starting to sound like boot camp.

"You'll get in the swing of it soon enough."

"Right," he said, unconvinced. "Goodnight."

He left them out on the porch. He could hear them whispering once inside.

If tomorrow was to be anything like today, it was liable to be strange. Sam stopped at the top of the staircase and glanced down the hall. Outside one of the doors was a serving tray with an empty plate and glass. He wondered about the man who apparently was beyond the door. If the place wasn't odd enough already, the mysterious Albert who hadn't shown his face yet wasn't only peculiar, but also kind of disconcerting. He could have sworn they had said they hadn't received anyone new in over two years. If that was the case, what was this guy doing here? Sam shook his head and went into his room.

He stood at the patio doors that overlooked the grounds and lake. The moon reflected off the lake, giving him a clear view of the water. It truly was a beautiful view. Sam breathed in deeply. He stretched out his arms behind his head, attempting to relieve the tension he felt in his body. His thoughts went back to Kate. What was he doing? Where was it all heading?

He sighed.

A few minutes had passed when he noticed a figure in the darkness moving towards the barn. A flashlight shone ahead of the person, slanting shafts of light into the pitch dark. A few seconds later a light come on from within the barn. Its amber light filtered through the gaps in the planks and flickered. He could hear the faint sound of music and see someone moving.

As he squinted to see who it was, his phone rang. He pulled it out, still trying to make out who was in the barn. He jabbed the front of his phone. It was Liam.

Finally, someone who was normal, if Liam could be classified as normal.

"Sammy boy."

"Liam."

"So where they got you penned up? I phoned Betty but they hung up on me."

"Typical. I'm in Walton."

"Where?"

"Ah, you don't even want to know. It's some backwoods town in upstate New York."

"Leave? It's never stopped you before."

"I wish."

"Don't tell me you are loving that group therapy, all that share your feelings crap?"

"They don't do that here, or at least I haven't seen signs of that yet. In fact, they don't look like they're the planning types from what I can tell."

"Are you serious?"

"Okay, get this. They don't check your bags, they don't refer to you as an alcoholic. It's truly bizarre." Sam reached over and poured himself another drink.

"Sounds perfect?" Liam said.

"I don't know, I have no clue what their idea of rehabilitation is. Hell, I'm the only guest here except for some guy who hasn't shown his face yet."

"You need anything?"

"Yeah, a get out jail card." He let out a laugh.

Sam leaned back on his bed and nursed his drink, giving Liam's question some thought.

"Think you could bring a few more bottles?"

Liam laughed.

"Oh, by the way, Liam. You heard from Kate?" Sam said, shifting the conversation to what had been niggling him.

Liam was silent for a moment.

"No, she's fallen off the radar at the moment, man. However, the good news is, the public seems to be siding with you over this. It's all over the Internet." He chuckled. "Let's just say she isn't exactly winning new fans."

"Well, that could change if they catch wind of where I am."

"Oh, don't worry, Eric has told them you are holed up with a friend, tending to a broken heart." He laughed.

"Liam," Sam said abruptly.

"Ah, c'mon, Sam, it's not like she meant anything to you, right?"

"God, you can be a dick sometimes."

"What?"

"Just remember to bring enough bottles. I'll talk to you later."

"Hold on. Hold on. You didn't say where you're staying."

Sam fished around in his pocket looking for the scrap of paper Eric had given him. Flustered and unable to find it, he said,

"Just ask for the Welland House, everyone knows it in town."

"Got it. Oh, and Sam, hang in there, buddy." Liam chuckled.

Sam rolled his eyes and disconnected. Staring at the wall, he wondered what Kate was thinking, what she was doing. Or better still, who was she with? He slapped the thought away and filled his cup with more bourbon, his thoughts circling back to Kate again. As crazy as it sounded and despite the photos, he still wanted to give her the benefit of the doubt. But she wasn't exactly helping herself by not calling.

The effects of the alcohol were starting to kick in. Like ambient waves of music rolling over him, the liquid lulled him into a drunken stupor and crowded out the noise and the pain inside that was showing its face again. Slowly but surely his eyes began to close.

* * * * *

On the second floor in the room directly above, Hailey

stepped out of the shower. A pile of soaking wet clothes lay heaped in the corner of the room. She wrapped herself in a warm towel and tiptoed barefoot over to her closet. The hardwood floors creaked with each step she took. She slipped on a fuzzy robe, took a seat in front of the mirror, and began blow-drying her hair. Despite it having been a gorgeous summer, she noticed that she was looking pale, at least paler than he was. He had the California glow to him; either that or it was a fake tan. It probably didn't help that most of her waking hours were spent cooped up inside, working at Maggie's and not returning home until the sun had set.

She brushed her hair and clipped it up at the sides. She took a handful of moisturizer and rubbed it into her arms and face. Her thoughts had drifted to him studying her in the kitchen when the phone rang.

Cassie, she thought. She had completely forgotten to tell her. Then again she probably already knew, as even the tiniest bit of gossip spread like wildfire in this town.

Hailey snatched up her cell.

Without even a hello, Cassie began ranting. "Okay, so today I'm cutting Jillian's hair, you know, Tom's wife? Well, you are going to flip when I tell you what she told me. Are you ready?"

"Do I have a choice?"

"She said that she is seeing this guy in the city. Can you believe that?"

Hailey said nothing.

"Apparently she found out her husband has been seeing someone behind her back, so instead of leaving him, she's found her own. I asked her if she was going to leave him. She's like … are you kidding?"

"Uh-huh," Hailey answered.

"Hailey, are you channel-surfing again?"

"Is that the only news you've heard today?"

"Why?" She extended out the word slowly. God forbid she had been kept out of the loop.

"Oh, nothing," she feigned.

"Hailey?"

"Oh, it's nothing that would interest you." She smiled, knowing it would drive her crazy.

"Spill the beans."

"He's here."

"Oh God, you don't mean Tommy. I will slap your legs if you gave into his—"

"No, no." Hailey cut her off. "No, I mean ... Sam. Sam Reid."

Laughter erupted on the other end of the phone, once again causing Hailey to pull it away from her ear. If she kept this up she would be deaf before she was thirty. She gave it a moment, and it went quiet. For a second, Hailey thought she had hung up on her. No such luck.

"WHAT?" she yelled so loud Hailey had to once again pull the phone away from her ear. "Hailey Marie Welland, if you are telling me a fib I'm going to do a number on your hair next time you come in."

Hailey laughed. "I'm serious. He's right below me."

"Wow, that's fast even for you."

"NO. I mean in the room below."

"I told you your Prince Charming would come along. C'mon, tell me I was right."

"He's a patient and not your regular kind. From what I'm told he's been kicked out of every other treatment center. No one will have him."

"You're kidding."

Hailey took a sip of her sleepy herbal tea that had now gone practically cold.

"So what's he like?"

Hailey pondered the question. "I'll let you know in two weeks."

"What's he taking?"

"You know I can't go into that. It's confidential."

"It's cocaine, isn't it? They all do it."

Hailey remained tight-lipped.

"Well, okay, at least tell me this. Is he as hot in person as he is in the movies?"

"Yes, Cassie, he's everything and more." She just wanted to move on from the topic; the idea of thinking of a patient as hot wasn't a thought she wanted to entertain. Everything to do with him had to be treated professionally, she told herself. She wasn't in the habit of flirting with patients and she wasn't going to start now, even if he was ... Before she could finish the thought, Cassie interrupted.

"I knew it! I'm coming over tomorrow."

"You can't be doing that."

"What, you get to ogle and keep him all to yourself?"

"He's not a toy, Cassie."

"I know, I know. But you can't fault a girl for wanting to play."

"Listen, if Sam is okay with it, we'll drop by the salon. How's that?"

"Phone before you come. I don't want to look like I've been dragged through a bush backwards when he arrives."

Hailey wasn't sure he would even be up for it, or even if her father would allow it. By the time treatment got under-way, few patients felt like traipsing through a town and overhearing the whispering gossip; never mind a big-time celeb.

"We'll see."

"Don't you forget."

"I said we'll see."

Cassie continued to mutter to herself about what she would wear and what she would ask him. Hailey rolled her eyes. Cassie was in a world of her own. Hailey flipped on the TV and as always began her nightly routine.

CHAPTER NINE

When morning came, the driving high winds had almost died down, giving way to a warm sun that peeked through an overcast sky. Hailey had been up for several hours, getting in her morning run. She listened to the world around her. The squawking of the American bitterns and ducks out on the lake surrounded her. The roads were empty and for the most part they would stay that way. In a few hours the place would come alive as locals went about their lives, but unless you lived in the area, you would imagine people rarely went out. She ran along the winding roads, occasionally switching it up and taking in the soft ground found in the trails that crossed through the fields to give her knees a rest from the hard streets. Despite her father's dislike of her choice to run alone, she always felt safe. Walton was a safe place to raise a family. Running allowed her to be alone with her thoughts. It was meditative and gave her that boost of energy for whatever the day would bring. She couldn't imagine running with anyone, talking, or even listening to music. She loved to watch the sunrise and take in the peace and solitude of nature.

Hailey remembered the morning her mother bought her first pair of running shoes. Initially she put up a resistance to the idea of running. Who in their right mind ran, unless they were being chased? Eventually she'd succumbed to her mother's pleas and joined her in the mornings. Over time, she caught the bug. Some folks referred to it as a natural high, a euphoria that only came from running consistently.

As she cut through trees and across the small wooden bridge that separated their property from the surrounding woodland, she glanced at the stream, noticing it was flowing faster than usual. She slowed into a jog as she came up on the house.

Outside, she took a breather, wiped the sweat from her brow with her forearm, and pulled her sweat-drenched top away from her body. Breathing fast, she bent over and placed her hands on her knees. She looked up at the house to see if the high winds had caused any damage; thankfully, everything was still intact. The winds were still high, but not as blustery as the previous day. But there was an uneasy tension in the air, as if Mother Nature had only given them a glimpse of what was about to come down the pipeline.

Scanning the house, she saw the curtains were still drawn in the guest room. She shot a glance at her watch: 7:15 a.m. Unlike other places, they had never followed a strict regime. They treated each person on an individual basis, depending on how they responded to treatment. Patients would go through a series of therapeutic sessions in order to uncover and heal the underlying cause of their dependency.

She wondered for a second how difficult Sam Reid really could be. What could he possibly have done that was so awful that centers wouldn't take him in? No doubt she would find out soon enough.

"M ... M ... Morning, Hailey."

She turned her head and saw Albert walking across the yard. He was a burly man who had been with their family since Hailey was seven, a Vietnam veteran who'd suffered a traumatic brain injury. Most would have assumed he wasn't smart because he stuttered and was slow to respond to questions. But Hailey knew that wasn't the case. He knew more about the world and life than anyone. His room was full of books and when he wasn't working his head was buried in one.

He was the type of man that worked hard and kept to himself. Their property was huge and continually needed maintenance. In the summer, you could start on one side of the house mowing the grass and by the time you had completed the other side, it was time to begin again.

"Hey." Hailey nodded, letting out a lungful of air, completely out of breath.

Still moving he continued, "I ... I ... hear, w ...w ... we have a new guest?"

Hailey looked back up at Sam's window before turning back to Albert.

"Don't remind me."

Albert smiled, shaking his head.

* * * * *

Hailey went inside and grabbed some orange juice out of the fridge. Charlie was seated at the table, paper open and sipping a hot cup of coffee.

"Morning, Hay."

Hailey swallowed a large gulp of juice and replied, "Is he not up yet?"

Charlie raised an eyebrow and glanced at her before returning to what he was reading. She took another pull on her drink and then placed it in the sink.

Let the games begin, she told herself.

She bounded up the stairs, skipping steps as she went; she was pumped with energy and raring to go, like an athlete who had just done their pre–warm-up. When she reached his door, she hesitated for a moment, wondering if maybe it was better to just wait. The thought lasted only a few seconds before she knocked. There was no reply. She gave it another hard thump; still no answer. She bit the side of her lip and turned to leave, but instead she turned back and entered the room.

Inside it was completely dark. The curtains blocked out all the light, making it difficult to see. She made her way over to the far end and threw them open. Light flooded in like someone had flipped on a switch. In a heap under the duvet there was a groan. An arm came out, grabbed the corner of the pillow, and dragged it over disheveled hair.

"Rise and shine! Time to get up."

He let out a muffled sound beneath the covers.

It was then Hailey spotted the empty bottle of Jack Daniel's beside his bed. She sighed, shook her head, and grabbed it up. She held it at waist level and dropped it into the trash can in order to create noise. The sound caused him to stir but not enough to reveal his face. He was buried beneath the duvet with only one bare foot sticking out. She left the room and returned a few moments later with a small bucket of ice. Dragging a chair over to the end of his bed, she set the ice on top. She lifted his foot and dropped it into the pail. The moment it disappeared beneath the icy cubes, he let out a yell. His foot flew upwards, sending the pail of ice cubes with it. He swung back the covers, his eyes wide open as if he had been given an electric shock.

"What the hell was that?"

"Oh." She feigned surprised. "You don't take it with ice? My bad."

He lifted his hands and pulled a face. "What?"

"Five minutes, by the lake. Wear something comfortable." She turned to leave, then spun back on her heels.

"And ... you might want to put some underwear on." She pointed down.

With a confused expression he glanced down. Quickly he covered his exposed cheek. With that she turned, grinned to herself, and walked out.

* * * * *

Thirty minutes later, Sam emerged from the house. Dressed in a body-hugging white T-shirt and sweatpants, he took a deep breath and held it in. With his arms stretched out he felt the tension in his muscles ease. The morning sun was already beating down, browning the tips of the grass and creating a blinding glare to everything in his vision. He cupped his hand above his eyes before the sun retreated behind a dark, ominous cloud. In the distance he could see Hailey beside the glistening water. Making his way over to the shoreline, he swatted at mosquitoes that attacked his arms and wondered what she'd planned. If it was anything like the last six treatment centers, he would likely be assigned a long list of chores, group therapy, and lectures. Yet it was nothing short of boredom and hours of mind-numbing psychobabble.

A warm breeze swept across his face as he got closer, bringing with it the scent of fresh-cut grass and the sound of water lapping. It immediately took him back to growing up in the countryside in the south of England, a memory that had been lost through the years of living in the smog-filled city of LA. Arriving, he noticed two blue mats were rolled out. A pair of sneakers was off to one side, and Hailey was going through a series of downright sexy stretching. *Now I could get used to this,* he thought. She wore dark black, three-quarter-length running bottoms and a black tank top with a band of aqua blue around it. Everything about it showed off how fit and firm her figure was. She wasn't skinny but she definitely looked healthy.

Hearing him approach, she turned then looked at her watch.

"So what are we doing here?" he muttered unenthusiastically.

Sliding her feet back into her sneakers, she said, "There is a Chinese proverb that says 'A journey of a thousand miles begins with the first step.'" She began rolling up her mat. "This, Hollywood, is the beginning of your journey towards healing."

"Tangling myself up like a pretzel?" he asked. "Doesn't sound like recovery."

She shot a glance back. "And neither does drinking a bottle of Jack Daniel's."

"Yeah, about that."

"I didn't tell my father, if that's what you're thinking."

He watched her with curiosity as she continued rolling her mat.

"Thank you."

Not responding, she simply put the mat under her arm and walked past him.

Sam whirled around, confused.

"I thought?" He motioned towards the edge of the water.

Hailey stopped in her tracks and looked over her shoulder. She glanced down at her watch again, making it painfully obvious before she headed off in the direction of the house.

Sam frowned. "What? Aren't we going to begin?"

"We already have," she hollered back.

Confused and frustrated, he kicked the dirt beneath him, picked up a few loose stones, and skimmed them out across the surface of the lake. He cast a glance over his shoulder, watching her as she disappeared into the house. He wasn't sure what to make of that. Why an earth would his manager send him here? They clearly had no idea how to treat addiction. Not that he had any intention of taking any of it seriously. And what was up with this girl? He inwardly groaned. Any other place and he'd be gone by now. But something was different this time.

He threw another stone across the lake.

It wasn't the consequences of leaving that weighed heavily on his mind. At this stage a jail cell couldn't be much worse than being confined to this place. No, he really wasn't sure what was keeping him here. Curiosity, perhaps?

CHAPTER TEN

"Two weeks is not long enough," Hailey shot back.
"Day one and you want to give up? You worry too
much."

Charlie was fiddling with the radio, tuning it to the local
station.

"I didn't say that," she replied as she buttered a piece of
toast and spread jam on it. "It's just ..."

"Just what?"

She huffed and changed the topic. "Are you going into
town today?"

"Why?"

"I need the truck fixed. It's still sitting outside Maggie's.
If you can deal with that, I'll take the next session with
him."

"Listen, why don't you go into town and take him with
you?"

"By him, you mean ... Sam?"

"Who else would I be referring to?"

"Are you serious?"

"Trust me."

"What about the process?"

"Ah, to hell with the process. I want to try something different this time. Get to know him. Observe him. Get under his skin. Find out what makes him tick."

Hailey raised her eyebrows in disbelief. Before she could reply, the sound of the front door creaking open was Hailey's signal to leave.

"Oh, and when you're there I could use a few more items from the hardware store. I want to be ready this time."

He scribbled on a scrap of paper and handed it to her. She cast a glance outside.

"Seems fairly calm to me."

Charlie raised his hand. "Shush," he said, as he tried to hear the local radio station's weather update. A few moments later he switched it off. "Looks as though we are going to get hit even harder. They're expecting a category four hurricane."

Hailey took the breakfast tray Charlie had prepared off the side.

"I'll take that up."

Charlie gave a sly smile of amusement.

"What?" Hailey smiled back as she walked out with a tray in her hand.

She passed Sam in the hallway as he came in. Their eyes locked for a brief moment. Sam looked steadily at her as if he was about to say something, but neither of them spoke; instead, Hailey looked away, not wanting to prolong the moment, and disappeared upstairs.

"I get the feeling your daughter doesn't like me," Sam said as he entered the kitchen.

"Ah, it's not you." Charlie grinned. "It's just the entire male population."

"Oh, that's a relief." He returned the smile. "I think."

"Coffee?" Charlie extended a cup.

"Yeah, thanks." Sam took it and sat down at the breakfast table.

Charlie set a plate of crepes, fresh fruit, and a bowl of granola with yogurt on the table.

"Help yourself."

"So what's the plan for today?"

Charlie leaned back against the sink. "Well, I'd like you to head into town with Hailey. She's got a few errands to run. If you don't mind, could you tag along?"

Sam shrugged. "Sure."

Truth was, anything was better than being stuck here. They hadn't mentioned meetings but no doubt if he didn't go he would likely be stuffed in a meeting or lumbered with some form of cleaning-up task.

"And Sam. Probably best you don't mention what I said."

"Mention what?" He grinned.

* * * * *

Hailey slipped behind the wheel of her father's truck and brought it to life. Beside her Sam snapped in his seat belt. As they rolled out, she switched on the radio. She could sense him looking at her, as if waiting to see if they would talk. The ride into town was short but long enough to make her feel uncomfortable. The thought of conversation after their morning was the furthest thing from her mind. Country music broke the silence, some sappy song; she changed the station only to land another. Eventually, she settled on an upbeat tune that didn't remind her of a past relationship gone wrong, her mother who had passed, or someone who had barely two cents to rub together.

The song had only been playing a few minutes when he leaned forward and changed the station. This time the music switched from country to rock. She shot him a sideways glance of disbelief. She changed it back. Seconds later he turned the dial back to the station he had it on.

"Problem with country?" she muttered.

"Can't stand it."

She gnawed on the inside of her cheek and then changed the station.

"Well, I like it."

That showed him, she thought.

No sooner had the thought passed than he switched it for a third time.

"Are you always this annoying?"

"Only when it comes to music and coffee," he said.

A few minutes passed on the song pretending to be music. It ended only to be replaced by a Lady Antebellum tune.

He began tapping his fingers and feet to the rhythm of the music while gazing out his window. She gave him a confused look and smiled.

"I thought you didn't like country."

"Well, I like this tune."

"What? This is country."

"Well, not exactly. It's borderline. You know, one of those artists that kind of crosses over into mainstream. Taylor Swift, Keith Urban … those types."

"Yeah. Country."

"No, country is that horrific, um …" He paused, as if trying to find the words. Instead, he began mimicking with a deep southern drawl a few lines from a Clint Black song.

Hailey let out a deep belly laugh.

"For someone who doesn't like country, you sure know the lyrics well."

He stopped, tilted his head, and gave a sarcastic smile. They were getting closer to town.

"So where we heading first?" He quickly changed the topic.

"The garage."

"You sound as if that's a bad thing."

"Well, the last guy I dated works there. It's not exactly where I want to be going but the nearest garage is further than I want to travel. Oh, and just a forewarning, please excuse what an ass he is."

"Hey, I can always do the work on it."

She gave a surprised sideways glance. "You're a mechanic, Hollywood?"

"No, but I've tinkered with a few cars in my time. I even have my own custom-built 1966 Chevrolet Corsa."

"How far did you get with that?"

He mumbled something under his breath.

She grinned.

"What was that?"

He threw his arms up. "What? I didn't have time. It's still in the garage."

"Don't you mean, still in the box?"

He smiled.

* * * * *

They pulled up in front of a garage that was part gas station and part wrecker's yard. A red and white rusting sign hung over the top. The words "Farlan's Auto" were emblazed into it, giving it a vintage look. Dirty water-filled glass lightbulbs hung above it and tires were piled up outside in columns, looking as if they hadn't been moved in years. Both of the garage doors were open. Vehicles were up on lifts and several mechanics were working away. One of them looked up at the shrill of the gas station bell. A young teen was filling up gas when they got out. He glanced over and gave a quick nod.

The same guy he'd seen at the diner the day before was coming out of the office. He wore blue overalls with one sleeve rolled up, and was wiping black grime from his hands with a dirty rag.

When they approached him, he shot a quick glance over at Sam.

"Hey, Hailey."

Hailey gave a brief nod. "Tommy."

"Wanted to take me up on my offer?" He gave a smug grin.

"Really? No."

Tommy spat a mouthful of chewing tobacco off to his right. Sam cringed. Could anything be more disgusting than spitting huge wads of brown goop all day? Tommy wiped the corner of his mouth with the same dirty rag.

"So what brings you in?"

"The truck. It's outside Maggie's. Can you pick it up and let me know the cost to fix it?"

"Sure, I can do that." His eyes darted back and forth between them as if he was trying to make a connection. He gave a nod in the direction of Sam. "Who's this?"

Hailey turned to Sam and then back, gesturing with her hand.

"Sam Reid—Tommy Farlan."

"I would offer you my hand, but you know."

Tommy showed both hands covered in grease.

Hailey handed him the keys, but as he took them he held on to her hand for a moment longer.

"So when can I take you out again?" He looked at Sam as if trying to make a point. Meanwhile, Hailey pulled her hand away.

"Give it a rest, Tommy."

The smug grin faded from his face before he chewed some more and spat again, this time slightly closer to Sam's feet. Sam's eyes dropped before returning a steadfast gaze. The whole incident made Sam feel as if he was rehearsing for a part in some corny western. Any minute now they would be drawing guns. He smirked, finding the whole moment too funny to take seriously.

"Right. I'll send one of the boys over and we'll be in touch."

As they drove away, Sam could tell she looked bothered by the whole interaction with Tommy. Even slightly embarrassed.

"Sorry about that. He doesn't let up. I know in some strange part of his brain, he thinks I'm still interested, but I'm not."

"Seems that way."

She glanced sideways at him.

"Do you have any annoying exes that you try to avoid bumping into?"

"Only a few, mainly the ones that spit tobacco."

She laughed. "I would like to see that."

CHAPTER ELEVEN

A s they drove through the main street, the morning sun was still attempting to forge its way through the clouds that masked what was left of the blue in an eerie-looking dark gray sky. Hailey rolled down her window, only to be met by a humid gust of wind that lifted papers her father had left on the dashboard up in the air. She quickly wound the window up, trying to catch her breath.

"The calm before the storm."

"What's that?"

"It's what my father is always harping on about. You can always tell when a storm is coming. Dark rolling clouds appear on the horizon, everything goes quiet, birds stop singing, and the air becomes calm. Nothing more than wind."

Sam turned his phone on and tilted towards her.

"Myself, I've always relied on the weather network."

She chuckled, shaking her head.

Hailey reached over and switched the air conditioning on. A cool gust of air rushed in, providing instant relief to both of them from the claustrophobic humidity. Moments later, they pulled up in front of the general hardware store.

"I have to get a few items for the house. Shouldn't be more than a few minutes."

"Can I give you a hand?"

"Sure."

When they exited the store, Hailey was juggling a bag of nails while Sam brought out the corrugated shutter protectors over the top of his head. After setting them down in the back of the truck, he wiped a bead of sweat from his forehead.

"I kind of get the feeling I should have stayed on the west coast."

"You've never been close to a hurricane?" Hailey sounded surprised.

"Nope."

In the past few years the country had witnessed its fair share of devastation and yet Sam had always been lucky enough to be either outside of or on the other side of the country.

"You're in for a treat then," she added sarcastically.

She nodded towards a store a little further down.

"Speaking of treats. They do the best ice cream in town. What do you say?"

Sam raised his eyebrows. "Sure, why not."

The air outside was warm and humid and despite the blustery weather, his shirt stuck uncomfortably to his back. As they walked down the street, Hailey gazed casually into a few of the windows and then looked back.

"Being an actor, you must get to travel a lot?"

"I live out of a suitcase."

"What's it like?"

"A lot of hotel rooms, bad food, and people following you."

"Sounds like you don't like it."

"Ah, I can't complain, I could be digging a ditch. It's the busy schedule that can wear you down."

"I guess I should take back those shovels I just bought." A wistful smile danced across her lips.

Sam chuckled. "What about you?"

"What?"

"Have you traveled much?"

"No," she said softly. He could sense she was a little embarrassed replying.

"Well, it's not all that it's made out to be. A lot of hype," he said, hoping to not make her feel as if she was missing out.

"I would love to see Europe."

"Europe?"

"Yeah, Amsterdam, Paris, Rome," she said. "I've always wanted to go."

"I think you would love it. Restaurants are open all through the night. Paris is something else. Mussels in garlic butter at midnight, wine and good conversation until the early hours of the morning, and watching some guy running around with a beer box on his head and nothing but his underwear on. Yep, you could say it's good."

"A guy in his underwear with a box on his head?"

He chuckled. "Yeah, I think it was his stag night."

"You hope." She grinned.

They continued to walk down the street. He became so caught up in seeing what stores lined the other side of the street that he didn't notice Hailey had stopped a few stores back. He turned and walked back to her. She was staring into a clothing store. Inside the front window was a revolving mannequin with an incredible strawberry-colored evening dress on it. It was strapless, had a low-cut back with a diamond design, and dazzling beaded embellishments on the front.

"A favorite store of yours?"

She was mesmerized by it.

"Have always loved this dress."

"Always?"

"It's been on display for the past year." She turned and smiled. "Things don't move fast in this town. Besides, not exactly a lot of places to go out and have a nice dinner. If you know what I mean."

"Why haven't you bought it?"

She scoffed. "Did you see the price tag?"

She walked away as he squinted through the glass—over two thousand dollars. It seemed odd, but he really hadn't given much thought to money, especially when he wanted something. If he saw something he like he just bought it. It wasn't as if his bank account was going to drain dry any time soon. Of course, there was a time he used to watch every cent he made. Waiting on tables, working in bars. Yeah—tips meant a lot back then. It dawned on him how much life had changed. He watched as she continued on ahead of him, her figure swaying, and he imagined for a moment what she would look like in it. *She would look amazing in that dress. Where did that come from?* he immediately thought. She looked back.

"Are you coming?"

He followed, deep in thought.

After they came out of the ice cream store, they took a seat on one of the benches and watched people stroll by. The warmth of the day was already making his ice cream drip down the side of his hand. Hailey handed him a napkin.

"Thanks."

"Sam, you never told me why other centers wouldn't take you in."

"You never asked."

She looked at him as if waiting for him to continue.

"Look, in all the time I've been in and out of these places"—he shook his head—"they've never once helped. They give you the spiel about ninety meetings in ninety days but everyone I know who's ever been there has fallen off the wagon, with or without those meetings. It's par for the course."

"That doesn't exactly tell me much."

He wiped the hand that was now practically covered in streams of ice cream.

"I get bored. Does that answer your question?"

She shook her head. "Bored?"

"Yeah, like thirty days is a long time to be stuck in one of those places. No TV, no Internet, no phone without their permission. Heck, you're stuck in meetings all day and listening to the same drab. All for what? To return months later? Please."

Hailey looked as if she was pondering what he was saying.

"Which reminds me. Why don't you follow the same format?"

She took a lick of her ice cream and then paused.

"I guess we got bored." She smiled.

He let out a laugh. There was something about her that

he liked; he couldn't quite put his finger on it. She was attractive, carefree, and had a relaxed attitude—that was, if she wasn't waking him with her Chinese torture games. He reflected on the morning's events with amusement.

She pursed her lips. "Okay, I have to ask you for a favor." He could tell she looked kind of embarrassed to ask. Her cheeks went a rosy red.

"Go on."

"I have this friend. And … I kind of said I would …" He could tell she was trying to find the words to say.

Finally, she blurted it out. "Well, I said we might drop in. She's kind of a big fan and she's liable to pester me to no end unless … I mean you don't have to—"

"Yes."

"Yes?"

"Yes it's okay. I didn't imagine I would fall off the radar for long. Even in a small town like this."

Her eyebrows rose. "Okay." She nodded, looking completely taken aback. Hailey motioned behind her shoulder. "Well, she works across the road. I have to warn you, though, she's a bit of a loon. Sorry."

"That's fine, I've met my fair share."

Suzie Q's was squeezed between Daisy's Bakery and a closed-down antique store. It had images of models sporting eighties hairstyles in the window, obviously displays they hadn't changed since it had opened. The bell shrilled as they entered. Sam put his sunglasses back on his head, resting them in his hair. Inside, there were two middle-aged women working on their clients' hair. One stylist had just finished placing an elderly lady under a hair dryer; the other lady was getting her hair washed. The look on their faces was priceless. It was like catching a deer in the headlights. He'd always enjoyed the humor of it all. It still amazed him that people got so enthralled by meeting someone who worked in film. He'd seen the look many times. Usually it was when he was attending events or spotted out in public. To him he was normal, but to them it was if he had come from another planet. It was always a mixed response. Some would approach him, and others would feign disinterest and pretend they hadn't seen him until they were close, and then they would pounce like a lion for an autograph. Few respected his privacy. But it came with the career.

"Is Cassie around?" Hailey asked the two dumbfounded women who stood with their mouths gaping. It looked as if she was going to have to repeat herself until one of them spoke.

Without taking her eyes off him, the taller one replied, "She's out ..." The woman was clearly at a loss for words.

Hailey nodded slowly, waiting for the next half while trying to help her.

"... Out?"

"Out back."

Hailey glanced sideways at Sam, smiled, and mouthed the words, *I'll go get her.*

Sam glanced around. It was a small setup, only a few ordinary chairs, mirrors, and hair dryers. The woman getting her hair washed couldn't make out what was distracting the other stylist, not only because her head was cocked back but because the stylist had froze like a statue and was now pouring water over the lady's face instead of her hair. *Earth to space monkey*, Sam thought. She spluttered and spat, causing the stylist to realize and shut off the water.

"I am so sorry."

A moment later Hailey emerged from the back. Follow-

ing behind her was a woman in her mid-thirties wearing far
too much makeup and carrying a steaming cup on a saucer.

"Of course I'm not a fool, I'll behave."

The moment she caught sight of him she dropped what
she was holding. Her eyes went wide and then a huge grin
spread across her face. She moved across the room in seconds, indicating quickly to one of the other women to clear
up the mess.

Then, like a speeding train barely taking a breath, she was
off. "Oh my gosh, I absolutely love you. Your role in *Raging
Hearts* was just amazing. I can't believe you are actually
here." She looked him up and down. "I always wondered if
you were as good-looking in person as you are in the movies and … Oh, I think I'm going to faint." She gripped one
of the counters to steady herself. Hailey rushed to her side.

"It's okay, breathe, and breathe," Sam said. He support-
ed her with one hand and dragged a chair over with the other. Cassie was looking at her own arm as if she couldn't
believe he was actually touching it. By this point the other
women had crowded around—a couple whispered, another
snickered.

"Okay, step back, ladies, we don't want any more of you
tumbling over," Hailey said, before getting a glass of water
and handing it to Cassie.

"I'm fine. I'm fine," she said.

"Ladies, as you were." She shooed away the women.
They returned to their workstations grinning from ear to ear
and whispering to each other.

"So you're Cassie?" Sam said. "Hailey has told me a lot
about you."

Hailey gave a surprised look; she hadn't told him anything.

"Hopefully good things?"

"Well, let's put it this way, I've been wanting to talk to you since I heard about you."

"No?"

"Yep."

He glanced at Hailey with a cheeky half smile. She smiled back.

The next thirty minutes felt like seconds as Cassie interrogated him at light speed about acting, travel, other actors, and what it was like to walk the red carpet. Hailey sat off to one side sipping on a coffee; he could sense she was watching him. He liked her friend. She was quirky, slightly erratic, but had a good sense of humor. Behind him he could hear the others talking among themselves.

"Ask him." A voice disrupted his thoughts.

"No, you do it."

Finally he felt one of them pat him on the shoulder. Sam turned. Behind him, holding a folded-up magazine, was an older lady with her hair wrapped up in a towel.

"Is it true?"

Sam frowned, expecting to hear some sordid rumor. "Is what true?"

"She cheated on you?"

She handed him a tabloid he hadn't seen. Front cover was a shot of him before he had left for treatment. A smaller image of Kate seen ducking behind a shirt was in the corner along with a statement expressing her regret in big bold letters across the page. Sam was still in disbelief that she'd chosen to issue a public apology before contacting him. His eyes fixed on the final words. *I still love him, I do.* Sam felt a sickening sensation in his stomach.

"Susan," Hailey said, apparently wanting to make it clear

how out of line it was to ask such a question.

He handed it back to the woman. Clearing his throat, he straightened up.

"Well … it was nice meeting you. I've got to go." Without another word he walked out, not thinking for one moment how rude it may have looked or even if Hailey was following. He simply needed space, a moment to take it in. It was then he realized he hadn't thought about Kate the entire day.

He'd only made it a few feet away from the salon when he heard Hailey's voice.

"Sam. Sam, hold up."

He kept moving across the road.

"Please."

He turned. A mixture of anger and confusion had welled up inside of him and without thinking he just let it out.

"What? What do you want to hear?"

"I just want to talk."

He continued walking for a moment before whirling back around and pointing towards the store, where by now the others were staring out the window like bewildered spectators.

"What was that? Did you put them up to that? Is this some sick part of you and your father's rehab game?"

Hailey stopped. "No," she said adamantly. She shook her head. "No," this time even louder, as if realizing what he was implying. "I didn't even know."

"Well you know now," he said.

They stood in the middle of the road for a moment staring at one another. He was half expecting a response but she said nothing.

"I just want to go. Can we go?"

She hesitated. "Yeah."

CHAPTER TWELVE

The journey home was filled with silence. Out the corner of her eye, Hailey could see him twitching. There was a slight shake in his hand as it rested on his leg. She knew the effect of withdrawing from alcohol wasn't easy, and with this clearly upsetting him, she would have to be more vigilant. Questions flooded her mind about what had happened and if this had been the cause of his drinking or just another reason for him to numb the underlying pain. Relationships weren't easy. It wasn't the first time she would have seen someone checking in because they were medicating to crowd out the pain of a failed relationship. Although she couldn't imagine he would have been driven to drink over a girl, would he? She didn't see a white band on his tanned finger, so that ruled out marriage. Whatever it was that was in need of healing it would eventually surface, and then they'd have to talk about it.

When they returned, Sam went off into the house without a word or a glance. By the look on her father's face when he came out, he'd clearly noticed that something had gone awry. It never seemed to faze him, though, maybe because he knew what he was doing. He treated every patient differently; it was the act of treating individually that made what they did so effective, he would say.

Hailey never questioned it. Her parents had a high success rate. And part of that success, he would say, came from not throwing patients under one blanket of teaching, like other centers did. Everyone responded differently, and what worked for one might not work for another.

The rest of the afternoon passed uneventful. Sam continued to look lost in thought.

It was hard to tell if a patient was responding well to treatment in the early stage and, no matter how many times they had done it, it was always worrisome. Their process took patients through a series of sessions with specialists in acupuncture, hypnosis, and meditation; talks with a psychologist; nutrition; and physical training. Each session was designed to be highly effective at targeting a different aspect of the patient. A complete mind, body, and soul approach. It was an all-in-one strategy that brought issues to the surface and rebuilt their sense of self—the part of them that they were before they began using.

It had always amazed Hailey, after all these years of seeing people come and go, that no matter how unclear their issue was, eventually, they'd always discover what was causing them to use. And every time, that dull look in their eyes would be replaced with a new spark of life. The problem was, with no staff around to help, all the work now rested on their shoulders.

Hailey had always been tight-lipped with her father about working at the center. She didn't want to give her father any more reasons to pester her about heading into the city, even though she did have a deep longing to make something of her life—to do something different—before it was too late. She wasn't sure why it felt like her life was slipping away, and yet a deep part of her felt unfulfilled. Maybe because she knew she wasn't getting any younger. Certainly, dancers didn't dance forever. Most retired in their early thirties, some of them going on to become choreographers or dance teachers. It was something that had crossed her mind frequently now that she was closing in on twenty-six.

On the other hand, working for the treatment center wasn't terrible. In fact, next to dancing, nothing gave her greater joy than seeing someone whose life was in pieces and watching them walk out clean and full of hope. But working at the center for the rest of her life? No, it wasn't exactly what she—or her mother, for that matter—had dreamed about. She knew she could get up and leave; heck, if she told her father he likely would have packed her bags and had her halfway to the city before she could mutter another word.

Yet she couldn't. She just couldn't.

He would go to pieces. Her mind drifted back to her father distraught and barely able to care for himself as her mother clung to the last strands of life.

* * * * *

The following days passed with only a few dark, looming clouds on the horizon. Sam no longer wondered when Liam would show up. With the weather warnings becoming more

frequent, he'd be lucky if Liam would show at all. The updates on the local TV channel served as a constant reminder
to the community that the storm of the century was about
to hit hard in a matter of days. That and the fact that half
the shelves were empty at the store, something Sam had noticed when tagging along with Hailey to stock up on supplies. People in town were already preparing, with store
windows boarded up even as the shops themselves remained open.

The routine trip to the store hadn't been easy. It seemed
ironic that among the lack of stock, the one item on the
shelves they weren't running low on was alcohol. And it
probably didn't help that Hailey had noticed him looking at
the bottles. But he appreciated the way she handled things;
it was a change from the hard-nosed personnel he was used
to encountering in other rehabs. Hailey's approach was sub-
tle. She simply distracted him by asking him to get an item
on the other side of the store.

Being with her was different. It felt comfortable, as if
he'd known her all along. When he was around her it almost
felt as if he could lower his guard. She didn't seem like other
women who were entranced by celebrity status. If she was,
she never made it obvious. She made him feel like a regular
guy. The way he felt before anyone knew his name. He liked
that.

As for treatment, well, each morning began the same.
He'd make his way down to the lake only to find Hailey either packing up or already gone for breakfast. There was no
denying it, he was struggling with the routine. Problem was,
it didn't seem to matter if he used an alarm clock or not.
Dragging himself out of bed at that ungodly hour wasn't
something his internal clock was used to, especially when he

had managed to sneak in a late-night drink, which only made him feel even groggier the next day.

What was the incessant need for treatment centers to wake up early?

Attempting to leave the comfort of a warm bed with the thought of doing yoga wasn't depressing, it was agonizing. It didn't help that inside he felt like a full-scale war was being waged between the desire to get sober and the overwhelming need to shut out the constant mind chatter.

It wasn't as if he hadn't tried to stop drinking. He'd done it one time before, but now, contemplating going back through the eye of the needle again was too hard. He remembered the year he'd noticed how serious it was getting. He'd blacked out in his trailer while on set for a second time. Thankfully, no one had found him like that. That summer he'd tried to kick it cold turkey from home using sleep and antinausea medications. The first few days were brutal. Sweating uncontrollably all day, tremors, the mind racing at night, and terror-induced nightmares were unbearable memories still fresh in his mind. The insomnia wreaked havoc on his body and only intensified the waking hours. It required every ounce of effort just to stay focused. The first time, he won the battle and stayed away from it for the better part of a year. The second, well, it was just easier to hide it. Surely if they knew how hard it was, they wouldn't expect him to try again?

The Wellands' approach to treatment was so different from anything he'd become accustomed to in all the centers he'd been in. They weren't like the others, bombarding you with a full day of lectures and then arranging meetings after to discuss how that lecture went. That wasn't treatment—that was more like insanity. Then there was the need to give chores a fancy name—"therapeutic duty assignments," he scoffed. They made it sound as if it was for his benefit. There was nothing therapeutic about chores. It didn't matter how they dressed up the name. In those centers you were nothing more than their slave for thirty days. Why should they hire a maid when you could pay them to come in and clean up their shit while they pretended to clean up yours? By the end of the day you either hit the pillow exhausted or you joined the antics of the other patients who were having sex with each other and smuggling in their drug of choice. Hell, that's where he'd gotten the whole idea of sneaking in alcohol in the first place.

Was it any wonder patients relapsed?

He shook his head—treatment? More like a joke without a punch line.

Sam stood beside the lake as the sun was swallowed by the horizon and watched as a flock of eastern bluebirds moved from tree to tree. The breeze had picked up, carrying with it an edge that chafed his skin. It was meant to be his form of meditation, a walk and time to nurture that inner calm. He could pick any place on the property, even one of the rooms in the home; instead, he picked the lake not because of how serene it looked at night, but because it gave him a chance to have a cigarette, another bad habit he couldn't shake.

A cool gust of air brushed against his skin, making him shiver. Truth be told, he longed to be back in LA, where the weather was akin to being wrapped in a warm blanket. He took a final drag and flicked his cigarette, watching the embers spark and fly before instantly going black as they hit the water. The whole holistic approach too was getting old fast. His patience was wearing thin and so was his desire to stay here. He zipped up his top, tucked his hands into his jacket, and glanced back at the house.

No, here it was an entirely different game and one that they had no qualms about changing the rules. He never quite knew what was coming next. They weren't concerned about routine, endless meetings, or tucking the big book under your arm. It was all about the one-on-one therapy. That wouldn't have been so bad if it didn't mean constantly being badgered with the same question: *Have you discovered why you are using alcohol?*

As if in some way they assumed he already knew the answer. Sam's reply was always the same. *Aren't you meant to tell me?* When that didn't work he would revert back to the only thing he knew to say. *It's a disease. I'm hooked on it.*

"No, that's not it," they would say.

He cursed inwardly, regretting ever telling them that he had kicked the need to take it once. That was all they needed to hear.

Charlie would shake his head. "No, there's more to this."

"Really?" Sam would say, rolling his eyes, knowing this was leading nowhere, fast. At least with the other centers they saw you as a hopeless case, forever doomed to attend daily meetings. This place didn't let up. They truly believed a person could be cured permanently. They were out of their frigging minds.

"Sam, you said yourself. You were off it for a year, no longer addicted and the withdrawal symptoms were gone, but you went back to it."

"Yes, I have a disease."

"No, Sam," Charlie would say adamantly. "Something beneath the surface is driving your addiction."

He snapped back to the present.

After a few minutes, Sam began making his way toward the house. As he crossed through a collection of trees he heard the side door open and noticed Hailey heading in the direction of the barn. She banged the flashlight in her hand and a shard of light shot out, illuminating the ground. Sam watched curiously within the trees as she disappeared into the barn. A light came on and again he could see movement and hear music.

On one hand, Sam wanted to seize the moment and sneak inside without being raked over the usual questions from Charlie as to what he'd discovered in his time of meditation, and on the other hand, he was curious. This had been four nights in a row he'd seen her enter the barn.

Boredom or curiosity, he had to know. As he rounded the corner of the barn he caught a glimpse of Hailey between the gaps in the wood. Her figure passed back and forth, fluid and unhindered. No one was with her as she moved to the music. Sam smiled.

Every so slowly he cracked open the large door. He realized as he slipped in unnoticed that he was intruding on what was a private moment of creative expression but he couldn't tear his eyes away. Beneath the numerous strands of illuminated lightbulbs, he saw a side to her she'd never mentioned. She was dressed in a beautiful white country summer dress, and he noticed the way her wavy blond hair flowed in rhythm with every move, like a conductor's wand leading a symphony orchestra. Except for the first day he'd met her, she'd always worn it up in a ponytail. He watched intently as she leaped and twirled with laser precision on the balls of her feet, completely lost in the music. The sound of her pink converse sneakers hitting the ground and sliding to the rhythm of the music was mesmerizing. Eyes closed, she navigated the room masterfully, as if knowing every ounce of it like the back of her hand. Over the years he'd seen his fair share of professional dancers perform in venues around the world and without a doubt, she was on par with them, if not better. Making use of every inch of the hay-covered floor, she spun with abandoned enthusiasm until she finally came to rest.

CHAPTER THIRTEEN

The sound of clapping startled Hailey as she spun around to see Sam stepping out of the shadows. He'd been watching. She wasn't sure if she should be embarrassed or angry. Attempting to catch her breath, she forced out a few words.

"How long have you been there?"

"Long enough," he said, drawing in close to her.

"Do you always spy on people?"

"No, I heard the music. I was just curious." He nodded. "You're really good."

Hailey moved over to the iPhone dock and switched it off.

"You didn't tell me you danced."

She turned back. "You didn't ask."

Sam picked up a book that was among her belongings and flipped through the pages. "You come out here every night?"

"Helps me remember." She looked around. "And it helps me forget."

He gave a confused look as she took the book from him and picked up the rest of her belongings.

Sam ambled around the room, taking it in.

"It's nice."

"Do you dance?" she asked.

"Dance? Me? No." He shook his head, amused at the question.

Hailey's lip curled. "C'mon, you don't dance?"

"Trust me, you don't want to see this"—he pointed to himself—"dance."

"You're saying you've never had to dance in a movie?"

"No," he said. "In fact, you know how some actors have nudity clauses? Well, I have my own; it's a dance clause. Yep, if there is any dancing involved, they bring in a dance double. Seriously, me dancing is not entertainment."

She laughed, setting her belongings back down.

"It's simple. Here … I'll show you."

Sam put up his hands in protest. "Hailey, no."

"Come on." She reached and took hold of his hands and led him out into the center of the barn. After some brief tugging, he reluctantly gave in. She turned the music back on and joined him, demonstrating a few moves.

"Now you try."

She bit her lip, trying to hold in the laughter as he tried to copy what she had done.

He flung his hands up in the air. "See, I told you, I'm a hopeless case."

"Poppycock," she said.

He laughed.

She smiled back. "What? What's so funny?"

"Where did you hear that?"

"I read a lot. That is what you say in England, isn't it?"

"Those must be outdated books. I haven't heard that word in years." He laughed louder. "Heck, I don't think they even say that anymore." He continued to roar with laughter.

"Okay, okay."

She changed the song that was playing to something slower. She took his hands and this time together they moved through a series of steps.

"Just follow my lead."

He stepped forward and trod on her toes. She let out a stifled yell.

"I'm sorry, I told you." He grinned, barely able to keep in his laughter.

Refusing to give up on him, and even more determined than ever, she took his hands firmly again. This time she counted out the steps.

Beneath the glow of the lights their bodies moved in unison, casting shadows on the walls, a graceful reflection of two entwined as one. He looked up from her feet and a wistful smile flickered across his face. Gazing into his eyes, Hailey wondered how long it had been since she had blushed around a man. She stepped back instinctively and managed to lose her footing. As she fell back he caught her, catching at the same time the breath that was leaving. As he scooped her up to his eye level, he held her gaze as their bodies pressed close to one another. Her heart beat faster as she felt the electrical charge building between them. As his gaze roamed her face, she studied him, feeling the anticipation of his words. Instead, not a word was uttered between them. And as quickly as it had begun, it ended. Hailey broke the silence.

"Can I show you something?"

He nodded.

They left the barn and Hailey led him through the darkness, beyond the old wooden bridge that arched the sparkling stream and past the weathered garden arbor. As they navigated their way through the woods, he continued his barrage of questions.

"Are we there yet?"

"How much farther?"

They eventually made it to a clearing at the edge of a farmer's field. The silvery moon brightly lit up the night, giving her a fairly decent view of what she wanted him to see. Just beyond the farmer's field in the distance was what looked like a giant white sign.

"What is that?"

"Let's go see." She grinned, knowing full well.

They made their way through the field of wheat until they reached the other side. As they stepped out of the crops, what had initially looked like a sign from afar was now clearly visible. Before them was a large drive-in movie screen.

"No way!"

She could see his eyes widen.

"What better way to see the stars than under the stars."

It was evident the drive-in had been out of business for years. The brush had grown and entangled around the rusted poles and speakers. Many were gone; others remained in a deteriorating state, with wires hanging loose where kids must have ripped them off. They walked between the remains of what once would have been packed with cars at this hour of night. Littered around were worn popcorn boxes and crushed pop cans.

"My mother used to bring me here when I was a kid to

watch old movies. We used to lie down in the back of the truck ..." Hailey paused.

"The one that's in the shop?"

"Yeah, my mother loved that truck. My father always wanted to buy her a new one. He said it had seen its day, but she wouldn't have it. To her it meant something more—it had sentimental value."

"Sounds like it still does." He must have caught the edge in her voice.

"Rumor has it that the owner of the farm had this place built for his wife."

"What happened?"

"They got old. When he lost his wife, he couldn't bear to see movies play here anymore. He closed it down sixteen years ago."

"Where do people go now?"

"Netflix."

He raised an eyebrow. "Figures."

Hailey stared at him, wondering what he was thinking.

"How did she pass?"

She shook her head. "No idea."

"No I ... meant your mother."

She was quiet before drawing a long breath. "Cancer."

He dropped his head. "I'm sorry."

Hailey walked over to one of the speakers; tied around it was a weathered pink ribbon. She gave a tired smile as she brushed off the debris and gently rubbed the silky ribbon between her fingers.

"This was our spot. Everywhere I'm surrounded by memories of her. Tomorrow marks exactly two years since she passed."

A mixture of fond memories and pain flooded her

thoughts. Her eyes welled up. She wiped them, not wanting him to see. Turning back towards him, she could see from his face that she hadn't hidden the tears as well as she thought.

His face registered compassion. "Why stay? I mean, you're really good at dancing, why haven't you pursued that?"

"Because my whole life is here. My father needs me and running from pain doesn't solve anything."

His expression was serious. "Neither does hiding your talents."

Hailey felt a few drops of rain splash on her arm.

"We'd better go."

* * * * *

A few drops turned into a light rain by the time they reached the house. Charlie rose from the porch swing as they came into view. Hailey noted his look of concern. As they got out from the under the rain, Hailey's wet clothes stuck to her skin, and she felt chilled to the bone. Her father returned with towels. Sam took one and rubbed it over his short dark hair.

"I thought you were in the barn."

"I took him to see the old drive-in."

Charlie glanced at Sam and then at Hailey.

Hailey could tell her father wasn't exactly thrilled by their late-night excursion. Sam must have sensed the tension, as he excused himself and went upstairs.

"What?" she quietly said.

"It's late. I think it's probably best we talk about this in this morning."

CHAPTER FOURTEEN

"Hailey, you know I want to make sure everything remains on a professional basis."

"I understand."

The whole conversation with her father that morning had been amusing.

Charlie sighed. "I can't believe it's been two years." He was rifling through mail on the side. "I forgot to tell you, you received another letter yesterday."

"Put it with the others."

Charlie shook his head.

Hailey took a sip of her coffee. It was Saturday and today marked the date her mother had passed. She was buried in the Walton cemetery on the south side of town. Hailey knew today was going to be hard. The first year was exceptionally difficult. She had prepared to go with her father to the cemetery, but she practically had to coax him into the bathroom and assist him in shaving off months of growth. A fresh shower, a clean set of clothes, and he was ready to go out the door. When the time came, he couldn't do it. She had managed to get him to the front porch but that was as far as he would go. She knew she couldn't go it alone—the thought of it was daunting enough. Instead, she stayed and consoled him on the front porch while he sobbed uncontrollably. She only hoped this year would be easier.

A lot had changed since that time; her father had gained some of the light back in his eyes. He'd even reminded Hailey that it was time to get the business going again. Yet she knew none of that would matter when it came time to leave for the cemetery. The feeling again was all too familiar. All she could do was hope for the best.

"Morning," Sam said, entering the kitchen.

Hailey smiled, rose, and made another place at the table for him. Outside, the wind howled.

"So no yoga this morning?"

"Nope. Consider yourself lucky," she replied, grinning.

Charlie sat quietly off to one side observing them both.

"Well, I'll go and get ready. Maybe you can fill Sam in on today's schedule."

Hailey gave a nod as Charlie left.

She poured some coffee into his mug and handed it to Sam.

"Slight change of plans this morning."

"Huh?"

"Were planning on visiting my mother's grave."

"Planning?"

She nodded towards the door with a pained expression on her face. "Yeah, I'm not sure if I'll be doing it alone. We should be back by the afternoon. That is ..." She trailed off. "It's possible even sooner if the weather takes a turn for the worse." She paused for a moment. "If the phone rings, would you mind answering it? Oh, and it's very likely I might need your help."

"Sure." He took a sip and relaxed against the breakfast counter, seemingly trying to decipher what that meant.

"Sam, I apologize that this all seems to have coincided with you being here. We'll continue treatment this afternoon."

He shook his head. "Nothing to apologize for." He gave a disarming smile that instantly reminded her of the previous night in the barn.

"Well, I better go make sure he's really getting ready."

She was about to leave when she remembered Albert's breakfast needed to be taken up. She sighed, returning to the counter.

"I'd lose my head if it wasn't screwed on."

"I can take that up. That's if you ... don't mind?"

Hailey hesitated. She had enough going on this morning, it certainly would help, but ...

"Ah, it's okay, I'll do it." She turned back. "Oh, and if you need anything, tea and coffee are in the cupboard, food in the fridge. Help yourself."

* * * * *

Sam stood on the porch nursing his coffee. He watched them as they drove out, leaving thin tracks behind in the water-soaked gravel. For a moment, he thought they weren't going to leave. He now understood why she had been so concerned earlier. It had taken them the better part of fifteen minutes to get Charlie in the truck. Hailey's shoulders had slumped and she looked as if she were bearing the weight of the world and a good measure of embarrassment. But eventually they got him in. The rain from the previous night had stopped, only to be replaced by the sound of rumbling thunder in the distance and high winds. Most mornings he could hear the faint sound of the American bitterns and ducks out on the lake, but today it was quiet. Not a sound could be heard except for the thrashing of water against the shore and the wind whistling between the trees. Sam went back inside, closing the storm door firmly behind him. This was the first morning he'd been free since he'd got there. He needed some more coffee, something to give him a boost to face the day.

Hailey reminded him earlier that morning that they wanted to arrange for one of his family to attend the family day. Just the thought of it made his stomach churn. Sam still wasn't sure what to do about that. Family day was meant to open up lines of communication, heal wounds, and give family members an opportunity to share their feelings and support them while in recovery.

Fat chance of that happening, he thought.

Though it wasn't family he blamed, it was himself. He hadn't opened up to Charlie or Hailey about his family; neither had he mentioned the ongoing problem or their lack of desire to have anything to do with him. If ever there was a reason to drink, that certainly played a role. Over the years, the whole situation had taken its toll on him. It was enough to wear anyone down, but there was little that he could do. They had made that painfully obvious.

And now she wanted him to get them to show up? He shook his head. Could it get any worse? He pushed the thought from his mind.

Sam went over to the counter and poured another cup. As he did, he noticed beside him a partially open letter lying on the side. The letter had been folded and only the top part was visible. The letterhead read: *The Juilliard School Dance Di-*

vision. Sam cast a glance over his shoulder, instinctively knowing that he probably shouldn't. But curiosity got the better of him. He took a sip of coffee and ever so casually pressed back one fold of the paper. His eyes scanned fast, trying to get the gist of what it was about. It was addressed to Hailey and seemed to be about ... acceptance? He furrowed his brow, sat his coffee down, and unfolded the letter. At that very moment the sound of a vehicle coming up the driveway spooked him. He quickly put the letter back where he found it, folded it neatly, and repositioned it so it appeared as if it hadn't been touched.

Tilting the curtain to one side, he noticed a dark red tow truck coming up the driveway. He remembered it vaguely; eventually it came into full view, pulling up in front of the house. Plastered on the side in large lettering were the words "Farlan's Auto."

* * * * *

It felt odd visiting a cemetery, taking flowers and talking to a stone. But at the same time it felt right. A way to acknowledge and remember the good times. She could have sworn she could hear her mother's voice as she sat beside the grave. It had taken as much convincing to get her father out of the truck as it had getting him in. For a while they sat there in silence, engine ticking over and the heater on full blast, giving them momentary relief from the colder weather outside. Her father stared off into the distance, while Hailey rested her hand on top of his.

"C'mon, Dad." She'd coaxed him out, keeping a gentle grip on his hand. It was every bit as hard for her as it was for him. She could have visited the grave numerous times over the past few years. But it just didn't seem right. Not without him. She needed them both to be there. That was the way she would have wanted it.

Hailey carried with her a large bouquet of bright, rich purple orchids. They had been her mother's favorite. She'd always had a vase of them in different areas around the house. Among all flowers, her mother said orchids were a perfect example of a ballet dancer; delicate in appearance and yet able to release the strongest of fragrance into the world. Simple beauty that might only be captured for a second, but its effect would echo throughout eternity.

She said it was the way she wanted to be remembered.

Hailey felt a lump build in her throat as she cleared away the roots that had grown up around the stone. She noticed the damage the elements had done in only two years. Pulling a rag from her pocket, she brought the shine back to the dark marble stone with a few wipes. She laid the flowers down, secured them in place with a few rocks, and stepped back beside her father.

For a long moment, Hailey said nothing; they both gazed at the stone as though hypnotized by finality itself. She cupped one ear with her hand as the wind nipped at it and looped the other through her father's, trying to comfort him and stay warm at the same time. She looked up. In the distance the sky was a light gray with spots of blue turning to darkness. It felt as though summer itself had been overcome by death, its ominous presence creeping closer, overshadowing and wrapping itself around the remaining blue skies. The storm wasn't brewing; it was rolling in upon thick clouds and as the tops of the trees bent, there was no doubt what danger it brought with it.

* * * * *

For a split second, Sam contemplated not answering the door. It wasn't that he felt threatened by Tommy; he simply had no desire to talk to him. Especially with everything else that was weighing on his mind. However, he assumed Tommy brought news about Hailey's truck and for that reason alone he'd decided to open the door. It had been a week since they'd dropped off the truck and he was only now getting back to her? Things certainly moved slowly in this town, Sam thought as he swung the door open.

"Huh." Tommy frowned at the sight of Sam. He scanned him just as he had before, clearly showing a level of distaste at seeing him at the house.

"Can I help?"

"Hailey in?"

"No." Sam didn't care to elaborate; his only interest was in ending their interaction.

Tommy sniffed hard, glancing around the property as if Sam were lying.

"Is the vehicle fixed?" Sam asked, hoping they could cut to the chase.

"Not exactly." He adjusted his ball cap, pulled it off for a second, and wiped his brow with it before placing it back on his matted hair. A huge dark wad of brown spit exited the side of his mouth before he spoke again.

"You know when she'll be back?"

Sam nodded. "This afternoon."

Tommy turned back towards his vehicle.

"Tell her I swung by."

"I'll be sure to do that."

It may have been something about the tone of his reply

or a need to get something off his chest, but Tommy paused and walked back. He cracked a smile as he waved his finger in front of his face.

"I know who you are."

Sam raised his eyebrow.

"You're that hotshot from Hollywood," he said. Tommy nodded. "Yeah, you're that guy that was dumped by that sweet piece of ass, what's her name?" He trailed off.

Sam's jaw clenched.

A smirk crossed his face. "Ah, it doesn't matter—who needs names, huh? When you've had one, you've had them all. Am I right?"

Sam wasn't sure what was holding him back from slamming his fist into Tommy's face. He knew he didn't like the guy—that was unquestionable. As far as he was concerned, his relationship with Kate was over. But there was something more. No, scratch that, there was someone more—Hailey. Emotions would surely be running at an all-time high with the anniversary of her mother's death. Besides, if the media caught wind that not only was he holed up at a rehab center but he'd gotten into a fight with a local, they would eat it up. No, if Tommy was attempting to get a rise out of him, there wasn't a chance in hell he was going to give him the satisfaction; at least not today. Sam remained composed.

"Have Hailey call me."

And with that he got back in his truck, shot a brief sideways glance, and drove away.

CHAPTER FIFTEEN

He didn't like it one bit, that was for sure. Tommy tapped his fingers against the wheel as he took one last glance in his rearview mirror. He'd rattled him, there was no doubt about that, he could see it in his eyes. He hoped he would have bitten, taken a swing, done something, anything. But instead he did nothing? *Weak*.

He chuckled to himself; Hollywood hotshot wasn't so courageous when he wasn't behind the cameras. They were all the same, full of themselves when the cameras were on, photo hogs, attention-seeking whores, but drop them in a small town, shine a light on their flaws, and they were nothing more than chumps. All the money in the world couldn't change that.

Tommy could see it, it was obvious to him, but it wasn't himself that he was bothered about. It was Hailey. He'd caught the glint in her eye when she looked at Sam the other day. No, this wasn't good one bit; the thought of them spending time together made him sick to his stomach. The thought of his hands all over her riled him up. And no doubt that little punk would try to put the moves on her. Who hadn't? He thought of the many guys who had tried to take her out. He knew what they wanted. Heck, he was a guy, and around these parts there wasn't much else to do. They weren't after a good night out, they wanted one thing—to get in her pants.

But she had that on lockdown.

Hailey had always been that girl, the one that had shot down advancements by all types of guys. As far back as he could remember, even when they were in high school together, most guys called her frigid. She was the girl that never went out of her way to attract men. Her clothes back then were nothing to stare at; not like the others who wore tight-fitting jeans and dresses. Yep, he knew what they wanted and he gave it to them. Oh, how easy they were. Oh, those were the days; he smiled with glib delight. But those days were long gone. Most of those girls had either left Walton or they were knocked up with a baby, and who the hell wanted that kind of baggage? Not him.

Now Hailey, she had done a complete one eighty and changed a lot since school. All right, she didn't have "you're invited" written on her ass but the glasses were gone and so were the unflattering baggy clothes. He remembered how mouth-watering she looked. Who would have thought that such a tight figure had been hiding under all of that? It wasn't as if she had decided to dress slutty like the others. She'd simply grown up and her choice of clothing and appearance now piqued his curiosity. She was the girl he had never had. And he was going to make damn sure it didn't stay that way. Nah, no hotshot Hollywood actor was going to sweep in and have first dibs on that bit of ass. It was all his.

He had plans. He was nearing thirty and well, the thought of having someone there when he got home was starting to look real good. It wasn't like he couldn't still dip his toes in other waters from time to time, but at least he would have something of his own. He didn't want to be alone any more than the next guy. Snagging her would be fairly easy. She wasn't going anywhere and neither was he.

His thoughts returned to the last date they had been on. God, how she made him sweat and beg to get her to agree. He had to admit he kind of liked the chase; it had made him even more eager.

And for a moment he thought he was in. All the lights were green and everything lined up perfectly. He had thought it all through beforehand. It was all about priming her, something he'd never had to do before because the others just did what they were told. But not Hailey, she was as stubborn as a mule. Though he would eventually break her. Had there been anyone else, he wouldn't have bothered, but times were desperate. Take her for a walk, hold her hand, give her some flowers. Girls loved that crap. Invite her out for a dinner, buy a bottle of wine, and slowly her defenses would come down. Before the end of the night she'd be like putty in his hands.

He relished in the thought for a moment before pushing it all from his mind as he recalled how quickly it had all flat-lined on him. What a wuss she was. Some things hadn't changed—she was still as frigid as ever. And as for him? So what, he liked to drink a bit. What guy didn't? But there was no denying it. He'd failed, but he wouldn't fail again. And this time he wouldn't take no for an answer.

He was hoping to give her a bit of time to cool off before he put the moves back on her, but with that Sam Reid guy around, it didn't seem as though he could afford any further delays. Who knew when big shot would make his move. Maybe he'd already made it. Tommy seethed with jealousy. What to do? What could he do to change this minor hiccup in his plans?

One thing was clear; he had to deal with the Hollywood hotshot. Where to begin? He couldn't just wait for him to leave. Who knew how long he was staying. Lost in his own thoughts, he swerved back into his lane just before he collided with another car coming the other way. Without even missing a beat, his mind rifled through questions like a Rolodex. He hadn't seen any news about this guy coming to their town. Hailey hadn't mentioned they'd be having another patient. It all seemed a little odd. Why show up here? There had to have been better places than the Wellands' rundown excuse for a rehab center.

Who cared? One way or the other, he figured Sam Reid would soon be out of the picture.

CHAPTER SIXTEEN

L ater that evening, as Hailey started to prepare supper, she watched her father and Sam finish up securing the last of the additional hurricane protection over the windows. Being further in from the mainland, it was uncommon for folks in their town to expect much more than flooding, and a few downed power lines and trees, but her father wasn't leaving anything to chance. The flooding in 2006 had been so severe that most of the town's businesses, bridges, and roads were washed out. It was unexpected and the devastation was overwhelming. No, with her father everything had to be just right. And in many ways she took after him—whether that was good or bad, who knew?

Hailey wondered if the need for everything to be just so had been the reason it had taken him so long to pick up the pieces after her mother's passing. He'd simply fallen apart when she died. Her mother had been his world. His routine revolved around her. Perhaps it was because of her parents that Hailey placed such a high regard on her own relationships. Noticing how much they loved one another, seeing how they finished each other's sentences and relished each other's company whether they spoke or not reassured her that it was true. Some people did stay together, even if it was rare.

The smell of the steaks on the BBQ permeated the air. With the wind at an all-time high and rain off and on throughout the day, her father didn't want her cooking outside but she couldn't resist it. In her mind, there was nothing better than the taste of grilled food. A large waft of smoke enveloped her, stinging her eyes. She wiped them and stepped back, watching the flames curl around the steaks.

She loved summers; they were a time when they would cook everything on the BBQ and unwind. Summers held fond memories for her; they were such a deeply ingrained part of her life growing up that she couldn't even begin to imagine her life without them. The family get-togethers, boating on the lake, afternoon cookouts, and lazy evenings swinging slowly in a hammock watching her mother tend to the flowerbeds. It was pure bliss. Her father usually cooked while her mother prepared salad and invited people in from the community.

She was amazed at how certain smells acted like a time machine, instantly taking you back to the special moments in your life. Though now the high winds weren't making it easy.

"Smells good," a voice said from behind.

Turning around, she locked eyes with Sam, who had cleaned up nicely. New jeans, a loose shirt, and hair that looked damp. Standing next to him even with the strong smells of the BBQ, she still caught a trace of his cologne.

She felt her insides react. It was something she had always appreciated about a man. Someone who smelled good and took pride in the way he dressed.

"Yes, it does," she replied, not talking about the smell of the cooking. "Hope you like marinated steaks."

She turned back to flip the meat, and fire shot up, the steaks sizzled, and a billow of smoke filled the air

"Hailey, I um … I wanted to apologize for the other day."

"That's okay." She gave a half nod as she continued to prod the steaks with a fork. It had been a week since his outburst, and to be honest, she really hadn't given it much thought.

"No, really, I unloaded my frustration on you without thinking. I'm sorry."

She could tell from the sound of his voice he was sincere. She had learned fast from her encounters with men when it was just a show—especially Tommy. It was like an inner bullshit detector that she wished she had tuned into much earlier when dating. It certainly would have saved her a lot of frustration and heartache.

"I probably would have done the same," she replied. She really couldn't blame him. She thought of how she might have responded if the person she loved broke up with her publicly and made her apology tabloid fodder.

Her reply seemed to set him at ease as he took a seat in one of the Adirondack chairs close by her. She looked down at his hand and noticed it was no longer shaking. She couldn't be sure if that was a good sign or if he had another bottle of bourbon stashed away somewhere. Her father's rule of not checking bags when guests entered wasn't something she and her father saw eye to eye on. In her mind, trust was earned and when a patient walked in the door, trust was at an all-time low. However, in all the years they had treated patients they'd only had four other incidents and they were minor. She often wondered if her father made that rule just to throw them off-keel when they arrived. Most expected to have their bags checked; not doing so certainly wasn't normal. She studied him, flipped another steak, and made a mental note to check his room later.

"If you leave them on the grill any longer, you'll be using them for kindle," her father joked as he brought out a bowl of Italian salad. She was so lost in thought that she hadn't realized the steaks were starting to resemble charred pieces of coal.

She quickly shut off the burners and brought them over to a table laid out with napkins, brown rye bread, and cutlery.

"You ready to eat?"

"Absolutely famished." Sam came over and sat down.

Hailey loaded up their plates with steak and slid the bowl of salad across to him.

"Help yourself."

"Well, I'll leave you to it," her father said, gripping Hailey's shoulders from behind.

Hailey turned in her seat. "Are you not joining us?"

"Not tonight, I'm going over to Danny's."

She pointed to all the food. "I just spent all this time."

"Yes, and I bet it will be lovely," he said, snagging a cucumber slice and popping it in his mouth.

"Danny's? C'mon, Dad." She knew what it meant and why he was doing it. "What about the weather, it's not safe."

"Hay, it's just a few wings and a chat. And besides, you

can take the time to show Sam around a bit more," he pointed out. "If you need me, just phone. Okay?"

Hailey didn't know what to say. Before she could protest or ask when he'd be back, he gave her a quick peck on the top of the head and left. She shook her head, leaning back around.

"Trouble?" Sam inquired.

"Don't ask."

"Well, I'm sure we can polish this off between us."

She smiled, watching him load more onto his plate. "Got quite the appetite, have you?"

"Haven't tasted food this good in such a long time."

"Don't you cook?"

"Yes, if by cooking you mean nuking takeaways."

She took a bite of her food, studying his physique. "For someone who eats takeout, you've done a good job keeping in shape."

He paused for a moment as if to consider what she said. She also realized how it might have sounded.

"I mean ..." She trailed off.

"Well, it might surprise you but I actually hate working out. But it's kind of expected in this career. If a role doesn't require it, you'd more than likely find my hand inside a cookie jar." He grinned.

"I always imagined that would be kind of neat."

"What?"

"You know, landing a role that required you to beef up like a Spartan." She tried not to make it obvious that she was looking at how well his shirt fit, the way it clung to his body making his lean muscular body clearly noticeable.

He laughed, nearly choking on his food. "Spartan? Yeah, glad I didn't land that role, you should have seen what they took those guys through. A friend of mine secured a spot in that film and let me tell you, he may have packed on the muscle but what they made him eat for months at a time would make your hair stand on end."

"Oh, I don't know, I imagine his phone was ringing off the hook long after."

He grinned. "Maybe, if he had kept it on. The next film he was in, he had to drop forty pounds. He dropped a forth of his body weight. Now that wasn't a pretty sight either."

"Do you ever feel like a puppet on a string?" She took a sip of her ice tea.

"All the time."

"Why do it then?"

"Same reason you work here."

She was curious to hear what he assumed about her. "And that is?"

"You're good at it."

"Um, let's have that discussion at the end of two weeks. You might change your tune then."

He laughed easily.

"Would you ever change careers?" she asked him.

"I think about it at times, usually at night when I'm shacked up in another hotel."

"Five-star hotels? The lap of luxury doesn't sound so bad to me."

"No, don't get me wrong, I'm very grateful for the opportunities that I've been given. There are actors that have been working longer in this industry than me and they're struggling to pay their rent." He took a swig of his drink. "You see, contrary to the way the media might portray us at times, there are only a handful who are considered to be at the top of the food chain, and we didn't choose to be there, the media puts us there. They're the ones that create the buzz, paint the stories, and well ... you're either the hero or the villain. There really is no in-between."

"That's ... a good thing, right? At least for you?"

"Yes and no. Being at the top you, don't have to fight so hard for the roles that you once groveled for—but more mud gets flung at you. You're under the ever-watchful eye of the paparazzi and in their eyes there's only one thing better than seeing someone rise."

"What's that?"

"Watching them fall."

Hailey nodded.

"What about you?"

"Uh ..." She wasn't sure she really wanted to get into it. The whole thought of sharing her innermost dreams, or unachieved ones at best, made her feel inadequate. They paled in comparison to his achievements. Truth was she hadn't seen pursuing dancing full time as a career change; instead, it seemed a distant fantasy that she'd had since she was young—a dream to follow in her mother's footsteps and make her proud. But now with her mother gone, it didn't seem to hold the attraction it once had.

Instead of answering, she changed the topic.

"Do the paparazzi know you're here?"

He grinned, eyeing the area around him. "I hope not."

At that moment his phone went off. He retrieved it and indicated with a raised finger that he'd be a moment. He walked a little way off as he put the phone to his ear. Continuing to eat, she glanced over and could see him pacing back and forth. Clearly distraught by the phone call, he raised his voice enough for her to catch what he said.

"How many times do I have to apologize?"

And then the phone call was over. He came back and sat down looking flustered and red-faced.

"Problems?" she asked.

He shrugged. "Family—nothing worth worrying about."

"You've not spoken about your family."

"Not much to say really."

He didn't seem interested in adding anything further, so she let it go.

As the evening wore on the sunlight shifted and waned. They finished eating, never returning to the conversation, and eventually they cleaned up the table and went inside. Sam praised the meal, saying it was some of the best steak he'd had in years. She wasn't sure if he was being truthful or nice. Either way, Hailey was relieved he hadn't asked for a hacksaw to cut through the burnt offerings.

"Would you mind if I put a pot of tea on?" Sam asked.

"By all means, go ahead, the tea is in the cupboard on the right."

"Do you want some?"

"Sure, I'll have the chamomile or I won't sleep."

Hailey went outside while Sam boiled the kettle.

A few minutes later Sam returned carrying a couple of steaming mugs. Hailey was sitting in the porch rocker with one leg up, slowly rocking back and forth. By now the temperature outside felt much cooler. The stars had emerged from hiding, lighting up the night sky. There was something serene about them sitting together, as if her whole world had stopped spinning and for a moment, she could see herself years on, sitting with the one she loved. She'd always imagined growing old with one person, having grandkids and telling them a unique story of how she met their grandfather. Another pipe dream, she thought.

She once again stole a glance at him while taking the cup. As he leaned in, she noticed how chiseled and defined his face was. He took a seat beside her and breathed out a deep sigh.

"So, what's the deal with the guy down the hall?"

"Albert?"

"Yes."

"He's been here for as long as I can remember."

"He's a patient?"

She screwed up her face. "Sort of."

"Don't you think that's odd?" he said. "I mean, isn't the goal to leave the place, not live here?"

"It's complicated."

"You want to talk about it?"

"Not really. I want to hear more about what happened with you and your girlfriend."

"Don't you ever get off the clock?"

"Not under these circumstances."

He shook his head.

"How did you meet?"

She could see him drifting back and forth from the past to the present.

"You must be the only one who doesn't know, as it appears our relationship is part of public domain now. We met on set. She and I had both just got out of a relationship. Honestly, I wasn't looking for anything. We just connected. Five years of working together can tend to do that." He paused and looked off into the distance before taking a sip of tea. "When you're around someone for that length of time, you're both working opposite one another and feeling a sense of emptiness, it was just a given that something would happen." He blew on the surface of his tea before drinking again.

"So what went wrong? I mean, other than the obvious?"

"Your guess is as good as mine."

"Has she spoken to you since?"

"Not a word."

"You've not tried to contact her?"

"Once."

"What did she say?"

"She never answered."

She realized now why he had been so upset. The thought of receiving an apology first and foremost through the media before contacting him was … Hailey couldn't even finish the thought. How could anyone do that? Why would anyone do that to someone they loved? If it wasn't bad enough to have it dragged out publicly, but to then not reply?

"What about since you saw the magazine?"

He put his cup down. "No. What do I say? Oh, you apologized so the whole world could read it, that makes it all better?"

"I guess not."

He yawned. "Anyway, enough about me, what about you?"

"Me?"

"Well, that Tommy fella seemed to have his eyes set on you."

She waved it off. "He doesn't understand the meaning of no. It's just a game to him. Not getting what he wants isn't what he's used to."

"Does he own the garage?"

"No, his father does, he lets Tommy run the shop when he's not around. Says he will be taking it over when he retires. Truth be told, he never had any intentions of sticking around these parts. At least that's what he says. Though I think when he didn't get a scholarship, he simply gave up."

Hailey shivered.

Sam noticed. He learned across and wrapped the throw that hung over the chair around her shoulders. She looked up at him and in that moment she saw something she hadn't noticed before. The colors of his eyes were a deep hazel brown and very warm. For a split second she could feel her heart beating a little faster.

He smiled at her and it was then she knew she'd held the gaze a little too long. She felt herself exhale, not realizing that she'd been holding her breath. She forced herself to look away, but the pull to look back at him was strong. She brushed a few strands that had fallen across her face back behind her ear. The warmth of the blanket was comforting; she hadn't felt this much at ease with anyone in a long time.

"What's the time?"

Sam glanced at his watch. "Ten-fifteen."

She frowned. "He's still not home."

"Does he have a curfew?" He smirked.

She shook her head. "No, it's just after today, well …"

The wind chimes jingled hard as the wind picked up. She wanted to stay longer but with her father's well-being looming on her mind, she decided to call it a night.

Taking off the blanket, she gave him one more glance before heading in.

"Goodnight, Sam."

"Night."

CHAPTER SEVENTEEN

When another hour had passed and he still wasn't home, she began to get worried. The wind was slamming so hard against the house, she expected at any moment the windows to break or the roof to be torn off. She had spent the last half hour on the phone with Cassie, calming her nerves over the incident. Cassie had felt like a complete fool and wanted to apologize in person to Sam. But Hailey let her know that it probably wasn't a good idea.

The sound of banging below her instantly disrupted her train of thought. It sounded as if someone was tearing apart the house.

"Cassie, can I call you back?"

"But I was just—"

She hung up, not giving her the chance to finish, and headed out to see what the racket was about. As she got closer to Sam's door she could hear him yelling. A door opened down the hall and Albert's head popped out.

Hailey waved him back in. "It's all right, go back in, I'll deal with this."

She knocked at the door and then without waiting, let herself in. Inside, the room looked as if it had been through a home invasion. The chair was turned upside down, the draws of the desk were halfway across the room, and the sheets were strewn all over the place. In the center of the room on the floor with his back pressed up against the bed, Sam was crouched down. His eyes were red and he looked exhausted. He immediately looked up.

"Where is it?"

She shook her head, knowing full well what he was referring to.

"Down the sink."

"You had no right to go rummaging through my belongings."

"No?" she said. "We have every right to do so. When you signed up to come here you willingly agreed to abide by the rules of the center. I told you it wasn't going to be easy. It wasn't our decision to work with you for only two weeks, that was your manager's. We only made a promise that we would try to help. It's far less time than we usually take, but if we have to do it that way, we are not going to mess around. We don't have many rules, Sam. Like we said, the only rule we have is one of trust and you already broke that. I could have had you sent back but I didn't."

"How did you know?"

"Your hands."

He regarded her. "I just needed a little to take the edge off. You know, it's not like I'm hurting anyone."

"You are, Sam. You're hurting yourself."

He shook his head and brushed his hand across his face. "I can't do this."

Sam stood up and began gathering his belongings together. He threw his bag on the bed and started haphazardly stuffing it with clothes.

"So walking out is how you plan on handling this?" she asked.

He didn't reply.

"Tell me, Sam, what was the phone call about earlier?"

"That's not your concern."

"Maybe not, but while you're here, you are, and if we're going to get to the bottom of what is driving you to drink, you need to be honest."

He didn't reply; instead, he continued packing furiously.

"Isn't it time you stopped running, Sam?"

He shot around.

"Well, that's what I do," he yelled.

"No, that's what you've done." She held his gaze. "It's not who you are, Sam."

He continued gathering his belongings.

She threw her hands up. "So you want to go to jail?"

He drew a breath. "I don't give a damn," he muttered.

She looked at him in amazement. "Then why did you come here?"

He stopped packing and for a brief moment gazed down as if searching for an answer.

"God, you are so self-absorbed."

He leaned around. "What is that supposed to mean?"

"You have the whole damn world at your feet. People would kill to be where you are and instead you would rather throw it away. Give up," she said. "Why?"

"You're the experts. Why don't you tell me?"

"Don't dodge the question."

He chuckled under his breath. "What, like the way you dodged my question earlier?"

"What?"

"Let me guess, it has something to do with that letter from Juilliard?"

"Who showed you that?"

"No one, it was on the counter."

"So you make it a habit of snooping through people's belongings?"

He shook his head. "It was open, in full view, and ... you're not exactly one to be lecturing on snooping."

"It's not the same."

"No?" he snapped.

The wind was whipping against the walls of the house, shaking the framework violently.

"Tell me, is choosing to stay here over pursuing what you are damn good at—not running away?"

"Forget it, you don't understand."

Without making eye contact, he continued to grab a few more items off the dresser. "Look, don't act as if you know me. You haven't got a clue. All you see is what the media shows you." He glanced at her. "I bet you think I should just shut up and be grateful because of what I do?"

"I didn't—"

"You didn't what?"

Hailey wrapped her arms tightly around her body.

"No, you're right. I don't know you. I don't know what it's like to be you. But I do know a little about wanting to run from pain."

"Okay ... yeah, okay, this where you give me the speech about having been there, right?" He zipped one of his bags closed. "Pain? You can't even begin to imagine what I feel. You want to know why I drink? You want to know what keeps me awake if I don't? You want to know my regrets and everything that reminds me of those I've let down? No, all you or anyone else sees is the glitz, the glamour, and a life full of privilege. You don't see the constant demands, you don't know the first damn thing about pressure. Holed up in this sleepy town, how could you?"

Sam moved with purpose down the hall and into the washroom, snatching up his wash gear. Hailey wasn't sure what to say as he brushed past her. His words stung, not because of his tone but because they held truth and truth that hurt. But this wasn't about her. She wasn't going to let him turn this around and make this about her.

As he came back into the room and continued packing, she racked her brain for anything to say that would make him stop. He was thinking irrationally, reacting from his pain. She groaned inwardly, wishing her father was around; he always knew what to say in these moments. He had a way with patients, a skill she hadn't quite gotten the hang of, despite what her father said.

With the wind battering against the shutters and the continual onslaught of torrential rain, it was virtually impossible to think straight.

"Sam, give it another night, at least until the storm passes. "

"No, I should have left days ago. Just sign off on the papers and I'll be out of your hair."

"No."

He shook head. "Listen, I know it goes against your rule books. But c'mon, what's a week? You sign off, I don't show up back in LA for a week, and we both win. You said yourself, two weeks wasn't long enough. And let's be honest, you weren't going to be able to sort this out. No one ever can, no matter how long they have."

For a brief moment, she wondered if he was right. Maybe he was beyond reaching? Maybe signing off would put an end to all this? They would still get paid and well ... She paused. But where would that leave him? Other centers would have been overjoyed to see him leave, but it only riled her up.

"No—if you want the paperwork signed you are going to have to stay here the full two weeks." As absurd as it sounded coming out of her mouth, she knew he wasn't going to get off that easy.

He heaved a big sigh. "Seriously. I'm giving you a way out here. I'm doing you a favor," he said.

She shook her head. "But you're not doing yourself any."

He looked steadily at her, and gave a brief nod. Shouldering one bag and grabbing the other, he passed by her, casting one final sideways glance.

"Sam," she hollered down the hallway.

He stopped at the top of the stairs and turned back.

"Hailey, you don't have to keep trying. Believe me, if you really knew me, you'd realize helping me isn't worth it."

He took another step.

"Everyone's worth it," she said.

* * * * *

Despite the weather, Sam couldn't begin to imagine staying any longer; he was surprised that he had stuck it out as long as he had. He wanted to be far away. A mixture of embarrassment, anger, and self-loathing welled up inside him, causing him to feel a throbbing ache in his chest. Outside, the wind was reaching epic proportions, bending back the branches of solid oak trees like they were mere twigs. Sheets of rain fell, soaking him through to the skin the moment he stepped out. The entire ground was a sea of large and small puddles. There was something about being caught in a heavy downpour. A sense that it could wash away all the wrong, all the lies and dredge that weighed a person down in life. He only wished it was that easy.

He threw his belongings in the back seat, slammed the door, and cast a final glance back over his shoulder before getting in. Thunder clapped and fork lightning lit up the night sky. Hailey stood beneath the porch roof as water poured over the gutters, almost hiding her from his view. An expression of concern, possibly disappointment or sadness, wrapped her demeanor. He hadn't stopped to think how his leaving would affect the Wellands. Where would it leave them? One thing he was sure about, she was right. He was running from the pain and it wouldn't get him anywhere except a stint in lockup. But at that very moment none of that mattered. All he wanted to do was get away, numb the pain, and sleep.

Driving toward the exit, he glanced back at her in his rearview mirror. He could barely make out her form through the streams of water now blurring his view. He should have told her about his family when she asked, and now he couldn't fathom why he hadn't. He figured she wouldn't have understood. He still didn't understand it himself. And to be honest, there was a part of him that wanted to stop, turn around, and explain it all.

But he wouldn't.

Of course he didn't want to go to jail, but she didn't need this crap. Charlie didn't want to deal with his antics and who knew when the media would descend upon this place. No, leaving Walton was best for all of them. Pulling a hard left out of the property, he wondered if she would eventually understand.

He could immediately tell that it wasn't going to be easy getting out of town. The road was now strewn with foliage and branches. It was only getting worse as he navigated along the dark country road. Water spread across the road and his headlights were useless even with his windshield wipers switched to full speed. He'd only made it a few yards out of the entrance when a crack of brilliant white light and a surge of wind brought down an entire tree ahead. Sam yanked the wheel to the right but with so much water on the road the car began hydroplaning. It was no use; he squeezed his eyes shut and braced himself for the inevitable.

Chapter Eighteen

"You think he'll be okay?"

"W… w … well, there's not much we c … c … can do tonight with the r … road out. Until this s … storm lets up, the best we can do is k … keep him comfy and get him l … l … looked at in the morning."

"Thanks, Albert."

From somewhere off to his side, Sam could hear the jumble of voices.

At first, he wasn't sure how long he'd been out, or even where he was. It took Sam a few minutes to get his bearings. Eventually the familiar sound of Hailey's voice was reassuring. Behind it he could hear the faint sound of wood popping and crackling along with the smell of burning embers. His eyes flickered, sending a kaleidoscope of images at him all at once. As his eyes adjusted, he noted the flowery décor, the mantelpiece, and photographs. He was back at the Wellands' house, inside one of the main rooms. Turning his head slightly to the side, he could make out Hailey kneeling close to the fireplace. She was drenched from head to toe and stoking the fire. She threw a few more logs into the fire, each one sending up a hiss. She brushed some of the red embers back into the fire and stood up, admiring her handiwork. Sam coughed, drawing her attention back to him. He tried to sit up until he felt his head throbbing.

"Whoa , steady, you got quite a knock there."

Hailey laid a hand on his chest. It felt warm and soft and it was then he realized he didn't have a shirt on. He was covered with just a thick, itchy gray blanket. It reminded him of the uniform pants he was forced to wear as a child in school.

"Where are my clothes?"

She stared for a moment before replying, as if recognizing the awkwardness of the situation.

She motioned toward the door. "They're hanging up to dry."

"Did you …?"

"No, Albert took them. They were soaked, we had to get you out of them. You also had a little bit of blood on the top."

He reached up with his hand to where he felt a twinge just beneath the hairline. It already had a Band-Aid on it.

"It's just a small gash. It doesn't look too serious but we'll get you looked at tomorrow. No doubt you have some whiplash."

"Actually, I don't feel too bad." He spoke too soon. Sam groaned as he tried to move.

"Yeah. Let's not be in a hurry to get up."

Hailey stepped back from the couch and sat across from him.

He glanced over at her. "What happened?"

"You don't remember?"

He coughed again. "I remember leaving here and ..." He trailed off.

"You slid off the road into a ditch. You were lucky, it could have been a lot worse if you'd hit that tree."

"How did you ...?"

"Albert brought you in."

Sam raised his eyebrows and looked around.

"You'll see him in the morning."

Sam gradually pulled himself up. Still dizzy but feeling less pain, he wrapped the blanket around his waist and shoulders to stay covered.

They were interrupted by the sound of a kettle whistling.

"I'll be right back," Hailey said.

A moment later she returned with two cups.

"Tea?"

Sam smiled as he took it from her. "Thanks."

He curled the mug in close to his chest, feeling its warmth. He took a sip and nursed it tightly. Despite the warmth of the tea and fire, he noticed he was still shivering.

"Do you need another blanket?"

"No, I'll be fine. Thanks."

For a moment neither of them spoke as they sat in silence, gazing at the fire as it swirled upwards. A golden display of autumn colors created dancing shadows on the walls around them.

"It was my sister—Jules ..."

"What?"

"On the phone," he added.

Hailey turned toward him, listening intently as he continued gazing into the fire. He wasn't sure he wanted to share it, but he did.

"Four years ago I was in Romania. I had just wrapped up the first of what would be several films." He took another sip of his drink. "There had been a bit of a misunderstanding, partly my fault." He grimaced.

"Anyway, the producers were in talks to have me replaced for the second film. You have to understand, landing that first one changed my career. I went from obscurity to a household name overnight. My manager busted his ass to smooth things out and he did. But you could say we were walking on eggshells from therein."

Sam set his drink down.

"Around that time, my mother had taken a turn for the worse. I knew she'd not been well but … at first, they said it wasn't serious. A few weeks later, Jules phoned to tell me that the doctors had given her a diagnosis of several months to a few weeks to live."

He stood up, tightly holding the blanket, and moved closer to the fireplace to stay warm. The fire spat out red-hot embers that quickly cooled dark on the stone-tiled floor. Mesmerized by the flickering fire, his thoughts drifted back.

"How was I to know? She'd always been so resilient in the past. You know … always bounced back. That was her—a fighter. I just … I just assumed it would be the same again. You know? I was in a tight spot, I had everything riding on this. They would have never believed me even if I told them. I just couldn't …"

He cast a glance at her sideways, hoping something, anything, in what he'd said was understandable. Hailey seemed to muse over his words, offering nothing more than a couple of affirmative nods.

"A week later, Jules phoned to tell me my mother had passed and they'd already had the funeral—without me."

He looked back into the fire.

"When we were done filming, I returned to England." He shook his head, closing his eyes to keep out the memory. "My father, Jules, and I had a huge argument. Things were said in the heat of the moment." He took a deep breath and sat back down, picking up his tea again.

"Let's just say they won't be visiting anytime soon. So that whole family bonding session you had in mind—not gonna happen."

After he told her, he anticipated questions. He wondered what she thought. He hadn't even shared this with Kate. In fact, he was surprised he'd been so honest with Hailey. Divulging his innermost thoughts wasn't his strong point. But something about being there, being with her, felt safe. It felt right. And in all honesty, he was tired of carrying it.

"Are they still in England?"

"No. When my mother passed, Jules took a job writing a column for the *New York Times*. She brought my father out."

Hailey nodded.

"Your father blames you?"

"That and more."

"And Jules?"

Sam exhaled. "Jules was always daddy's girl."

"Has it always been strained?"

It took him a moment to respond.

He raised his eyebrows. "My father, yes. He never really saw the whole acting thing as a sustainable career. It was always 'when are you going to get a real job?'" Sam took a final swig of his tea and set it down. "Jules—" He chuckled under his breath. "We were inseparable growing up. Being her little kid brother, I always had her to look out for me.

She was the one that stayed home from school when I was ill, the one who walked me to school. Never once did she complain." He smiled as he remembered with fondness. He continued to share stories of his time growing up in England. He mentioned how Jules had on more than one occasion taken the fall for pranks he'd done, mistakes he'd made, and problems he'd caused. She was always the one that could get their father to give in.

"After the success of my first couple of films, things changed." He shook his head slightly. "I don't know why. She became distant. We began to talk less and when we did, she had little to say."

"You think she might have felt as if her life paled in comparison to yours?"

"Well … yeah, I guess. I mean I tried to not talk about what I was doing—you know, I was more interested in what she was getting up to—but she never seemed to want to tell me what was going on in her world …" He sighed and paused for a moment to collect his thoughts.

"God, I've been so self-absorbed."

"Sam—"

He shook his head. "No, you were right. I've been so caught up in holding on to what I thought mattered that I've neglected the only ones that really mattered."

Hailey bit the side of her lip.

"Anyway, they won't be coming here, that's for sure."

"Well, tomorrow's another day. That's the thing about a new day, you get the chance to start again."

She sat up and took his cup. "Can I get you another drink?"

"No, I'm good, thank you."

As she walked away, he had one last question.

"Why?"

She turned back, looking steadily at him.

"Why what?"

"Why are you so determined to help me?"

"I told you—"

"Yeah, I know you need the money with the place and all, but if money was all you wanted, you would have jumped at the easy way out and signed the form."

She blew a strand of hair that had fallen across her face and was about to reply when Hailey felt her phone buzzing on her side. She put down the cups and slid the lock on the phone. Her father was on the other end.

"Hay, are you okay?"

"Yeah, I'm fine. I'm more concerned about you. Why didn't you answer? I must have left you at least eight messages."

"I know. I know. I thought I was going to be able to make it back but with the weather being so bad, the roads are blocked."

"I know."

"What?"

"Ah, nothing. I'll fill you in tomorrow."

"But you're okay?"

"Yes, Dad."

"How's Sam doing?"

She glanced over at Sam, who was huddled up beside the fire."

"Good."

"Is there something I should know, Hailey?"

"I'll speak to you tomorrow."

Hailey swore her father would have made an excellent detective; he had a knack for picking up on what a person wasn't saying. She was sure it was what made the Welland House popular at one time. Sure, their methods weren't exactly orthodox and they knew many centers saw their approach as a joke, but there was no denying the results they got with people. Many times it was in the eleventh hour that the light would come on, even with the most stubborn patients.

She glanced over at Sam.

Her father had always been adamant that he would never turn away a person if they truly wanted to get well. Where other centers would convince patients that they would suffer with their disease for the rest of their life, her father would question it. When other centers would tell patients they needed months of ongoing therapy, her father knew different. It wasn't as if he tackled addiction with empty theories. He'd seen the results many times. He'd say that once the underlying condition had come to the surface, and the person truly wanted to get well, it was only a matter of how fast the individual wanted to get well.

Hailey knew that other centers didn't resent them because their approach was different. They resented them because their long-term success rate was higher than any other center. Still, her father never boasted about it, he never wrote it on their website or shoved it in the faces of those who disliked them. Ultimately, it wasn't what they said about themselves that made them stand out. It was the patients. Yeah, word of mouth was a powerful thing and if anything would bring the place back to its feet, it would be the same again.

Hailey watched Sam as he stoked the fire, bringing life back to its dying embers. She wondered if Sam would be the catalyst that would reignite the embers of what had once thrived. And yet, more than that, she couldn't help wonder if he would rekindle something more.

"I can't stop shaking, but I don't feel cold," Sam said, wrapping the blanket tightly around his body and pacing back and forth.

"It's not the cold. You're withdrawing. Detox is going to be tough. Do you ache?"

"Yeah, all over."

"You feel nauseated?"

He nodded.

"Where did you put the pills?"

"What?"

"Well, if you're feeling this now, you would have gone through this in the first couple of days. Obviously I found the alcohol, but not the pills we gave you. Now I can give you some more, or you can tell me where you hid the last lot."

"Beneath the side dresser."

Hailey went off to retrieve them. She was glad to see he didn't put up a fight. By the look of his condition, he didn't have much fight left in him. She saw something different in his demeanor. Her father would always say that at the moment a person wanted to get well, you could see it in their eyes. The lies, the façade, and the games would end and finally, the healing could begin.

By the time she returned she could hear him retching in the washroom. She gathered a few warm blankets, a damp cloth, and a large bottle of water. Outside, the wind howled. A sound tore through the air like the cry of a trumpet on the battlefield, a stark reminder of the war that was being waged outside between Mother Nature and all of society.

Inside, their battle had just begun. Either way, they were in for a rough night.

Sam came out of the washroom looking like death warmed up. His complexion was a sickly pale and he was breathing heavily. Hailey wrapped one of the warm blankets around him and he curled up on the floor. She sat with him, keeping him hydrated and every now and again wiping his forehead with a moist cloth. The following hours were filled with little sleep and a lot of restlessness. He made multiple trips to the washroom and clung to the toilet as if holding on for dear life to a buoy in a turbulent ocean. She wiped the sweat from his face and rubbed his arms, holding him close. As he groaned, she tried to comfort him.

She thought back to the times she'd seen him on TV and in films. He'd always appeared so well presented, and she wondered how many others had seen him in this state. Right at that moment, she knew that she was seeing him for the first time. Sure, it wasn't what she imagined it would have been. But nevertheless, it was him she was seeing; his flaws, his secrets, out in the open—the man behind the lights and stardom.

She shook her head, thinking of how society had made celebrities. They placed them on pedestals, set them up, fashioned them as almost the gods of this world. They were the untouchables who didn't need saving. They were the ones that saved us. Saved us from the gloom, the mundane, the boring parts of our lives. Was it any wonder why so many wanted to be them? But how many of them had ended this way? How many had broken under the pressure of the spotlight? Admired as they rose, praised when they entertained, and yet somehow people assumed they were immune to weakness. Yet given the right circumstances, even the strongest could fall. And now sitting beside him, she could see the irony.

Even they needed saving.

Eventually the trips to the washroom lessened until finally they both fell asleep in front of the fire.

CHAPTER NINETEEN

H ours passed. When Hailey awoke her body was
pressed tight against the sofa with her arm slung over
Sam. He was strewn between her legs with his back against
her chest, still asleep. She glanced at the clock. It was a little
after six a.m.

A beam of morning light filtered through the curtains,
offering a glimpse of what the day had become, following
one of the worst storms they had experienced in years. She
glanced down. Some women may have imagined the
thought of waking up with one of Hollywood's hottest actors to be more than fortunate and yet Hailey knew the
truth. After the night they'd gone through, it was far from
being sexy, romantic, or in any way something to be desired.
Anyone else may have savored the moment, but the only
thought going through her mind was stepping under a hot
shower. She slid out from underneath him, hoping her
movement wouldn't wake him. He stirred but remained
asleep.

It felt refreshing to get cleaned up and throw on some

fresh clothes, and even better to see that the house was still intact. It was surprising to say the least. She had envisioned waking up to find the roof gone and half of her neighbor's property in her kitchen.

From her makeup bag, she pulled out some foundation. Just a touch would hide the bags under her eyes. She exhaled deeply, gazing at her reflection. Nothing short of plastic surgery would sort out the way she looked today, she thought. She stretched her neck side to side, contemplating sleeping a little longer. As she crossed the room, she considered going for a run. It would give a boost. Lying back on her bed of fresh sheets, she tugged on a sneaker. Swallowed up by the puffy duvet it only took seconds to dash that thought from her mind. She couldn't have been there for more than ten seconds before she drifted back into a slumber.

She woke up abruptly, running her hand over her face. Gazing over at the clock, she realized she'd been asleep for an hour and half. She groaned and dragged herself off the bed, knowing if she stayed there any longer the day would be completely shot. *Coffee!* she told herself. Nothing but the strongest would do it.

Trying not to wake him, she tiptoed around the kitchen. Opening a cupboard, she moved aside a jar to reach the coffee. Her hand caught the edge of a cereal box as she pulled it out, causing it to drop with a clatter onto the counter. Cereal went everywhere. She flinched and rolled her eyes.

"Isn't that always the way?"

She whirled around to see Sam standing in the doorway.

Hailey furrowed her brow. "Sorry, did I wake you?"

"No I've been awake awhile."

"How are you feeling?"

"I've felt better," he replied, rubbing his head. "Hope it doesn't last long."

"It tends to get worse before it gets better. Though it shouldn't be more than two to four days of detox. Everyone is different."

He pulled out a chair and took a seat. "Thanks for reminding me."

As soon as he said it, he knew what she was going to say.

Hailey raised her eyebrows slightly. "How long ago?"

Sam glanced sideways and met her gaze. "A few years back. In the summer."

"And?"

"I was off it for a year."

She paused, thinking about it.

"Coffee?"

Sam nodded with a smile. She took out some cups, boiled the kettle, and added the water when it was done. She handed him a cup, a plate of toast, and some headache medication.

"Toast will help with the acidity."

"Thank you."

"You're welcome."

"About last night." He lifted the toast to his lips. "I feel like a real jackass, the way I blew up and stormed off."

She leaned against the counter. "If it's any consolation, you're not the first."

He smiled then bit into his toast. "Do you sit with all your patients?"

Hailey gulped her coffee and looked at him over her cup, conscious of what he might be getting at. She could tell by the expression on his face that it was more than pure curiosity. She could feel her face going a slight shade of red. "Well … you … um … I just thought—"

"Either way, I appreciate it. Thank you," he cut in.

She nodded slowly, and offered a smile. In truth she appreciated it far more that he interrupted, as she really didn't want to finish her sentence. In all honestly, she felt like a bumbling idiot and at a complete loss for words.

"So, we'll get you seen to this morning."

"Umm." He didn't sound too keen on the idea.

"Well, better to be safe than sorry, right? Can't be sending you on your way today looking as if we've beaten you. Can I?"

Sam shrugged. "Well, I ... was kind of thinking of staying a little longer. If that's okay?"

Hailey sipped her coffee and fixed her eyes on him.

"Till the end of the week?" she asked.

"Actually, I was thinking of staying a few weeks longer. Might as well do this right."

She hesitated, surprised at his response. "If you stay, no more drink."

He nodded in agreement.

She shook her head. "No more games. You do it our way."

"Yeah, I promise." He nodded again. "I mean it."

Hailey let out a sigh. "Forgive me if I'm not entirely convinced."

"Rightly noted."

From outside, they heard the sound of a vehicle pulling up. Hailey set her cup on the side.

"Charlie?" Sam asked.

Hailey peered out the window and gave an affirmative nod.

"If you want to take a shower, there are fresh towels in the cupboard in the washroom, and your bags are back in your room."

Sam stood up to leave, only to turn back and offer a look of concern.

"I guess you'll be filling him in on last night's events?"

She caught an edge in his voice.

"Leave it with me. Oh, and soon as you're ready, I'm taking you in to the hospital. No arguments."

A moment later, Hailey watched Sam head up the stairs before she went out to meet her father and check the property for storm damage.

Stepping out into the bright morning light, she shaded her eyes with her hands before greeting her father, who looked deeply concerned. He gestured over his shoulder. "Is Sam okay? They just hauled his car out of the ditch. What happened last night?"

"Yeah, he's taking a shower and then we're going to get him looked at."

"What? Looked at?"

His voice was getting louder by the second.

"Calm down. Are they towing it back here?"

He shook his head. "I don't know. It's probably being towed to the garage —"

She groaned, cutting in. "Not Tommy's?"

"More than likely—Hailey, it doesn't matter. What happened?"

Hailey hesitated for a moment. She wasn't sure what he'd do if she told him the full story. Despite his zeal to get the place going and take Sam in, she knew full well his patience had grown thin over the past few years. He acted as if could manage the ups and downs of running the place, but a lot had changed since then. He'd changed. She could have sworn it was her mother that had kept him together all those years.

"He was leaving."

"Why?"

"Why does anyone want to leave?"

Charlie tilted his head to one side, an expression that let her know that it was going to take more than that before he let this one slide.

"Okay, he's been drinking. I found the bottles. Got rid of them and well ..."

"That's it." He threw his arms up. "Once we get him checked out, he's gone."

Charlie moved past her, and she spun around.

"Dad."

He continued walking, either oblivious or ignoring.

"DAD."

Charlie stopped and looked back.

"Give him another chance."

"What? No, I should have listened to you when he first arrived."

"I was wrong. He wants to change and I believe he can."

"No." He shook his head. "I don't know what I was thinking."

He turned to head back into the house.

"Mother never gave up on you."

Charlie stopped in his tracks and looked back over his shoulder, scanning her face before sighing.

"Look, you always said that you could see it in their eyes. That moment. The moment they were ready, right?"

He nodded.

"I saw that. I saw it this morning. I know I can help him."

He breathed in deeply, then rubbed the back of his neck. She could see he was weighing it in his mind.

"You know we only have a week left?"

"Well, it seems he's willing to stay longer," Hailey said.

Charlie nodded slowly before breaking into a smile.

"You know I miss your mother, a lot." He stared off. "There isn't a day that goes by I don't think about her. But having you here ..." He trailed off, smiling. Hailey thought she caught his eyes tearing up.

"I know, Dad."

"Whew, a lot of dust kicking up." Charlie wiped his eyes. "I think I'll head in."

Hailey smiled and watched him disappear inside.

* * * * *

Sam could have stayed under the water forever. Its warmth wrapped him like a blanket and relaxed his aching muscles. Yet even the shower couldn't ease the anxiety, shakiness, and difficulty he now felt trying to think clearly. A flood of memories was now at the forefront of his mind, tormenting him with how hard it would be to withdraw from alcohol. His mind flashed from Hailey, to Kate, to his father, and then to his career. It felt like a heavy weight crashing down on him. Irresponsibility, pain, and epic failure swirled and fought for control.

Sam pressed his hands against the tiled shower walls, feeling a mixture of emotions welling up inside of him. Streams of water poured over his face mixing with his tears and diluting their saltiness. He wasn't one for crying, but now that was all he seemed to be doing. This wasn't part of withdrawal, he thought. His thoughts flashed between the past, the present, and the future. An onslaught of regrets, anger, and what-ifs over his mother's death, missing her funeral, and the breakdown of his relationships bombarded his mind.

Eventually he closed his eyes and breathed in the steam from the shower, trying his utmost to mentally push the past out the only way he could. By replaying the previous night in his mind. By thinking about her. Within minutes he couldn't stop thinking about her. It had worked. He couldn't remember when someone had believed in him as much as Hailey. Someone who seemed to see beyond the smoke and mirrors, the flaws, masks, and walls he put up; someone who really was concerned for his well-being instead of their own agenda. Her honesty was refreshing in his world of lies. Her tenderness and touch were something that made him want to linger longer. It had been a long time since he had thought about anyone else the way he had about Kate. He didn't think that anyone else would be able to capture his attention the way she had. But with Hailey it felt different. He wasn't sure what it was. There was a gentleness and deep strength to her that complemented the other. And when she smiled ... he found himself smiling just at the thought of the way her lip curled up.

After drying off he slipped on a fresh set of clothes and continued patting his damp hair. He opened the doors to the outside patio, pushed wide the shutters, and was bathed in golden sunlight. He leaned against the wooden railing. Looking out across the lake with the towel around his neck, he breathed in the morning. He was about to turn when she came into view. Hailey was walking the grounds picking up items that had blown away in the storm. He felt his chest tighten at the sight of her. He couldn't pull his eyes away. It was like seeing her in a new way.

It was then she looked up and noticed him. She gave a slight wave. Sam casually nodded back.

She smiled and gestured to him. "C'mon."

"I'll be right there."

Stepping back in, he sprayed on some deodorant, checked his breath on his hand, ran some hair wax through his hair, and gave one quick glance up and down in the mirror before leaving. *Urgh*, he groaned. After minimal sleep, vomiting all night, and pain medication he wasn't exactly feeling like Don Juan. Though after last night, this was a vast improvement. It would have to do.

CHAPTER TWENTY

Hailey stood back and assessed the house. Though it had fared well, the rest of the property hadn't been so fortunate. Parts of the barn roof had been torn clean off and dropped on the opposite side of the lawn, chairs had toppled like tumbleweeds to the far edge of the land, and a large majority of the fencing had collapsed under the weight of fallen tree limbs. While the forceful winds had given way to a gentle breeze, it still had not entirely gone. It would likely be a day or two before things returned completely to normal.

Hailey was turning a chair upright when he came out. He was wearing jeans and a white T-shirt and had his hands tucked inside his dark blue hoodie.

"Hey." She smiled. "You're looking ..." She trailed off.

He grinned and rolled his eyes. "I know, like crap."

"Well, I wasn't going to say that but ... yeah." She smirked. "Well, are you ready to go?"

Sam nodded, and they left for the hospital.

By the time they made it to the spot where Sam's car had slid off the road, they could see that workers had cleared away the debris and the only indication that he'd been there were two deep skid marks that disappeared over the grassy shoulder into the ditch.

"It's at the garage if you're wondering," Hailey said, keeping her eyes on the road ahead.

"Huh," Sam mumbled under his breath.

He shook his head. "That reminds me. Tommy came by yesterday, looking for you."

Hailey grimaced.

Sam chuckled. "Yeah."

"Did he tell you if he fixed it?"

Sam raised an eyebrow and gave her a look. It was enough.

She frowned. "What a guy."

Reaching across to turn on the radio he caught a trace of her perfume. It had almost a sweet candy-like scent to it. The rest of the journey into town was filled with comfortable silence and the faint sound of the local radio station giving updates on the storm.

Hailey hadn't shared much about her past relationships, besides Tommy. Sam didn't want to pry but nevertheless he was curious to know why she wasn't in a relationship. It wasn't that he thought all women needed to be in one. It was just that she was attractive and he couldn't imagine anyone not wanting to date her. Sure, she was somewhat stubborn but so was he. For whatever reason she was still single, he was kind of glad.

Along the way they observed the town's damage. Most homes only had flooding in their yards while others weren't as fortunate. Several electrical lines were down and two houses must have caught fire during the night as they were now covered in soot and sending up thick smoldering smoke into the air. Turning into the main street, they gave way to an emergency vehicle that was heading out at breakneck speed. The morning sun had already begun to dry large patches of the roads while smaller off-roads resembled tiny rivers. A blanket of moist mist crept its way between the homes, giving everything an eerie appearance that seemed to play tricks with Sam's eyes. Driving through the town, they noticed the older homes had been affected the worst. Their foundations and driveways had been swept away, leaving nothing but soiled rubble. Homes stood preciously balanced like a deck of cards, only held up by temporary foundations. Ruined belongings and various types of debris lined the sidewalks. Store owners milled around probably discussing the storm. A few removed plywood and steel shutters while others wandered aimlessly in what could only be a state of shock.

Within minutes they were at Walton Hospital. Sam had his reservations about going in. Not only would people be staring, but also he knew there would be families waiting to be seen with far worse injuries than his. He only agreed to go out of respect. He was their guest and he'd caused enough trouble already. The last thing he wanted to do now was rock the boat any further, even if it did seem trivial.

Sitting in the waiting room, he could hear people whispering between themselves and gazing over. Hospitals, waiting rooms, and, more than anything, people staring made him feel uncomfortable. It wasn't exactly the staring that bothered him as much as it was wondering what they were thinking. He was never one for being treated differently, yet it happened. Truth was, depending on where he was in the world, his celebrity status did provide a level of attention that others wouldn't get. At first he thought it was cool—who wouldn't? Getting into places for free, being escorted through airports, and getting random gifts were common. Though over time, he had to admit the novelty had worn off. Some days he felt like standing on a chair and announcing, *I'm just a guy. Cut me, I bleed just the same as you. Now go about your day!* Instead, he would smile politely and look anywhere else except in the direction of the curious onlookers. It probably didn't help that every table in the waiting room was lined with tabloid magazines where the front-page photos were his face or Kate's.

Before Sam could turn any redder in the face than he already had, Hailey had found the largest paper she could find, opened it, and suggested he hold the other side to avoid the constant staring. *Yeah, like that's going to fool them. What is she thinking?*

It wasn't long before she was snickering to herself. Every time he looked at her, she stopped. Once he turned away it began again.

"What's so funny?"

To which she laughed all the more.

"Seriously, what is up with you?"

She nudged him and motioned for him to take a look. Sam slipped the paper down slowly and peered over the top.

Three people in the room were reading through the same tabloid magazine with his face splashed across the front, their heads perfectly hidden behind its pages creating the illusion that his face was theirs. If that wasn't odd enough, along the bottom of the magazine a headline read: "Will the real Slim Shady please stand up."

He turned to Hailey with a sarcastic grin. "Are you sure you don't want me to get them to check you out as well?"

She smiled and dug him with her elbow. "This is all too surreal."

Right then his name was called.

After a thorough inspection, a series of repetitive questions, and a request to scratch his autograph on a blank medical note for the doctor's daughter, he was given a clean bill of health and sent on his way.

* * * * *

"I can't believe that was it. I could have sworn you would have had at least suffered a concussion."

"I guess I got lucky."

Hailey pondered his answer driving past trucks loaded with debris.

"Do you ever think that life places obstacles in our way, to set us in a new direction? To keep us where we are until we're ready to move on?"

Sam rubbed his forehead.

"Hailey, I know I didn't suffer a concussion, but at this time in the morning that's a tad too deep for my brain. Give me another cup of coffee, a few hours to clear the cobwebs out of my head, and I'll get back to you on that."

She liked his response, but even more than that she enjoyed the way he looked at her. She felt comfortable with him; there was even an odd sense of familiarity that she couldn't quite figure out. Nevertheless, she was just glad he was okay.

Maggie's Diner was packed with young and old locals. It had become almost a central hub for folks in town to swap stories over how they had weathered the storm. The smell of bacon, toast, and eggs filled the air along with the clatter of cutlery and the regular sound of Danny's music drifting out of the kitchen.

Danny was the first to acknowledge them, giving a brief nod before handing off an order to Carol. Maggie was manning the till and repeatedly banging the side of the ATM machine that was known for playing up. Hailey always joked with her that banging it probably didn't help. But Maggie was convinced it was the cure for everything—especially faulty technology. If it doesn't work, give it a kick. If it still didn't work, hit it with a hammer. It kind of explained why she had a reputation for driving out customers who bellyached about service.

"You want to get a table?" Sam asked.

"Yeah —"

As she said it, her eyes flashed to the far side of the restaurant to where Tommy and several others were seated. Thankfully, they hadn't noticed them yet.

"Ah, maybe we should take it to go."

Sam followed her eyes and realized why the sudden change.

"Don't we have to see him anyway?"

Hailey winced at the thought.

"Yeah, but—"

"Hailey," Tommy called out.

Too late.

Hailey rolled her eyes before turning towards him. They grabbed their coffee and crossed the room. Tommy was sprawled across the booth looking as if he had just won the lottery. He hushed the others' conversation with a flick of the wrist and they leaned back. Each of them wore identical grins, as though they were privy to some inside joke.

"Just the woman I wanted to see."

Hailey really wasn't in the mood for his childish games today. *Keep it brief,* she told herself.

"Sam's vehicle, we'd like to pick it up," she told Tommy.

"Yes, whatever happened there?" He shot Sam a gleeful look, sliding closer to Hailey.

"None of your business," she answered.

He pulled a face to the others and then smiled.

"Maybe. However, there is going to be a little fee to retrieve it. That's if you can even drive it away. Looked pretty banged up to me. Didn't it, boys?"

Hailey scowled, knowing full well where this was heading and wondering if he had done any further damage, just out of spite.

"How much?" Sam asked.

Tommy shook a sugar packet, ripped it open, and added it to his coffee.

He stirred it. "Well, let's see. We have the cost of towing, storage overnight, and of course today …" He turned to his coworkers. "Um, hasn't my father just increased his prices?"

"Yeah, I think so," said Luke, giving a sly grin.

"Umm, yeah. Well, how about you drop by this morning and I'll give you an exact figure."

Hailey's eyes darted between him, Luke, and the others.

"Fine," she said, turning to walk away.

Tommy caught hold of her wrist, firmly pulling her back.

"Oh, I forgot to mention. Your engine is going to need a rebuild. It's gonna be pretty expensive."

"Let go." Hailey tried pulling her wrist away, but his grip only tightened.

"Now, I could be persuaded to do it for free." He tugged
her closer.

"Let go," she said louder.

Sam stepped in. "I think you need to listen to her."

Tommy shot him a glare and Luke stood up.

"Is there a problem here, fellas?" Maggie pulled up
alongside them. Tommy released his grip and Hailey re-
coiled.

He shook his head.

Not taking his eyes off Sam even for a moment, he said,
"No, Maggie. We were just leaving." He wiped the corner
of his mouth with a napkin and tossed it onto the plate.
They passed by, offering a final look of defiance.

"I never liked that wee laddie," Maggie said in her thick
Scottish accent.

Hailey rubbed her wrist, which burned and was lined
with a red mark.

"Thank you," she said to both of them.

"C'mon, let me take a look at that." Maggie rubbed Hailey's wrist and to her embarrassment gave it a loving kiss as
if she was tending to her own child. But even that couldn't
distract Hailey's thoughts from what this would all mean.
Just how much trouble was Tommy planning to cause?

After they decided to stay and have their coffee Maggie joined them, bringing over some of her newest
homemade dessert, called Clootie Dumpling. This
brought no end of laughter as they both took guesses as
to what was in it and who in their right mind would give
it that name. Maggie gave them both a short lesson on
traditional Scottish desserts like the Edinburgh Fog and
Tipsy Laird, which she was quite quick to point out
would not be best suited for the guests at the Welland

House, due to its high content of the alcoholic beverage, Drambuie.

By the time they left, they were stuffed.

"I couldn't eat another bite."

"Me too."

As they made their way over to Farlan's Garage, the atmosphere in the truck became tangible. They didn't say much on the way, Hailey wondered if he was thinking what she was. At the best of times, Tommy knew how to be a royal pain in the ass, but now?

"Maybe we should come back later. Give him time to cool down?" he suggested.

"You don't know Tommy, he doesn't cool down. He either gets what he wants or he finds a way to make it difficult for you."

CHAPTER TWENTY-ONE

Without any other option, they pulled into Farlan's Garage. They could see Luke and a few of the other men working beneath the cars. Hearing their engine, they immediately looked over, and one of them whistled to the other. Tommy was busy inside finishing up with customer when they rolled up in front of the office.

"Why don't you wait in the truck, no need for both of us to have to deal with him again," Sam said.

"No, I think it's best I go in."

The mingled odor of oil, rubber, and rusted metal hit them as they walked into the office. The whole place had a grimy feel to it, as though it hadn't been cleaned in years. A small cabinet of dusty trophies and faded Little League photos were displayed prominently near the front of the doorway, making anyone who entered clearly aware of their involvement in sponsoring the local kids. Torn clippings from the local newspaper were tacked to the wall highlighting news about the garage over the years: one of them was the announcement of Tommy becoming joint owner with his father, Monty. Beneath the headline was a proud photo of them both sticking out their chests.

Shrouded behind a cloud of gray cigarette smoke, Tommy eyed them over a customer's shoulder. His expression became animated when he saw them. Waiting in line, Hailey shifted her weight from one foot to the next, feeling awkward. Finally it was their turn.

"Uh—" Before she could say anymore, Tommy grunted.

He skipped the small talk; instead, he tapped on a few keyboard keys before twisting the screen around for them to see.

"Your bill comes to eighteen hundred."

"What?" Hailey stammered, knowing full well that it didn't cost that much to tow a vehicle a few miles and keep it overnight.

He stuck his finger in his ear and shook it. "Like I said, prices have gone up. Cost of inflation and whatnot."

"This shouldn't be more a couple of hundred."

"Hailey, don't worry. I'll just pay and we'll get going," Sam interjected, taking out his wallet.

Maybe Sam was fine with it, but she wasn't going to have it.

"No. He's taking us for a ride."

Tommy yawned. "Have it your way." He turned the computer back around and casually flipped through a smudged sports magazine on his desk. Hailey was fuming; she could feel her anger rising at his smugness. The muscles in her jaw clenched. Part of her wanted to leave immediately. Unfortunately, it would have only meant returning later.

"You know what, Tommy, I'm tired of your crap."

Tommy didn't even raise an eyebrow as he flipped another page. Seeing him ignore her only infuriated her more. She slapped the magazine out of his hands. Tommy jumped up but before another word could be said, his father, Monty, stepped in from out back.

"What's going on here?"

For a moment neither of them said anything, Tommy and Hailey exchanging icy glares.

"Hailey, how's Charlie doing?"

"Good." She didn't hide her look of disgust for his son.

"Now what appears to be the problem?"

"Your son is trying to rip us off."

"Oh, c'mon, Hailey, I'm sure you're over-exaggerating."

"I'll tell you what's over-exaggerated. Eighteen hundred is over-exaggerated."

"Tommy?"

Tommy smirked. "It's nothing, Dad, go back out. I can handle it."

"Son, step out of the way."

Tommy reluctantly moved to one side.

Monty shuffled past him, pulled out his spectacles from his chest pocket, and peered at the computer. He was a large, burly man who had known Hailey's family for years. He had always been the one to do the repairs on any of their vehicles. He and her father had known each other since school, but then again most of the folks in town knew each other. Monty was an odd guy; you never quite knew how he was going to treat you. He rarely smiled and when he did, you kind of wished he hadn't. Most would have assumed he was exactly like Tommy, yet that couldn't be further from the truth. He was from a different generation. The kind that believed in an honest day's work and occasionally helping you out when you didn't have enough to pay a bill right away. Hailey couldn't recount the number of times she'd brought that old truck into the garage only to have him do work on it for free. Tommy said it was because his father knew how much Tommy liked her. But she knew different. Monty treated everyone equally. It was why his business did so well. People felt like they could trust him. And knowing him, that was one principle he would make damn sure his son learned before he handed him the reins of the garage.

He tapped the keyboard a few times. Hailey looked at him then back at Tommy, who was now looking uncomfortable. The smirk was gone from his face and in its place was an annoyed expression. A printer behind them kicked in, spitting out a couple of pages. Monty collected them and put them on the desk.

"That'll be three hundred and twenty-five dollars."

"Sounds more like it," Hailey said. "Thank you."

Monty cast a glance over his shoulder at Tommy, giving him a look that she knew would mean they'd be exchanging words later. "The front end grill is caked up with soil and grass, so you might want to get it cleaned, but other than that it should run fine."

"Thanks, much appreciated," Sam replied.

"Hailey, say hello to your dad for me."

"Will do. By the way, do you know what's the deal with my truck?"

"I already told you," Tommy piped up.

"Settle down," Monty reprimanded him.

Hailey wouldn't even look at him. In her mind he had told enough lies. She wasn't going to give him anything else to hold over her head.

"I'll get one of the lads to go see," Monty said.

After paying they were led out back, where Sam collected his vehicle. Hailey watched as he drove it out. It seemed as if it had shared the same good fortune that Sam had. The bumper was scratched up and there were chunks of earth squeezed in the grill but it had come through the crash remarkably unscathed.

Monty spoke with Luke. Hailey had a hard time hearing what they were saying but Monty didn't look too pleased. Luke disappeared into the back of the yard with a set of keys in his hands. Monty came over, wiping oil from his hands with a dirty cloth.

"Hailey, it appears there have been some engine problems and while those can be fixed, there's more bad news."

He briefly hesitated, obviously recognizing her concerned expression.

"The storm last night brought down a branch and your truck was among the few that got damaged. Now I want you to know we'll cover the cost of that if you still want to fix it, as it occurred on our property. So you have nothing to worry about. It might take some time, though."

Hailey stared. She couldn't believe what she was hearing. If Tommy's actions weren't bad enough, but now this?

"Well, of course I'm going to want it repaired. Why would you think otherwise? What about the engine?"

"That's the thing, Hailey." He shook his head. "It's going to be costly. With the history and age of the truck, I'm not entirely sure it's exactly worth rebuilding. Parts for this are hard to come by. Besides, you have it in here more times than you have it on the road, right? Maybe it's time to get a new one?"

Hailey's shoulders sagged. She knew they were tight for money as it was, with the cost of getting the Welland House up and running, the anticipated expense of hiring staff again, and repairs from the storm. She groaned. Even with the money they'd get from having Sam they would barely manage.

And no doubt her father would side with Monty on this one. In his mind it would all be about priorities. He'd wanted to get rid of that old truck even when her mother drove it. To him, it was a hazard. It was old and not worth a dime. He was forever chiding her about putting so much money into it. *All the money you've spent on that damn thing you could have bought yourself a new one*, he would say. He didn't understand and neither did Monty. It wasn't about owning a new vehicle. It wasn't about the money she'd put into it to keep it on the road. None of that mattered. It was her connection to her mother. It still carried her scent, makeup, and driving license. It was the one memory of her that meant more than money could buy. Letting that go—no, she wasn't ready for that, at least not right now.

Sam's car idled up beside them; she could tell from his expression that he knew something was up.

"You okay?"

She replied fast. "Yes, fine. Go ahead, I'll be a few minutes behind you."

His eyebrow rose. "You sure?"

She nodded, feeling as if she was about to burst into tears at any minute. The day had all been too much and it had only begun. The fact that she knew Sam was wealthy only made it worse. He probably could have bought every car that was in the lot and it barely would have scraped his bank account. She didn't want him to know what her situation was. It wasn't as if it was his problem or as if he would have done anything anyway. The thought flashed through her mind of him offering to pay and that just made it all that more humiliating. No, that was not going to happen. She felt another wave of embarrassment.

She turned back to Monty and listened for the crunch of gravel as Sam drove away. Even Monty was looking perturbed as she stood in silence. She gave a final glance to make sure he was gone before telling Monty that it was probably best if he just towed it back to her place. He apologized and said if she changed her mind, he would try to shop around for cheap parts.

Hailey dragged herself back to her father's truck and sank into the seat. She wanted to sit there and wallow in her sadness, but seeing Tommy glaring from the office was making her uncomfortable. She pulled away, not wanting to stay a minute longer.

CHAPTER TWENTY-TWO

S am was having a conversation with her father on the front porch when she pulled up. She really didn't want to rehash the whole incident again, so she hoped Sam had filled him in. Thankfully, her father went back inside while Sam made his way over.

"So?"

She furrowed her brow. "They'll drop it off."

He nodded. "Good."

"You want to take a walk?" she asked. "I need to check the rest of the property for damage."

While it was true, she really just wanted to avoid the million and one questions from her father and then admitting the truck wasn't going to be repaired. She thought she would postpone it—at least until she could shake off what she was feeling.

He shrugged. "Sure."

They walked side by side towards the shoreline where a

rack of kayaks had been overturned. There was a beauty to the morning that seemed to permeate everything. The sky was a deep blue with only a few clouds in the distance and the scent of fresh-cut fields hung in the air. Hailey flicked at a mosquito buzzing around her ear. The mosquitoes were already out in full force.

"Your father seemed … surprisingly chipper this morning? I'm gathering you didn't mention the whole fiasco last night?"

"No, I did."

"And?"

"You don't need to worry, unless of course you were thinking of reneging on your promise."

He shook his head. "No. Of course not." He swatted a swarm of tiny flies around his head.

"How do you put up with all these insects? I would go crazy if I had to deal with this every summer."

"Ah, you get used to it. The mossies aren't bad, it's the black horseflies you need to watch out for." She tapped the air with her finger. "Now those will take a chunk out of you."

His eyes widened.

Drawing closer to the lake, she tried to contain her laughter as she eyed him trying to dodge flies. Finally, she couldn't resist it any longer and she slapped his arm.

"Heck, what was that for?" he cried, stopping to check himself.

"Black horsefly!" she replied, smiling and walking ahead knowing full well there wasn't anything there.

They paused beside the water's edge and stared at the overturned rack. The kayaks were floating in various places around the wooden dock and further out on the lake.

"Okay, I'll get those out there, if you want to pull those in." Hailey indicated to the ones closest to shore.

"I can go out and bring those in."

She smirked. "You sure, Hollywood?"

"Stop calling me that. I'd have you know I used to work with kayaks in the summers."

"You did?"

"Well ... one summer, that is ... when I was a kid." He tapped his leg. "Until I was fired for falling asleep on the job ..."

She nodded, smiling, never taking her eyes off him. "Go on."

"... And letting people go on without paying, and ..."

His trailed off, grinned, and then bit the side of his lip.

Her eyebrows rose. "There's more?"

And then he spat the words out fast. "And I kind of set the place on fire."

She burst into laughter. "Well, in that case, I think you deserve an opportunity to redeem yourself."

* * * * *

It took them all of forty minutes to gather up the boats, restack them, and get the place looking usable again. Much of that time was filled with laughter as Hailey watched Sam balancing precariously in a boat while attempting to tie the kayaks behind it. She couldn't believe he didn't fall in.

As they continued to make their way around the grounds, there were moments they walked in silence. She wondered if she should make use of the time and dive further into his background with his family, but knowing how tired both of them were, she decided against it. Occasionally she would point out parts of the property that he hadn't seen yet. She was surprised at how comfortable they both were in saying very little. It didn't feel awkward as she imagined it would. There was a natural ebb and flow to their conversation that seemed almost effortless.

* * * * *

They made their way over the bridge. Sam noted the way the stream below had risen higher since the previous night's downpour and had now soaked the surrounding banks. On the far side, close to the water, was a cedar pergola arbor that looked as if it had seen better days. It was covered in brambles and ivy. Stone slabs led up to it, each one barely visible beneath the dirt, overgrown weeds, and leaves.

Hailey leaned part of the broken trellis back up only to see it fall back down again. As the storm had ripped its way through the grounds it carried integral parts of the arbor away on the wind as they were nowhere to be found.

"Where have I seen this place before?" He furrowed his brow, looking around at the paving on either side of the path.

"The photo on our mantel?" Hailey replied.

"Yeah, there were chairs here."

Hailey held a broken piece of the trellis in her hand and brushed it clean. "Yep, it's where my mother and father were married."

In that moment, looking at her against the backdrop of the sun and lake, which acted like a canvas of glorious colors, he registered the way the wind blew strands of her hair across her face and against the tops of her bare shoulders. She probably had had less sleep than him, and yet it didn't seem to matter. At that very moment she stole all words from his mouth. He was so taken by her that it took a few seconds to realize that she'd glanced back in his direction. He coughed, bringing his hand up and looking casually away. He could feel himself going a slight shade of red; inwardly he hoped that she hadn't noticed him observing her but when he looked back her wistful smile confirmed she had.

"Hey, I wanted to thank you," he said.

"For what?"

"Back at the garage. Speaking up. Holding your own."

"I just hate to see people take advantage of others," Hailey said.

He chuckled. "New York City is full of them, you should go there sometime. There's always someone trying to sell you something; No other place like it. I love it."

"You like the city life?"

"There's something for everyone. When I can't sleep at night I sometimes leave early and go into Washington Square Park and play chess with some of the old-timers. They never seem to be bothered by life. I like that."

"You didn't get mobbed by all the tourists?"

"No. Even in the city that never sleeps, tourists don't generally wander through the park at that time in the morning."

"And you do? Got a death wish?"

He chuckled.

"Maybe."

They made their way back and paused on the bridge, watching the water rush beneath them.

"Do you miss it?"

"I don't miss all the crowds—"

"No, I meant England."

A brief smile flickered across her face.

"At times." He nodded. "I mean, I've been here so long now I've kind of got used to it. And working constantly, well ... I can't say I really get enough downtime to dwell on what I miss."

"Tell me something about England you miss."

"Well, there is a number of things."

"And?"

He took a little step forward and leaned on the wooden railing.

"It's kind of the little things, you know? Certain foods, humor, and well ... It might kind of sound stupid. But ... the smell of the air after a hard rain ... There is nothing else like it. I've been in a lot of countries in the world and it's not the same. It's strange, I always get a sense that it's like life's way of giving everything a fresh start. Like hitting reset on a computer, you know?"

"You ever wish you could hit reset?"

"I think we all do at times, right?" Sam replied.

Hailey smiled and nodded. "Right."

He liked the way she smiled. It had been a while since he felt so at ease with a person. More specifically with another girl other than Kate. But this felt different, though he wasn't sure why.

CHAPTER TWENTY-THREE

The following three days and nights felt like a roller-coaster ride of emotions. A battle was being waged within him, like a caged lion trying to tear its way out and gain control. Detoxing with natural medication helped but it did little to alleviate the nightmares. Sam suffered all the usual cold sweats and anxiety that came with facing the memories that alcohol had so easily made him forget.

A routine was established. Each day was filled with acupuncture, yoga, meditation, eating the right foods, running, and long walks. He found himself opening up far more than he had with any other person. Talking with Hailey felt natural. Being around her, he knew he could let his guard down. And for once in his life, it felt safe and grounding at the same time.

His conversations with Hailey felt more like chatting with a friend than psychotherapy. The more time they spent together, the more he began to see her as more than a counselor or someone to confide in. She was special. She never judged him, which was refreshing after feeling as though he had been raked over the coals in previous centers. He started to notice her ability to pick up on the times when he was skirting an issue. They talked more about his family, his past, and his relationship with Kate. Whether she knew it or not, she had a gift for getting a person to open up.

More days passed. It took all of one week before he was sleeping well again. Everything about the way he felt when he woke up felt physically better. He even noticed the thoughts that pummelled him endlessly at night were no longer causing the trauma he'd become accustomed to. It wasn't like he had resolved them; they were still there. His family was still broken, his relationship with Kate was still in ruins, and soon he would have to return to his normal life and all that had once contributed to the stress.

But now those weren't at the forefront of his mind. He felt a glimmer of hope; she made him feel that there was a way out. There was light at the end of the tunnel and it didn't require him to surrender to a life-long disease, self-medicate, or run from pain. It only required him to remember who he was before the drink. Before the pain and heartache. To reconnect with the person he was beneath the glare of the lights and behind the wall he'd put up to protect himself.

As each day passed he found himself being peeled like an onion. Each morning he awoke excited about what the day would bring. More specifically, he looked forward to being with Hailey. She was the first thing on his mind when he woke up and the last when his eyes closed. By day he would enjoy her company. At night he would relish their conversation as they sat drinking tea on the porch and watching the fireflies flickering on and off. Many nights after retiring to his room he would see her make her routine trip into the barn from his window. Through the darkness and the light that filtered through the cracks he would watch her silhouette dance freely. Free, he thought. That was how he felt when he was with her. She made him look at things from a different perspective—a lighter side. He could be honest around her, let down his guard and be who he was before it all. Before the fame, before the pain and the emptiness he had tried to fill.

* * * * *

By the following weekend, with only one week left in his stay, he no longer felt the harsh effects of detox, and things were looking up in all manner of ways. Charlie had suggested to Hailey that she should take him into town on Sunday and introduce him to some local culture.

"A shindig, a celebration of sorts, is being put on by the town," she told him. There really wasn't any other way of explaining what it was. It was a mix of everything.

For a time, it looked as if the town wasn't going to move ahead in light of the storm. However, efforts over the past week had been stepped up in order to make sure that the event that had never been postponed would go off without a hitch. Despite the devastation that the hurricane had brought to parts of the town, much of it remained untouched and any part that was left in ruin was quickly cleared and tended to by crews and local families—everyone pitched in. The whole town had worked hard to prepare for the annual Delaware County Fair, and not even Mother Nature was going to sway them off course.

Over the years the turnout had grown larger, with companies sponsoring the event and the draw of big-name bands and artists scheduled to play. It had run for as long as Hailey could remember. The variety and fun that people had there was what had put their little town on the map. Families would come from miles away to attend, which only helped Walton's economy even more. It would start on a Sunday and run for the entire week, from morning till night. It was a large community event and people loved it.

* * * * *

The morning had started like any other, though now Hailey was used to Sam joining her in morning runs and yoga by the water. She had crammed as much as she could into every hour of the day, knowing that while they had made massive progress, there was little time remaining. She knew the odds, statistically, how people fared when they left any rehab. Fifty to ninety percent would relapse but that hadn't been the case with their methods.

Maybe that's what had gotten them blacklisted by those in the rehabilitation community. They didn't like how different their methods were to theirs; they didn't like that people had once flocked to the center. In their minds it was clear that any addiction was a disease and one that a person would have to manage for the rest of their lives. Yet at the Welland House they never saw it that way. And their results proved they were right. Still, they never took chances with anyone that passed through their doors, and Sam was no exception. For her, it had become personal. She couldn't let him fail.

"Where are you taking me again?" she asked.

"I told you, if I tell you it wouldn't be a surprise, now would it?"

The sun was close to peaking and thankfully the heat wasn't too unbearable. It was a perfect day with hardly a cloud in sight. Sam walked with her towards the lake. In his hand he carried a wicker picnic basket.

"We should really keep digging in, we have less than seven days left."

"Hailey, look at me. I feel the best I've felt in months. You said yourself I looked healthy."

"I know, but detoxing is one thing. There is still a lot to be done inside you, Hollywood—and besides, we're already going to be taking the evening off to go to the fair."

"C'mon, you can still psychoanalyze me where we are going—you always do." He grinned. "And anyway, your father said it's fine."

"You asked my father?"

"Of course. Who do you think gave me the basket?"

She frowned. "And he said yes?"

He nodded.

"Now I'm worried," she said, smiling.

He laughed. "C'mon, let your hair down, let's take a break. We've been at this for three weeks now. An hour isn't much to ask, is it?"

"Two weeks, to be exact, and let's be honest, the other one was shot."

Sam gave her a look. She laughed.

"All right—an hour."

Once they reached the dock, Sam sat the basket inside one of the larger cedar canoes and hopped in, causing the entire thing to wobble from side to side. Recognizing her hesitation, he extended his hand.

"Are you getting in or going to wave to me from the shore?" He smiled.

"You don't have any matches in that basket, do you?" she jested.

He grinned. "I'm not going to live that one down, am I?"

She stepped in, balancing carefully before taking a seat opposite him. She watched him as he untied the rope and pushed out. As he rowed she saw the muscles in his arm tense. They glided through the water with ease; the only sound was the waves lapping up against the canoe. She stared at the beauty around her. The trees along the edge hung low over the surface of the lake and the birds darted in and out of the reeds. Everything about the sounds and sights seemed elevated. She breathed in deeply, taking in the fresh air and drifting back to all the times she had come out on the lake. Sitting across from each other, their eyes would occasionally connect, each time igniting a forbidden thrill of being alone with him that she hadn't felt up until now.

"You look as if you could get used to this," she noted.

He pulled hard on the oars. "Maybe. I must admit it's beautiful and peaceful." He hesitated. "But don't you go stir crazy? I mean not hearing much more than nature around you?"

She cocked her head to one side. "Tell me, what are you thinking about right now?" she asked.

"Well … nothing. Just us, the water."

"Calming, therapeutic even, isn't it?"

"Do you always do that?"

"What?"

"Answer every question with a question?"

"Do I?"

He laughed, and she joined in.

Hailey went to lift the top on the basket but before she could catch a glimpse of its contents, Sam said. "Hey, no peeking."

Hailey raised an eyebrow. "Okay, now you really have me wondering."

"Trust me, it will be worth the wait."

Dotted along the lake and barely visible behind the trees were cottages. Many were empty, summer retreats only used for short periods of time. Most of the owners were city folk looking to get away on long weekends or a month. When the summer people were here, the town was busier than ever and when they left, traffic on the roads was practically zero. In the past few years, however, a lot of the cottages had become abandoned and derelict. Kids in the area with nothing better to do had been known to break in or smash windows.

Finally, Sam pulled in the water-soaked oars and they floated slowly along with the mild current. Lily pads broke apart, sending up a flurry of waterborne insects.

"Okay, now close your eyes," he said.

"Do I have to?"

"Yes."

Reluctantly, she did as requested, wondering what on earth he was up to. She could hear the creak of the basket lid being lifted.

"No peeking."

"I'm not."

"Okay, I want you to take a bite out of this and tell me what you think."

"Oh no, is this going to be gross?"

"Live a little."

She hesitated for a brief moment and then took a bite. It

was like biting into a pastry pie but instead of fruit filling it
was meat. She chewed it around before swallowing.

"So?"

Hailey mused, moving her head from side to side.

"What was that?" she asked.

He laughed.

"It's called a pork pie. Did you like it?"

"It was tasty."

She could hear him chuckling to himself.

"Okay, now keep your eyes closed."

She smelled a savory morsel close to her lips.

"Go ahead."

The next bite tasted like breadcrumbs initially and then
soft in the middle. She immediately recognized its taste. It
was an egg. She opened her eyes to see what he was holding.

"Now that was tasty. But what is that?" she asked.

"It's a scotch egg. The staple diet of any true Englishman
or Scot."

"Scotch egg, pork pie, I know you didn't raid our pantry
for those. Let me guess—Maggie?"

"Yes, who would have guessed? She makes it all." He
waved the pork pie in the air. "You know how hard these
are to find over here? Your dad picked them up after our
last chat."

He then continued to reel off a series of food and drink
that Maggie was able to make, like an overly enthusiastic
food connoisseur. He continued pulling out strange foods
she had never tried along with a dubious-tasting fizzy drink
that apparently Maggie had also concocted.

"Why did you want to do this?"

"What?"

"Come out here?"

"Just wanted to do something nice for you. You've been through a lot lately." He met her eyes. "Why, you not enjoying yourself?"

"It's not that. Let's just say that when guys in the past have done anything nice for me, there was usually some ulterior motive going on."

Sam's eyebrows went up. "Oh. No. Um, if this makes you feel uncomfortable…" He motioned to the shore. "We can go back."

"And let this food go to waste?" She smiled.

Thirty minutes later, after a lot of laughter and a lengthy food-tasting session and more discussion about what he would do when he left the center, Hailey leaned back, slowly dragging her hand through the water while studying him.

"So what do you do, Sam, when you're not traveling and doing movies?"

"What, besides sleep and dodging the paparazzi? As I do a hell of a lot of that, when I get downtime."

"I mean for fun—for you."

Sam looked as if he was stumped by her question.

"Seems to me if you have to think about it, something's out of balance," she said.

He smiled. "I never used to work a lot. But the last five years have been really busy. It's one of those things you either ride it or you vanish."

"Does that worry you? I mean losing the limelight?"

"I think it worries Eric more than me."

"Eric?"

"My manager."

Hailey took another sip of her drink.

"And you?"

Sam didn't reply. He simply gazed off, appearing as though he was contemplating the question.

"Here, let me show you something." Hailey slipped down off her seat and lay back in the canoe.

"What are you doing?" he asked.

"C'mon, lay down."

He raised his finger. "Okay, just to let you know. If you have some ulterior motive going on—" He laughed while slipping down beside her. She nudged him, smiled, and shook her head.

"Now just close your eyes."

Both of them lay still within the boat and allowed the current to take them, neither one saying a word. It was if they both knew speaking would spoil the moment—and the stillness. As if even one utterance would somehow interrupt what nature was doing around them.

Ever since she was a kid, one of her favorite things to do was to lie back in a canoe and just let it carry her downstream. She couldn't begin to recall the number of weekends she would wake early while there was still a fine mist on the lake and venture out. It had become her escape, a place to clear her mind, read, dream, and well, to be honest, at times she did it simply to get out of a stack of chores. There was nothing like lying back in a canoe and letting the flow of the water carry you. Yet in all her years, she had never shared the experience with anyone else. And here she was with no other than Sam Reid. It felt surreal, intimate, and special.

Several minutes passed before she spoke. "Do you think you'll try and get back in contact with Kate when you go home?"

Sam twisted a water reed he'd broken off between his fingers.

"I hadn't really thought about it, to be honest."

She heard the surprise in his voice as he spoke.

"Did she drink a lot?"

"Everyone does. If it's not drink, it's prescription drugs. Uppers, downers—you name it." He let out a faint laugh. "Kind of sad really, isn't it? I mean most desire to be where we are and yet when you get there, you just want to be back where you were. You crave anonymity. But the money train keeps going and there isn't exactly an easy way to deal with it. Nothing prepares you for it. And there are few that get off without injury."

Hailey mused.

"Do you still love her?"

He turned to face her, his brow furrowed.

"Sorry, I shouldn't have gone there—"

"No, it's okay." He was silent for a moment. "I still have … feelings for her … if that's what you're asking. Kind of hard to switch them off after so long, but …" He trailed off.

"But what?"

He breathed in deeply. "It's over. That's the past. She's changed. I've changed. Maybe some relationships just aren't meant to last. After the ones I have been through, I'm kind of thinking most don't."

"I don't know about that. Some do."

He turned back and smiled. "Ah, the optimist. There's always one. Tell me, for someone who seems so sure and, if you don't mind me saying, looks so pretty, why hasn't someone tried to—"

"It's not that they haven't tried," she cut him off, slowly smiling at the thought that he considered her pretty. "I guess it's more me than them."

He raised an eyebrow and gave an amused look. "Ah, have some skeletons of your own, do we, Ms. Welland? Do tell."

She shook her head. "No, I mean. Probably will sound silly to you, but … I kind of have always thought that when you meet the right person … it will be freeing … and yet grounding at the same time." She paused. "I guess … I haven't met the right person yet."

She shot him a glance and then waited for him to make a joke, but to her surprise he didn't.

"No. It makes sense." He smiled. "You're a deep one, Hailey Welland."

She laughed. "You make me sound like a teacher."

"You've taught me a lot."

She studied his face as he continued to twirl the reed in his hand. Flattered by his comment and dwelling on it for a moment, she could feel herself becoming flushed.

A few more minutes passed, and as they lay gazing up under the warm sunshine it was hard for Hailey to imagine that only days earlier they had been through the worst storm in years. Drifting along, she became aware of how close they were, their bodies tightly pressed up against each other. Her mind began to wander thinking of how far they'd come. Yes, it had only been three weeks, and yet they'd been together every day and while it seemed short, so much had changed between them in that time. She no longer saw him as the A-list celebrity, the untouchable, or widely desired public figure that originally walked into Maggie's. He was just Sam, a guy with flaws and a history much like her own.

She even had to admit she had grown fond of being with him—not that she would announce it. No, she would never hear the end of it and well … she didn't want to make things awkward. And yet—so much had changed in three weeks. She felt as though she'd been wrong about him. How easy it was to prejudge and make assumptions about someone. The career they held, the way they looked, the words they spoke, or the actions they took. And yet behind it all was someone far deeper. Her father was right—*"Be kind to all as you never know the baggage they are carrying."* And oh, what baggage they both carried. Pain could change a person, affect their attitudes, and fuel the way they came across. She was no different. She carried her own. Had he prejudged her the same way? What did he think of her? Did he think of her?

She barely had that thought when she felt his hand brush up against hers. She felt her stomach tighten. Other than the time she'd sat with him through the night, she hadn't been this close to him in a while. And well, that night wasn't exactly the best circumstances to be close.

Where were these thoughts coming from? She couldn't think like this. He was her patient. She had to stay professional, she reminded herself. But it was useless; her mind was telling her one thing but her heart was winning. She could feel a deep longing inside of her that she hadn't felt before.

Before she could think to pull her hand away, he'd taken it in his—lifting it upwards. It felt so natural, as if he had held it many times before.

He squinted one eye, looking at the silhouette of their hands cut into the sun.

"Wow, your hand is small."

She glanced his way, determined to say something, but surprisingly nothing came out. Her rational side was berat-

ing her to pull her hand away fast while the other was saying, linger awhile. If it was a war the rational side was losing
miserably and she was glad. She gazed at their fingers entwined and then at her hand. He was right; her hand fit
snuggly in the center of his. For a moment, only for a moment, she chose to forget who he was, why he was here, and
that she was his counselor. Instead, despite all good judg-
ment she allowed herself to enjoy it, to enjoy that moment;
more specifically, to enjoy him.

All at once, she knew where this would lead if she left it
any longer. If he wasn't going to make the choice, she
would. She had to. There had to be a line in the sand and
she for one wasn't going to let him step over it. And anyway, he'd be gone in a week and where would that leave
her? Even more despondent than she was before he arrived,
she told herself. Nope that wasn't happening. Like mental
ping-pong, she couldn't believe she was having this conversation with herself. She released her hand from his and sat
up casually.

"Well, I think we should head back." She nodded, lacing
her fingers together in her lap.

"You okay?" He scrutinized her face, still lying back in
the canoe.

"Yes. It was nice to be here with you, thank you." She
feigned a response the best she could. It wasn't as if she was
lying but she didn't want him to think she was bothered.
She could have sworn she caught a look of disappointment
on his face before he sat up.

He shrugged. "Okay."

Circling back to the dock in silence, occasionally she
would glance at him and point out things, hoping to steer
their conversation or any further questions to anything ex-

cept what she assumed he might say. Was he going to say anything? Ah, it didn't matter. In all honestly she really had enjoyed her time more than she would openly admit. But it was for the best. She had done the right thing and besides, what if she was reading it all wrong. *Oh that would be* … She couldn't even finish the thought.

As they reached closer to the shore, Hailey shielded her eyes from the glare of the sun. From where she was sitting, she could make out the silhouette of a figure waiting at the end of the dock but couldn't quite make out who it was. When they'd gotten a little closer she could tell it was a woman she hadn't seen before. Dark hair tied back with a dark red band. A long, flowing summer dress. After a moment, Sam must have noticed her squinting over his shoulder, and he turned to see what she was looking at. The moment he did, his rowing slowed. He shot her a look but said nothing. By the expression on his face he knew the person on the dock but he wasn't saying anything.

CHAPTER TWENTY-FOUR

A s they drew up alongside the dock, Hailey stepped out
of the boat, pulled up with the assistance of the
stranger.

"Thank you."

"You're welcome."

Hailey recognized the voice immediately. They looked
each other over before the woman turned toward Sam, who
was tying off the rope.

"Hello, Sam."

"Jules."

There was an awkward beat while he exited the boat and
joined them.

"Is Dad with you?" Sam asked.

"He's waiting in the car."

"What?" Sam peered over her shoulder, trying to get a
better look.

She put her hand up. "Yeah, it's probably best you don't
… go over."

"No surprise there then," he said. "Why would he even come up if he's not getting out?"

She tilted her head and didn't answer.

He shook his head in disbelief. "You didn't tell him."

"You think he would have gotten in the car if I had?"

Sam looked over at Hailey, who was observing. He motioned to her. "Jules, this is Hailey. Hailey this is —"

"Your sister, yes." Hailey smiled politely.

Again there was an awkward moment, and Hailey felt as though she was intruding on a meeting meant only for Sam and his sister. Hailey gestured over her shoulder. "Do you want me to put some coffee on?"

"No thanks, we won't be staying long," Jules replied, her eyes darting back to Sam, who was wiping his hands on the sides of his pants.

"Well, I think I'll leave you to it. It was nice meeting you, Jules." Hailey shook her hand.

"Same."

Hailey cast a final glance at Sam, checking to see if he was okay. He nodded, and Hailey turned and headed back to the house.

* * * * *

Sam and Jules began walking around the property. Sam cast a glance over at the car. Behind the tinted windows he could barely make out his father. He wondered what he was thinking.

"You think he's going to get out?"

She shook her head. "No."

"So ..." He trailed off.

"You know, Sam ..." She paused. "The past few years

haven't been easy for any of us. Being stuck between you and him—I don't get any pleasure out of it. It's not what I wanted."

He ran a hand through his hair. "Could have fooled me."

She stopped in her tracks. "Look, you haven't exactly helped yourself," she snapped.

Sam turned to her. "Look, Jules, did you come all this way to lecture me?"

"No, I —"

"Seriously, I don't need it. I know I messed up, I don't need you to remind me."

They continued walking. A gentle breeze blew in off the lake, carrying with it a soft summer scent of freshly cut grass.

"How have you been? You're looking better."

"Feeling better."

"Are you clean now?"

"Detoxed and the meds are helping."

"Good."

Sam took her over the old wooden bridge.

"Do you remember Carl Gordon?"

Sam cocked his head. "Who?"

"Yes, it was a long time ago. You were eight. He was my first love …"

"Oh, I know …" He started laughing.

"Ah, now you remember."

"Wow, that was ages ago. What a douche he was."

"You warned me, but I never listened to you."

"Whatever happened to him?"

"Last I heard he was divorced with four kids."

"What a guy."

"You remember what you did."

"The coat hood. How I could forget, that was classic. He needed a new coat after that."

"I still can't believe you did that. He was six years older than you. You tore that hood right off his coat."

"He spun like a spinning top."

She laughed.

"He deserved it," Sam said.

They stood on the edge of the lake, looking out across the water. Jules' laughter died down and was replaced with a serious look.

"That's the thing." She paused. "You always were there for me. I ignored you, made sure you got in trouble when it was me. And yet despite it all, you always looked out for me. I treated you terrible. Why?"

"You're my sister." He chuckled under his breath, nodding. "You were a pain, but who else did I have to look up to? I admired you."

"You admired me?"

"More than anyone."

"Really?"

He nodded, and the corner of his lip curled into a smile.

As they continued their walk, a peaceful silence surrounded them. Somewhere across the lake the call of geese broke the stillness. The water lapped up against the shore, bringing with it all manner of weeds. The breeze was warm and inviting. Sam noticed it all, every sound and sight mixed with the words his sister had said. He was pleased she'd come up, but a part of him couldn't help feel disappointed. The decision hadn't been his father's and the fact that he hadn't stepped out of the car since arriving meant he still hadn't forgiven him.

Would his father ever accept his apology? A part of him

had become so accustomed to being snubbed by him and having Jules as the mediator, he wondered if it was even worth trying. Maybe it was best to just stay clear of him. Though he knew doing so would only mean forcing a stronger wedge between him and Jules, and he wasn't ready to let that happen. If there were one relationship he would fight to maintain it would be with his sister.

But even now, seeing Jules walking beside him, he questioned if that was what she wanted or if this was just another ploy to make herself look good, something he'd become accustomed to her doing.

"Sorry to hear about Kate," Jules said.

"Ah, you know, I seem to have a knack of driving people away."

"Don't be so hard on yourself. Sometimes people just need time."

"Is that what Dad said?" Sam eyed the car.

Either not wishing to answer or not hearing, she continued without missing a beat.

"So how long will you be here?" Jules asked, as they came back around to the parking lot in front of the house.

"Another week. I return back to the city on Sunday. They're actually holding a form of graduation on Saturday," he said.

"Graduation?"

"Yeah, strange, eh? But ... you're welcome to come if you can. I'd love it if you could be—"

"Sam ... I'm not—"

"I know, it's fine." He dismissed what she was about to say with a wave.

"Look. I'll speak with him again. I can't guarantee anything. He usually shuts me down the moment I try to bring up the topic of Mom or any mention of you. But I'll try."

Sam nodded.

Jules turned towards Sam and gave him a loving hug. It had been a long time since they'd hugged, and it felt good to have his sister back in his life, even if it was only for a brief moment. She made her way back to the car.

"And Jules," Sam quickly added.

She looked back before getting in.

"Yeah?"

Sam squinted. "Thanks for coming."

"It's not me you need to thank. Thank Hailey."

Sam's brow furrowed. Jules smiled and disappeared inside the car. Within minutes they were gone, leaving behind nothing more than a cloud of dust. As the dust settled a flurry of thoughts went through his mind about what Jules had said and about his father not stepping out of the car. His father knew full well why Sam was there, and yet it didn't matter. To his father, he had failed. He'd not only let his family down but his own mother.

And the truth was his father was right, it wasn't just about missing his mother's funeral. There had been many times when his mother had been ill and he wasn't there. If he had been, maybe things would have been different. He wouldn't be at odds with them; he wouldn't have felt so low that turning to drink seemed like the only solution. He wouldn't be here. At that final thought, he turned and walked inside.

* * * * *

Hailey was pouring coffee when he passed by her. Charlie sat at the head of the table eating his breakfast and reading the local paper.

She glanced over her shoulder.

"Hey, how did it go?"

Sam, heading upstairs, paused to reply, "You called Jules?"

"Yes."

"But I never gave you her phone number."

She could tell by his expression that he wasn't going to let it go. Charlie glanced up, his eyes darting between them, also eager to hear her response.

"I looked at your phone. The other night when you were ill."

"You know you had no right to do that?"

Hailey glanced at Charlie, thinking that he might intervene. But he looked surprised to be hearing it himself. It wasn't protocol. And she knew she'd get an earful for stepping over that line. But ...

Her eyes lowered. "I know. I'm sorry, I only wanted to—"

"I appreciate it." With that, he turned and went upstairs.

Hailey stared after him, dumbfounded. She had been sure he would blow his top. She'd seen his father in the car, heard what Jules said, and well ... she never expected to hear that.

He appreciated it?

She felt like pinching herself. She knew he'd find out eventually, but she didn't ask him beforehand because there was a good chance he would have been against the whole idea. But he appreciated it? She smiled to herself and then looked at her dad. Charlie cocked his head, shrugged, and carried on eating. Hailey absorbed Sam's words before sipping her coffee, feeling her shoulders relax. Maybe the day wouldn't turn out so bad after all, she thought.

CHAPTER TWENTY-FIVE

"Okay, so tell me again, he did what?" Cassie asked.

"Held my hand," Hailey said loudly, trying to be heard over the noise.

Ten minutes earlier she and Sam had pulled into the Delaware Country Fair parking lot and met up with Cassie and Matt. The place was packed as usual. Kids darted in and out of parked cars chasing one another while parents attempted to juggle coolers, folding chairs, and cans of bugs spray. It was one of those beautiful summer evenings. Perfect temperature, light breeze, and streaks of red and orange stretching across the sky. In the distance, she watched Sam and Matt order a couple of ice-cold fruit smoothies. Dressed in jeans, a loose white shirt, and shades, Sam occasionally glanced back at them and smiled.

Hailey smiled back at him, remembering the conversation they had before leaving. With so many people showing up at the fair, there was a good chance that a number of them would recognize him and turn into crazed fans. Hailey had offered him a moth-filled wig she had used in an old school play when she was six. To which he laughed and actually attempted to put it on to see what it looked like. Instead of looking inconspicuous, he would have more than likely attracted attention. He looked like one of the members of the BeeGees, Hailey joked, saying it would have been perfect for the karaoke contest the town held every year at the fair.

Now, staring at him from afar, she felt like pinching herself. It seemed all too surreal. She almost felt like a teenager again with butterflies in her stomach. She took a deep breath and reminded herself to stop fantasizing. To stop thinking what it would feel like to have him close again.

"Hailey. Hailey, are you listening to me?"

Hailey blinked, snapping back to reality. "Yes."

Cassie followed her gaze.

"I knew it. You do have a thing for him."

"No. No, I'm wondering how he's going to cope when he leaves here next weekend."

She squinted. "Hailey Welland, you might be a good counselor but you're a terrible liar."

Before she could grill her any further, Sam and Matt came back. Matt wrapped his arm around Cassie and she took the drink from his hand.

"Seems Sam and I have a lot in common. Don't we?" Matt said.

Sam shook his head, smiling, and handed Hailey her drink.

"Like what?" Cassie said, rolling her eyes.

"Movies. He says he's keen to work behind the camera. And I was telling him how I studied directing. I could teach him a few things."

"Oh please, Matt it was a one-day workshop held at the Walton theater and you never even completed it. What was your excuse for leaving after an hour? Oh right, you needed air!"

"Well, it was a long day. My creativity was stifled."

"It was eight hours, Matt!"

"Yes, that's a long time," he insisted. "You can't force creativity, and anyway they say you're most creative every thirty minutes."

"Who said that?"

Hailey caught Sam looking at her, and she could tell he was trying not to laugh. They sipped their drinks, feeling like spectators to the insane banter between Cassie and Matt, which didn't look like it was going to end anytime soon. Anyone else would have wondered why they were together but Hailey knew they loved each another. They were like two peas in a pod. She envisioned them both when they were sixty years old bickering over two flies on a fence post.

"Shall we meet back up, say ... in one hour in front of the stage? I thought I would show Sam around," Hailey said.

"Really? I was thinking—"

Before Matt could finish his sentence Cassie stepped on his foot.

"Sounds good. You two have fun." Cassie's eyes widened, to which Hailey rolled her eyes. She knew what her friend was thinking.

Sam and Hailey navigated their way through the crowds. Some stared and a couple whispered while pointing at Sam.

"Told you, you should have worn that wig. Those sunglasses just aren't doing it." Hailey laughed.

"I guess not." He lifted his sunglasses and she caught his

eyes sparkle under the lights. "If you had your way, I would have shown up here in lipstick and a dress." Sam grinned.

"Now that would have been an eyesore."

"You bet."

The smell of burgers and fried onions wafted through the air, making her stomach rumble. The delicious home-made baked snacks being offered at every other stall only strengthened her desire to grab a bite to eat.

"Did you ever visit many fairs in England?"

"Yeah, when I was a kid there was one that used to drift into town every year for a couple of weeks."

"Drift?"

"Gypsies run them. They were never there long before they moved on to the next town. We'd spend all our money within minutes of getting there on slot machines and rides. Though I'm pretty sure they had the entire place rigged."

"Ah ... nailing down the wooden bottles trick." She smiled.

Surrounding them were stalls for as far as the eye could see. There was a booth for everything you could imagine. Raffle tickets were being sold for artwork, live chicks were hatching from eggs behind glass, historic items from the railroad were on display, and jars of maple syrup were being offered. Every year there would be new booths, it's what drew people out—enticing treats, the events they put on, and of course the live bands.

"You've got to see the butter sculpting."

"Butter what?"

Hailey threw the remainder of her drink in the trash and grabbed him by the arm. "Let me show you."

They walked a bit further before rounding a corner to a stall where a large crowd had gathered. Squeezing between the people, they made their way to the front. There before them was a sculpture of a life-sized lamb and a little girl. A sign nearby said the entire thing was molded out of eight hundred pounds of butter.

"Impressive," Sam said, arching an eyebrow.

"Ah, that's nothing, you wait till you see the fire-eaters and magicians."

She spent the next half an hour taking him around various stalls, each one equally impressive and bizarre. Eventually, after trying and spitting out a number of exotic foods and taking a short ride on the Ferris wheel, they wound up making their way over to one of the main events of the evening—the demolition derby.

"You into this?"

"Yeah, I love it. It's a metal-to-metal jousting match, where whoever is still moving is given the title of winner," Hailey said.

"What?" He gave a skeptical look. "I'm surprised."

"Why?"

"I just never imagined you to be the smash 'em and crash 'em type of girl."

"There's a lot that you don't know about me, Hollywood."

Their eyes held for a moment before she forced herself to turn away. She continued to watch him from the corner of her eye. Was this the same guy that walked in only three weeks ago? Was she the same girl, noticing how comfortable she felt around him?

Sam's eyes lit up like a kid as the engines roared to life. The sound of metal crunching and cars colliding while they spluttered and skidded around in the water-soaked mud only seemed to add to his enthusiasm. No sooner had she turned back to the action than two cars came dangerously close to the barrier only to swerve out at the last minute. As their wheels spun away, mud splattered all over them and a number of other spectators.

Their hair was drenched, their faces caked with mud, and as for their clothes, they were completely covered. Sam and Hailey stood like statutes, not daring to look at the other. Slowly turning their heads in unison, they looked at the mess the other one was in and immediately broke into laughter. Sam playfully flicked some of the mud at Hailey, and she returned the favor. What may have annoyed others had no effect on the atmosphere they shared that night. Hailey had to admit she'd never felt so alive in that moment. She forgot all the times she'd wanted to leave Walton. She forgot the bad dates. She even forgot the one thing that had not left her mind in over two years—the death of her mother. It wasn't that none of it mattered. It all mattered. It was just in that moment, none of it was at the forefront of her mind. For the first time in a long time, she was no longer living in the past or future; she was fully present and loving every minute of it.

Hailey lifted her hands. "We skipped the hog wrestling and still ended up covered."

"Hog wrestling?"

"Yeah, they do it every year, kind of cruel, I think, but that's small towns for you."

Hailey wiped her face with the back of her hand.

"Um …" Sam gave a wry smile as he nodded towards her.

"What?" She wiped again with her sleeve, only smearing more mud across her cheek.

"Yeah, I think it's going to take more than your sleeve to

get rid of this."

"Let's go get cleaned up," Hailey said.

"Ah, leave it. I'll shower when I get back. Anyway, now I have the perfect disguise." The side of his mouth curled, cracking the now drying mud on his face.

"Do you mind if I go get cleaned up? You know, being a lady and all that."

He chuckled. "No, go ahead."

"I'll be right back."

* * * * *

Sam watched Hailey walk in the direction of the re-strooms, thinking that she had changed a lot over the last few weeks. Or maybe it was him? When she wasn't hidden under thick mud, he'd noticed how attractive she looked. She wore little makeup and yet it didn't seem to matter; she had a natural beauty that didn't rely on it. She was less defensive around him and today proved that. He noticed that the more he was with her, the more he wanted to be with her. She wasn't only good at drawing out of him the very things he buried, but her conversation was without pretense. He never got a sense that she was trying to impress him. So many girls he'd been around, whether he was dating them or not, always seemed to try too hard—but not her.

There's a lot about me you don't know, she had said. To any other it might be a passing comment, one that most would overlook as something anyone would say to another stranger, and yet it left him wanting to know. Her life felt so different from his. So ordinary, and yet something about that was appealing. Something about her was a mystery, an alluring mystery that made him want to spend time discovering. It went beyond the way she looked. It was what she did and who she was. He still couldn't get his head around why someone so full of talent would stay in Walton.

* * * * *

Hailey slipped through the crowds, noticing that she hadn't stopped smiling since leaving him. She wondered if he had looked at her as she walked away. There was something sensual in that realization, and for the first time she let that feeling soak in. Three weeks ago she never would have imagined feeling that way, especially with someone who was a patient. She'd counseled many men over the years and many who were good-looking, but she had never seen them as anything more than patients.

She knew her father wasn't a fool. He knew it was possible that someone would eventually take a liking to her, and that's why he'd always made it clear that relationships were to remain professional at all times—before, during, and after treatment. He never wavered on that rule, and she hadn't wanted to either. Yet here he was encouraging her to spend time with Sam beyond treatment hours? Now, of course, they weren't exactly overwhelmed with staff that would usually share the weight of the work, but still ... if she wasn't mistaken she could have sworn her father was secretly hoping something would spark. Weeks ago she would have pushed the very thought from her mind, but now ...

A few feet from the door to the restroom, she felt someone take hold of her arm and spin her around. Startled and partly blinded by the glare of one of the floodlights, she finally realized it wasn't Cassie or Sam but the last person she wanted to see—Tommy.

CHAPTER TWENTY-SIX

"I need a word with you."

Tommy gripped the back of her elbow tight and pushed her forward

"Let go, you're hurting my arm."

He didn't answer; instead, he forced her into a gap between two tents.

"What's the deal with making me look like a fool in front of my father?"

Hailey was repulsed by the smell of alcohol on his breath.

"God, Tommy you're drunk."

He scowled at her. "Answer me!"

She pried her arm away from his vise grip and attempted to leave but he put an arm either side of her.

"Let me go. I'll scream."

He gave a smug grin and began to scream himself. "Go

ahead, everyone is screaming—as if anyone is going to hear you."

"What do you want, Tommy?"

"What's up with you, Hailey? Haven't I treated you good? Haven't I shown you that I care? What, you want me to take you out again? Give you gifts? 'Cause I can do that."

"Tommy, you don't know the first thing about treating anyone right. Look at what you're doing now."

"Oh, I get it," he said. "It's him, isn't it? Yeah, I've seen the way you look him. He's your ticket out of here, isn't he?"

"You're drunk, Tommy."

"I thought you liked drunks, isn't that what he's in there for?"

"It's none of your business."

He gave a sly grin. He ran his finger through her hair and Hailey cringed. She tried to slide underneath his arm but he quickly stopped her.

"Yeah, I bet you've already done the dirty with him, am I right?"

He licked his lip and slid his finger down her face, neck, and across her breasts. Hailey swatted his hand off her and slapped him hard enough that his cheek burned a ruby red.

"Really? You like to play rough? My type of girl …"

With that he grabbed the back of her hair and yanked it back, then forced his mouth on hers. He pressed against her so hard it didn't matter how much effort she mustered, she couldn't push his foul body off her. She did the only thing she could do.

He let out an excruciating yell and fell to the ground, holding his groin. As she moved past him, he caught her ankle and she hit the soiled ground. He yanked at her jeans and inch by inch he began pulling her back towards him while cussing her. She had the wind knocked out of her but she wasn't going to let him get the better of her. Furious, she kicked at him with all her might and called out, hoping that someone, anyone, would hear her, but the noise from the crowds, amusement rides, and music smothered her cries.

* * * * *

Sam had been waiting for what seemed like an awful long time. The day's sun had all but vanished. He wasn't sure how many times he'd checked his watch or glanced over his shoulder but it had been one too many. Did the washrooms have showers? He wondered if she'd bumped into Cassie and got trapped in another Matt and Cassie drama.

Eventually, he decided to go check on her, and at the same time he'd wash the dry mud that was now irritating his skin. It wasn't bad when it was wet but now it was itching like mad. People were making their way towards the main grandstand where a blues band was playing. It felt like he was back in the city as an onslaught of people moved in every direction with little regard for whom they bumped in-to. Outside the restroom, he couldn't see any sign of Hailey. He continued looking around, and for a split second he thought of peeking in the restroom and calling out to her, but that might have been a little weird if she was fine.

Still, something didn't feel right.

* * * * *

A few tents down, Hailey felt as if she was fighting for

her life. She slammed her leg into Tommy's arm with such force that she was sure it would break. He was still immobilized by the swift knee to the groin, but he wasn't letting up either. He still had a firm grip on her jeans.

"Would you stop it, Hailey?"

"Let go."

Exhaustion or pain, she wasn't sure, but when he finally released his grip on her jeans Hailey dragged herself to her feet and stumbled out.

He hollered, "Hailey, you think you can do better than me. You're just another slut who isn't getting out of this town."

Hailey stopped in her tracks. She wasn't sure what riled her up more, the way he treated her or the comment. It took everything she had to resist turning back and slapping him. But he wasn't worth it. She wouldn't stoop to his level.

"Watch me," she mumbled.

And with that she stepped out from between the tents into the flow of people.

It was at that moment he spotted her—wobbling, still covered in mud, and slightly unsteady on her feet. He pushed his way up through the crowds like a fish swimming upstream. She didn't spot him until he had hold of her.

"Hey, you okay?"

Breathless, she flinched at his touch. As she looked at up at him, her face a mask of surprise and fear, he found himself wondering what on earth had happened.

"I want to leave."

"Sure, let's go."

Sam wrapped his arm around her, sensing her need for comfort. On their way back to the truck, Cassie and Matt spotted them. Instinctively, Cassie knew something was up as within seconds she was there taking hold of her hand.

"Hailey, what happened?"

"I'll speak to you later. I just want to go home."

She glanced at Sam as if he held the answers. Sam shrugged.

"You want me to take you?"

"No, Sam will."

"You sure?"

"Positive. I'll phone you later."

* * * * *

Miles from the grounds, Sam could still hear the faint noise of the fair. Hailey had spent the past few minutes explaining what happened. Everything in him wanted to turn the truck around and go back and find the jerk. Forget police, or the thought of Eric dragging him over the coals. He wanted to give the guy a black eye. No one should get away with treating someone like that, especially women and certainly not Hailey.

Sam realized in that surge of emotion that the way he felt about her had changed. She had become far more than just a friend, his counselor, or another woman. He felt protective of her. And the thought of someone treating her badly made him grip the wheel so hard his knuckles went white.

"Did he?"

"Oh god, no," she replied.

"We need to report this to the police."

"No." She shook her head.

"No?"

"Just forget it."

"Your father at least—"

"I don't want him to know."

"But Hailey—"

"Please. Really, I'm fine. Just a little shook up."

He was bewildered that she wanted to pretend it hadn't happened. Was this something that occurred often? Had this happened before? Still—to do nothing just didn't make sense, he thought.

"Listen, I know you mean well. But saying anything in this town is about as useful as shouting for directions in the middle of New York City. No one cares."

"Someone would—"

"No, you don't get it. If I was to say anything, I might as well place a trail of gasoline up to our house and set it on fire. Nothing happens in this town without consequences. Trust me. Just leave it."

He studied her face.

"I'm fine, honestly."

Hailey couldn't bear to go into the house when they returned home. She couldn't face her father, at least not until he would have expected her to return home. They would have been at the fair for hours had it not been for the incident, and they still had several hours to kill.

By now, the sky was as dark as the northern seas. Only the light from the full moon and the stars gave them any indication of where the driveway entrance was. Instead of driving up the long winding path, Hailey directed Sam to pull up close to the lake. The reflection of the moon on the water shimmered, giving them a beautiful view of the dock that jutted out. They got out and Sam noticed Hailey looking back at the house. The lights inside glowed yellow and they could see Charlie's figure pass by the window several times.

"Are you sure you don't want to go up to the house?"

She turned. "Not yet."

CHAPTER TWENTY-SEVEN

The long wooden dock creaked as they walked down to the very end of it. Boats tied up securely were bobbing around on the gentle flow of the water. A pleasant damp smell that immediately reminded him of their time out on the lake lingered in the air. Hailey took a seat on the edge of the dock, dangling her feet and calves in the warm water that mirrored the star-pricked sky. She tucked her hands under her legs.

"You going to take a seat? We'll probably be here awhile."

The light of the moon hit her face and shadows danced off her features. Still covered in dry soil, she reached down and began to splash some water across her face and wash it clean. Sam sat beside her. What a state they must have both looked, heading out of the fair. Every part of them was covered from head to toe. Sam joined her. He cupped water in his hands and rubbed his face. He ran the cool water

through his hair, noting how solid it felt, as if he hadn't
washed it in months.

"We're never going to get this off. It's like a thick skin."

Leaning forward to dip his hair in, he felt a nudge that
nearly sent him off balance. He turned, smiling. "What was
that?"

"Sorry, there's not exactly a lot of room here."

Sam glanced around, recognizing there was tons of
room. He chuckled to himself and proceeded to lean forward. Again, he hadn't had his head down a few seconds
before he felt her elbow nudge him almost off balance. He
glanced up, this time grinning from ear to ear. He noticed a
flicker of a smirk on hers.

"Okay."

With that he cupped some water and tossed it across at
Hailey. He smiled.

He could tell she was trying her best to hide her amusement as she reached down, slowly cupping water with both
hands. He knew what was coming and yet he had no intention of moving. Sure enough, a splash of cool water hit him.
Hailey sat looking very pleased with herself. He laughed.
Within seconds of attempting to gather up some more am-
mo she had already pushed him. This time he fell off the
dock and head first into the lake.

Seconds passed and then a minute.

He waited just long enough beneath the surface to see
her curiously peering over the edge. Trying to make out why
he hadn't come up, she splashed the surface of the water.
That was all it took. He reached up from within the darkness and grasped her wrist, pulling her in.

When both of them came to the surface they laughed so
hard, they thought they would never stop. As they playfully

splashed one another back and forth like two teens, Sam felt alive. It felt like freedom. As if someone had unlocked a heavy chain around his neck. It had been a long time since he'd experienced something so easy, so natural and enjoyable.

"At least we won't need a shower," Sam said, pulling off his mud-caked top and throwing it onto the wooden dock.

"Hey, hey, Hollywood, this isn't skinny-dipping." Hailey smirked as she followed suit, throwing hers close to where his landed.

Once their laughter subsided, they stared at each other. As the water streaked down her face onto her bare shoulders, he noted how striking she was. Her crystal blue eyes were hypnotic. For a while they simply studied the other's face, only occasionally looking away while treading water. Everything in that moment felt good. The cool drips of water rolling down his face, the warmth of the summer evening, being with her. The only sound filling the air was the slow movement of their bodies in the water and a chorus of tree frogs. Moving in closer to her, he could see the reflection of the silvery moon in her eyes. She bit the side of her lip. He thought for a moment he'd caught an edge of nervousness in her expression but it was soon replaced with a smile. Under the natural light she looked every bit as beautiful as the day he saw her standing beside the garden arbor.

"You missed a bit," he said softly, motioning to her face.

"Oh?" She reached up but he gently took her hand.

"I can do it."

Sam slowly wiped the part of her forehead above and around her eye. Her skin was soft and cool to the touch. He brought up another handful, and Hailey closed her eyes as the water ran down her cheeks, lips, and then back into the lake. Sam could feel his heart beating rapidly; his chest rose and fell fast. Every touch felt intimate and new.

"You know ... it's okay to let someone help you, for once."

He moved in closer until he could feel her chest against his. Her eyes opened and what he saw in her expression was enough to tell him that she was feeling the same way; she felt the same longing.

In that instant he wasn't her patient and she wasn't his counselor. They were two imperfect people discovering each other for the first time. As each second passed, he anticipated she would pull away, as she had in the canoe. But to his surprise, she didn't. All at once, it was hard to breathe. He wanted desperately to kiss her but he felt torn. Was it over between him and Kate? Was it really over? And then there was the fair, the last thing he wanted to do after ...

Before he could finish that thought she moved in, pressing her soft lips against his. They held for a moment, completely lost in one another. He breathed her in deeply. A sweet taste lingered on his lips—the remainder of her lip gloss mixed with the water that ran down her face. The touch of her hand wrapped around his neck and the warmth of her body pressed against his felt electric. Beneath the water, he wrapped his hands around her waist, drawing her gently closer, catching the faint scent of her perfume. With every passing moment their kiss became more passionate as their bodies swirled slowly under the illumination of the moon. He felt her tongue against his as he ran his hands through her hair, down her neck, until he traced his way down to the small of her back.

He wasn't sure how long they remained in each other's arms. Time seemed to vanish and with it the world around them. He just knew there was nowhere else he'd rather be.

Afterward, they swam back to the dock. Hailey grabbed a blanket from the truck and wrapped it around them. They sat with their feet dangling in the water, their arms coiled around each other in contentment. Talking and laughing some more, they lay back on the blanket gazing up into the night sky. Hailey pointed out the constellations and named each one, while Sam pretended to make out he could see them.

"Yep, the Big Dipper, I see it."

It took her only seconds to realize he hadn't a clue after she named a few that didn't exist.

She nudged him.

"What?" Sam said, smiling.

She smirked. They lay there long into the night, watching the fireflies flicker around them, flashing on and off and seamlessly blending in with the stars.

CHAPTER TWENTY-EIGHT

"What time did you get in last night?" Charlie muttered, putting a dab of butter on his toast.

It was Monday morning and Hailey had stumbled into the kitchen to grab some fuel before her morning run. She pulled a banana and a cold bottle of water out of the fridge before answering.

"A little after midnight."

Charlie cocked his head.

"What? We hung out with Cassie and Matt after." She yawned, feigning ignorance. Inwardly she regretted lying.

"Nothing. I just didn't hear you come in." He smiled before taking the final scoop of cereal out of his bowl. "Anyway, did you have a good time?"

She smiled, fondly remembering the previous evening.

"Absolutely." She stared off into space and ran her fingers over her lips.

Charlie raised an eyebrow as he poured a cup of coffee.

Noticing he was studying her, she said. "Well ..." She thumbed over her shoulder. "I should go wake him."

"He beat you to the punch."

"What?"

"He's been up for over an hour."

"Huh?"

He looked up from his morning paper and paused while chewing toast. "He's down by the lake. Um, what did he say?" Charlie looked thoughtful. "Oh yeah, I think he said he's finishing off his morning yoga." He grinned.

Hailey tucked a strand of hair behind her ear. "Well, how about that?"

* * * * *

During the following days before Sam's departure, Hailey tried to spend as much time with him as possible, far and above their usual daily routine. And even though she felt happier than she had in a long time, eating away in the back of her mind was a nagging thought of what it all meant. What did it mean to him? Where was it all heading? Had she been rash in kissing him? Had he simply kissed her back out of kindness—pity even? Wasn't he used to having women throw themselves at him?

She sighed.

Who was she to think she was any different? That it would be any different? If he had thought it was a mistake he wasn't letting on, as he was still his jovial self and affectionate whenever they would steal a moment. Long walks, chatting on the dock, and humorous attempts to teach Sam to dance in the barn filled every moment of the little spare time they had in the evenings.

Conversations with Cassie on the phone before sleeping remained as funny as ever. Hailey never did tell her about

her scuffle with Tommy on the night of the fair. She trusted
her friend but knew she had a way of letting things slip
when talking with clients. Instead, she told her about the
night in the lake. That was all Cassie needed to hear. She
cackled wildly and so loud through the phone, Hailey had to
pull it a safe distance away from her ear. Every night she
would fish for new and titillating morsels of information on
what they had done. Sometimes Hailey exaggerated, making
it sound steamier than it was, if only to get a rise out of Cassie before telling her she was joking.

Hailey had to admit she liked being able to talk about a
guy who hadn't let her down, hadn't tried immediately to
get in her pants, and hadn't so far been a jerk to her.

But the truth was, the daytime hours were the hardest.
Trying to concentrate on his treatment in those final days
took everything she had. There was no denying it. That
evening had changed her relationship with him. Of that she
was sure.

Her father as usual was right. It no longer felt professional; instead, it left her feeling like a teenager again, doing
something illicit behind her father's back. Each second of
the day felt painfully slow, as if she was biding her time.
Watching the hands on the clock tick over, she couldn't wait
until they could be alone and undistracted; until she might
feel his touch and kiss again. She hadn't felt such strong
emotions for someone in a long time, and every moment
alone with him only intensified that. When they couldn't
physically be close to each other, their eyes, gestures, and
movement would reveal what the other was feeling.

And yet still in it all, she longed for clarity. To clear the
air; find out how he really felt. His actions conveyed one
thing, but was that how he truly felt? She'd known guys who

did all the right things at the start, but when you cornered them about their innermost feelings, well, that's when they either clammed up or ran for the hills.

Yet he was different from any other man she'd met. Wasn't he? At least that was how it seemed. It wasn't just the fact that he was a celebrity, a leading man known all over the world. It was more. She couldn't quite put her finger on the pulse of what it was, but clearly he wasn't Tommy—thankfully.

Would this whole thing amount to nothing more than a frivolous act of passion or a senseless mistake? It wasn't as if they had jumped into bed together. It was a kiss—several, now she thought about it. Was she just being a fool, reading too much into it, or was he playing her along?

No, times together in the evenings were real, sincere, and loving—weren't they?

"Urgh," she groaned. The mental mind games were taxing on her energy. It hadn't helped that Charlie had stepped up the number of hours in the final week and taken on more of the sessions, making it virtually impossible to discuss it with Sam. She wondered for a minute if her father had known. Maybe he'd seen them down by the dock? Or picked up on the way they looked at each other in sessions?

She shook her head. For God's sake, she was a grown woman, she shouldn't have to slink around or justify her actions, she reminded herself. But it wasn't that. Had it been anyone besides a patient, her father wouldn't have batted an eyelid—heck, he would have probably given her an advance wedding gift. It was the principle. There were few rules that he was a stickler for, and getting romantically involved with a patient was one of them. It was out of the question.

No, she didn't want to force the issue or smother him.

They hadn't jumped into bed with one another, and he had no obligation to her. She was the one who moved on him. So maybe he'd think she was taking it too seriously. Blowing a beautiful moment completely out of proportion. Making it something that it wasn't; something that it would never be. The thought pained her. She had to accept that this wasn't any ordinary relationship and the probability of being let down wasn't just high, it was more than likely to happen.

Some of the most memorable and at times awkward moments in those final days felt the best. It was like a balancing act and one where she wasn't too good at deciding which way to lean. In those days, she couldn't keep track of how many times they rode into town to pick up supplies. Both knew it was just an excuse to be alone and yet neither of them said it out loud. In the truck he'd slide up close, his warm arm around her, running his fingers lightly over the back of her neck. Goose bumps prickled her skin and made the blood rush to her cheeks. Other times he'd simply hold her hand, tracing his thumb slowly across the back of hers. She relished every second of how good it felt, knowing that in a matter of days it more than likely would be over.

She could have sworn her father gave her a strange look when they returned each time. Then again, there were only so many cans of beans one could buy in a given week before it looked a little odd.

* * * * *

By late afternoon on Friday, the day before Sam's graduation, the sun was still beating down mercilessly. The temperature had soared into the high eighties and whether they were inside or out it was unbearable. It was something he noticed about New York summers, compared to LA. It wasn't the temperature that got you, it was the humidity. Where in Southern California it was a dry heat and you always felt as if you were wrapped in a comfortable blanket, in Walton, you felt as if you were sitting in a sauna fully clothed. Sam pinched at his shirt, pulling it away from his body and flapping it to get even a smidgen of relief. From inside the sunroom he could see heat waves vibrating off the surface of the lake and though the windows were fully open he couldn't feel even the slightest breeze.

Hailey came in bringing a tray of iced tea. She looked up briefly and smiled as she poured his drink, followed by Charlie's. Sam had grown used to the routine of each day and now it was nearly over. It was hard to imagine he'd been there almost a month. He would miss the place, but most of all he would miss Hailey. He'd never felt so torn. He glanced at her golden curtain of flowing hair as she dropped down into the seat across from him, pulling her feet up and rotating the glass of tea in her hand.

There was so much about her that intrigued him. It wasn't that she was attractive; he'd seen lots of pretty women. There was more to her. A lot more that he had only just begun to discover. A hidden strength, intelligence, and quick-witted humor that made being around her feel effortless and all the more appealing.

Though he'd noticed over the past few days she'd been a little less herself and more withdrawn—preoccupied. He hadn't been blind to it, despite what she may have thought. And it wasn't that he was trying to put off the conversation that he knew was coming. He was still processing that evening and their time together. Still trying to make sense of the way he felt about her. The logistics of how it would all work. He'd never been in a relationship with anyone other than a celebrity. It would be new, strange even. And yet he'd never been with a woman who knew his innermost feelings as Hailey did. Kate only knew what he wanted her to know and even that was minimal. One thing for sure—he didn't want to rush into anything. It had been hard enough coping with Kate's betrayal, his family discord, and making it this far through treatment. But he knew she deserved to know. He couldn't begin to imagine what she'd been thinking.

Another idea passed through his mind. Maybe he'd get the whole court thing behind him and then invite her out to LA. Another thing he was sure about—whatever had started between them, he didn't want it to end.

"So tomorrow you graduate, how do you feel about that, Sam?" Charlie said before taking a sip from his glass.

He cocked his head. "Mixed emotions." His eyes drifted to Hailey's.

"So any family or friends going to be attending?"

"Not that I know." He shook his head. "And I don't expect them to show."

Hailey interjected. "I did make a call but got an answer machine."

"Yeah, story of my life."

"Sam, Hailey gave you the after-care plan I put together for you, right?"

His eyes darted to Hailey and then back to him.

"Yes, I got it, thanks."

Charlie leaned forward. "Sam, I have to admit I had my doubts about you when you first arrived. But I've watched the way you've changed. And … I want you know that it's been a privilege to have you here. Just know this, when you leave on Sunday, you are not the errors of your past; you are not what you do or don't achieve in the future. You are whole, free, and in control of what you do next. But remember in that freedom the choice to slip back down is only one choice away. Make good choices. Take it a day at a time."

Sam nodded. "Thank you, Charlie."

Charlie stood up. "Well, I'm going to speak with Albert and see if there's anything I can do to help him with tomorrow."

After he left they both sat awkwardly sipping their drinks, waiting for the other to say something, Sam was the first to break the silence.

"Oh, um ... I have something for you."

"You do?"

"Yeah, hold up, I'll be right back."

A few minutes later he returned carrying with him a rectangle-shaped white box with a red ribbon tied around it. He handed it to Hailey and took a seat. He watched tentatively as she began untying it. She only looked up to smile and give a slightly perplexed look. Lifting the top off, Hailey pulled back the thin purple wrapping paper and then her jaw dropped.

Inside was the strapless, strawberry evening dress.

Sam stooped his head to see her eyes. "Well? Do you like it?"

"I—I love it," she stammered.

He could see her eyes well up with tears before she wiped them quickly.

She slowly put the top back on.

"I can't accept this."

"That is the one, isn't it? The one you were looking at in the window, right?"

"Yes, but ..."

"But what?"

Hailey dropped her legs down and leaned forward to hand it back.

"Thank you, Sam, but I just can't."

"C'mon." He tried to hand it back to her. "It's my way of saying thank you for everything you've done."

She shook her head slowly.

"It's just a gift." He held it out. "It's not like I'm asking you marry me."

"Well, that's the thing. As beautiful as it is, you leave in two days and I'd only be left with something that would remind me of you."

Still holding the box, his arm dropped limp.

She sighed. "And anyhow, who would I wear it for?"

"Well ... I thought me."

She looked back up at him inquisitively.

"After graduation tomorrow, I wanted to take you into the city. That is, of course, if it's all right with you?"

She paused. "And then?" Her voice was soft as she met his eyes.

"Well." He held the box back out to her. "I thought we could take it a day at a time." He smiled and watched as the remaining resistance faded.

She hesitated briefly before accepting the box.

"It would be a shame to see such a beautiful dress go to waste." A sparkle returned to her eyes. "Thank you, Sam." She leaned across and kissed him, her lips gently brushing against his while her hand caressed his neck.

"My pleasure."

* * * * *

Everything about the rest of that afternoon together was beautiful. There was simplicity to it all from what Sam could remember. They were invited to Maggie's for a farewell dinner, where Danny and Maggie sang an embarrassing yet hilarious karaoke rendition of "I've Walked Ten Thousand Miles" by The Proclaimers. They all ate more than their fair share of scotch eggs and Clootie Dumpling, on which Sam nearly choked from laughing so hard as Maggie shared her stories of running the restaurant. He watched Hailey join Danny in a series of comical dance moves and it was then he was reminded of how different he now felt. Relaxed, as if he'd come home to a place his heart had longed to be. He'd arrived as an outsider, bruised and guarded, and yet in time he'd opened up, healed, and with it grown as a person. He'd grown to love the quaint little town of Walton, its slow-paced life, the unusual people, Maggie's cooking, and most all of the woman who stood across from him.

Upon returning that evening they went out in the canoe and watched the sun go down. They held each other and gazed in awe at the shades of fiery red and orange. He savored every moment of it, knowing somehow that after tomorrow life wouldn't be the same.

CHAPTER TWENTY-NINE

T he following morning, Hailey was nursing a cup of
coffee out on the porch. A flock of starlings broke
through the ghostly morning mist that hung on the surface
of the lake. The sun was barely up and yet between the pine
trees, which rose toward the sky like upraised fingers, she
could see a couple from one of the cabins dragging down
their canoe. There was a crisp freshness to the air that was
unmistakable. Tourists who frequented the area knew the
best time to get out there in the summer was early, as once
the sun was fully up, you'd be eaten alive by mosquitoes and
the humidity would fill you like you were sucking in water.

She hadn't slept much that night. Her body ached and
her stomach felt tight. She guessed it was a mixture of excitement and uneasiness over what the day would hold. The
thought of venturing into the unknown robbed her of what
little sleep she tried to get. Instead, she tossed and turned,
trying not to imagine the worst. She wanted to remain fo-

cused, happy, and not set her hopes too high. *Just get through this, just get through this day*, she repeated to herself. She was startled when she heard the front door creak open behind her. She half expected it to be Sam, but instead it was her father.

"Hey," Charlie said, bringing out his own cup of coffee. "You're up early."

"Couldn't sleep." Charlie took a seat beside her on the porch rocker.

"Me neither." Hailey stared out.

They both sat taking in the morning rays. Neither spoke for a while; neither felt the need to. Both were preoccupied with thoughts.

Eventually, Charlie breathed in deeply and exhaled. "Always loved mornings here. Your mother was always up before me. You know, she'd wanted this place from the first time she laid her eyes on it? It was the wraparound porch that overlooked the lake that sealed it for her."

Hailey raised her eyebrows.

"When you were tiny we used to sit out here and dream about what the future held. We wondered what you would do when you grew up. We wondered what type of man you would meet. God, your mother loved you. I miss those times."

Hailey listened while running her hand down the side of her cup.

"Look … um …I know it's none of my business, Hay. But I couldn't help notice how close you and Sam have become."

Hailey shot him a sideways glance and then took a large gulp of her coffee.

"When did you know?"

"I would like to say it was the excessive end-of-the-world stockpile of canned baked beans in the cupboard. But I kind of came across you both the other night ..." He trailed off, giving a wry smile.

"Ah..." Hailey said, not attempting to hide her slight embarrassment. "It doesn't worry you?"

"You're my daughter. Of course it worries me. Look at the bags under my eyes. You've always worried me." He chuckled. "But you've grown into a beautiful woman and it's to be expected."

"You know he bought me ... the dress."

Charlie's brow furrowed. "What? The one in Darcy's Gowns?"

"The one."

He raised his eyebrows. "Wow."

"He wants me to go into the city with him this evening."

"That's ... good, right?"

"Yes. I ..."

"Hay, if I knew all it took was a dress to get you to head back to the city, I would have bought it for you months ago." He grinned.

Hailey nudged him and he wrapped his arm loosely around her shoulder. She leaned into him.

"I would have thought you would have been thrilled," Charlie said.

"I am, it's just it still seems to surreal."

"Why? You deserve every bit of happiness you can get, Hailey." He sighed. "I mean you've certainly had your fair share of letdowns."

"And what if it doesn't work out?"

"You won't know unless you try. If there was anything your mother taught me it was that there is nothing certain in love. Look at your mother and I. Two completely different people from opposite sides of the track, we fought each other like cats and dogs, and yet we loved each other intensely. I don't know where I would be today if it wasn't for her. She was my rock."

Hailey was reminded of the conversations she used to have with her mother. The times she shared how she'd met her father. The stories she had about him struggling with addiction. He was the reason she started this place. She'd tried every form of traditional treatment and still he'd fall off the wagon. She eventually took matters into her own hands.

Charlie turned to her. "One year, one month, one second together. If you love one another, you'll find a way to make it work."

She chuckled. "You make it sound so easy."

Charlie nodded. "I know, hon, but these things have a way of working themselves out."

They continued sitting there enjoying each other's company until the sun came up. It didn't matter how old she got. Her father would always be an anchor in her life, the one sure thing that she could rely on to be consistent no matter how many curveballs life threw at her. The smell of fresh pine and earth combined with the kick of caffeine brought Hailey's senses to life, and in that instant she wondered how many more moments with her father she would get like this.

After they'd finished breakfast, and once they made sure they had everything ready for the graduation ceremony, Hailey returned to her room to take a quick shower and pack her suitcase. She'd hadn't asked Sam if they were staying overnight but she assumed by the time they got there and enjoyed the evening it would likely be too late to drive back. She wondered what he'd planned. She liked the spontaneity of it all. She was definitely one for having the guy plan out a date. *A date.* She paused. *That's what it is.* The corner of her lip curled as she relished the thought. For once this was one date she was looking forward to. She stood in front of the full-length mirror and smiled, holding the strawberry evening dress against the front of her. It was exquisite. Words couldn't begin to express how much she loved it. The only thing that could be any more exciting was the thought of him holding her in it.

A knock at her door jolted her out of her daydreaming.

"You ready, Hay?" Charlie hollered.

"Yeah, just give me a few minutes, I'll be right down."

She laid out the dress on the bed for later and smiled to herself, giving it one final look before getting ready.

* * * * *

By midafternoon, the sky was an ocean blue with only a few wisps of clouds in sight. It was time for Sam's graduation. He wasn't too sure what to expect as he stepped outside into the warm sunshine. Hailey was in the courtyard wearing a beautiful light brown summer dress and flat sandals. To his surprise Cassie, Matt, Maggie, and Danny had shown up.

Hailey was the first to step forward, the gravel crunching beneath her feet as she leaned in and motioned over her shoulder. "I hope you didn't mind, they really wanted to be here for you," she said softly.

"Of course not."

She briefly talked him through what they would do. It

was very relaxed and informal. Usually family would have a chance to share, but with no family in attendance, they would give Sam a chance to speak and then move into saying a few final words. Finally, Charlie would present Sam with a heart stone in honor of his achievement.

As they turned to make their way to the graduation room, they heard the sound of tires and spitting gravel. Slowly coming up the driveway was Sam's sister. Sam's eyes widened, and he indicated to Hailey that he would be along shortly. He watched as she led the others off behind the barn.

He turned back as the car came to a halt in front of the house, its darkly tinted windows hiding the occupants. The driver's door opened and his sister stepped out. She paused and smiled.

As Sam was about to step forward to greet her, the passenger door swung open and out stepped his father. Sam felt his emotions well up inside. For what seemed like minutes they simply stared. Before him he no longer saw the strong father he'd known growing up. His father was a thin man; he looked as if the years had sucked the life right of him. His father offered a strained smile, something Sam hadn't seen in a while. It had been far too long. His father closed the door and walked towards him. Sam met him halfway and without saying a word they embraced each other. For someone who looked so weak, his strength hadn't failed him. He could feel his father's firm grip on the back of his collar as they held each other tightly. Sam felt warm tears roll down his cheeks. He didn't for one minute expect the years of broken communication and a strained relationship to be solved in a day—that would be hoping for a lot—but in that moment all that mattered was his father was there. It was a beginning and one that he welcomed.

Jules joined them and Sam hugged her too.

The graduation room was located behind the large red barn further out on the property. It was nestled between two ancient oak trees and raised up slightly. Old cobbled stones led up to a beautiful octagon-shaped gazebo made from thick pine logs. It was the kind of place that could easily have been used for hosting summer dinner parties. The inside was large enough to hold twenty-five people. Directly on the opposite side was an incredible stone fireplace, and above it hung a heart-shaped sculpture made from forged iron. Panes of glass from the ceiling to the floor let in warm bands of sunshine, making every color in the place appear more vibrant and alive. Cushioned seats were positioned in a wide circle and everyone was deep in conversation when he pulled open the doors.

As Sam entered with his dad and sister, a deep sense of pride in being able to introduce his family to the others washed over him. After introductions, they took a seat and Hailey sat beside him. He reached over and placed his hand on hers and she glanced at him. Charlie opened, welcoming everyone for coming. Briefly he shared the original vision he and his wife had when they first opened the doors to the Welland House. His eyes lit up as he spoke about the years and the many men and women with various addictions who'd passed through and left whole. He admitted his initial reservations in taking in Sam and yet how something about him reminded Charlie of someone he once knew. He recalled the first graduate being one of the most troublesome people you would ever come across—then confessed it was himself.

A few people let out stifled chuckles.

He shared how after all the years of running the place, nothing brought him greater joy or satisfaction than to see the looks on families' faces when they could recognize the person looking back at them was the one they knew before addiction.

Jules glanced over at Sam and smiled.

At that point, Charlie gave Sam the opportunity to say a few words. Hesitant at first, he stood up and turned to face them. He'd stood in front of many people throughout his career—Broadway audiences, cameramen, actors, producers, directors—and yet he'd never felt as nervous to speak as he did right then. His palms felt sweaty and his throat felt like the Gobi Desert. Sam coughed a few times to clear his throat.

"Well, um ... before coming here, I never even knew what graduating a rehab meant. This is definitely a first and it feels good." He looked towards Charlie and Hailey. "I wouldn't be standing here if it weren't for both of you. I owe you more than I could ever say in a few words. Thank you. You showed me that no matter how many mistakes a person makes, today is always a new opportunity to change, to turn things around and heal."

He turned to the others. "Matt, Cassie, Maggie, and Danny, thank you for being here and treating me like one of your friends. Your laughter and weird antics made it easier to be here."

And finally he turned to his family. "And, my family ..." Sam faced them both square on. "Having you here today ..." He paused, trying to stay composed. "Let's just say that I haven't exactly been the person you once knew. I could blame my career, the alcohol, and point the blame in many directions, but I realize that the buck stops with me. I'm deeply grateful you came today and I'm deeply sorry. Sorry I can't turn back time, though I wish I could. I can only offer you this … that I will do everything I can to show you how much you mean to me from this day forward."

Sam returned to his seat. Hailey squeezed his hand tight.

Charlie gave the opportunity for anyone else to speak. As he was about to close the ceremony, Sam's father stood up. He gestured that he would like to share a few words and moved to the front.

"I know that most of you here only know my son as the film star, the actor, the face that's plastered on billboards, magazines, and online, but I've known him since I could hold him in my arms." He paused. "At some point the kid I knew disappeared. I saw his face but that wasn't him. I heard him on TV but that wasn't him. Until a few days ago, I had no intention of coming here. My daughter had tried to convince me as she had attempted to countless times before."

Sam glanced at Jules.

"But being old, stubborn, and set in my ways, I refused to listen. Then a few days ago I checked the messages on my answering service." He glanced over at Hailey, who was staring at the floor.

"Someone whom I had never met and had never spoken to before managed to break through this crotchety old exterior. Which my Jules can tell you is quite a feat." He faced Charlie and Hailey. "Thank you. Thank for giving my son back to me."

Sam wondered what Hailey had said. He'd thought his sister had managed to wear his father down, but apparently she hadn't. Maggie wiped a tear from her eye and Sam's father took his seat again.

Charlie closed by presenting Sam with a ruby heart stone and then invited everyone to join him over at the house for a bite to eat.

As they were leaving, Sam pulled Hailey to one side.

"How did you do it?"

She smirked. "Wouldn't you like to know?"

"No, c'mon, what did you say to him?"

She looked up and smiled.

"I'll tell you one day. For now, let's go eat."

He shook his head and smiled to himself.

CHAPTER THIRTY

Later, after everyone had said their farewells and she had cleared up dishes and leftover food, Hailey returned to her room, removed her clothes, and took another quick shower to get rid of the sticky afternoon humidity. Next she slipped into the strapless strawberry dress. It felt a little loose, but not enough that it would need to be taken in. And better than being too snug! Not bad, she thought, considering he didn't know her size. She turned sideways in front of the mirror, smoothing out the front and back of the dress, eyeing her figure. She had a firm body but that didn't mean she threw caution to the wind. Checking her figure had become second nature, especially when going on a date. She rarely wore much makeup and when she did it was a little mascara to bring out her eyes, a touch of foundation, and a light lipstick or gloss.

Next, she pinned up her long wavy blond hair. Lifting it up and off the back of her neck felt refreshing after the day's heat. She put on the bracelet her mother had given her and snapped in a pair of gold hoops. A final spray of her favorite light, green tea perfume and she would be ready.

This was it. She had been anticipating this all day and longing for time alone with him. To go off to the city with the promise of a romantic night out, just the two of them, made her want to squeal with delight. She slipped her feet into a pair of black high-heeled pumps and took one final look to evaluate herself. Perfect, she thought.

Her stomach still felt queasy. She wasn't sure how the night was going to go and if anything did go awry it wasn't like she could jump in a cab and be back at home in ten minutes.

She took a sip from a bottle of water on the nightstand, zipped up her small suitcase, and then left the room.

* * * * *

As she descended the staircase, Sam was standing in the foyer in deep conversation with Charlie. Hearing the clatter of her heels on the burnished hardwood steps, he turned and glanced up. When he saw her, desire ignited. She smiled at him. Mesmerized, he followed her down with his eyes. He wasn't sure what stood out the most, the dress or her eyes. Either way, she was gorgeous. For a split second he felt like a young kid experiencing all the emotions that first love brought.

As she reached the final step he moved forward to help her with the suitcase. Extending her hand out she stumbled slightly and he caught her and the case. His arms wrapped around her curved waist, supporting her.

"Not used to wearing heels," she said softly, her skin flushed red.

"No?" He smiled, staring into her blue eyes. "I thought you wore them well."

They were silent for a moment, lingering in the embrace and fixed on each other. Charlie cleared his throat behind them and they snapped out of their gaze.

She stepped down and removed her heels.

"Maybe I should slip on something that's slightly easier to walk in, at least for the journey down."

Sam's eyes darted to Charlie and then back to Hailey. "Sure. I'll put your case in the car and wait for you outside."

She gave a nod and Sam headed out.

* * * * *

Her eyes flicked from Sam to her father. Charlie had an expression of amusement on his face.

"Don't you say a word." Her lips pursed then curled.

He lifted his hands. "I was just going to say how beautiful you looked, darling."

"Sure you were."

He laughed.

She knew him too well. He never missed an opportunity to find the humor in her most awkward and embarrassing moments.

"No, I'm serious, you look lovely."

"Why, thank you."

He gave her a huge hug.

"Okay, Dad, I have to get going."

She dashed upstairs to find more comfortable shoes. It was a quick choice. She looked down at her sandals, a pair of lower heels, and her pink All-Star Hi Converse. She grabbed the Converse and put them on. She tied them up and dashed back down. Comfortable yet still cute, she thought.

"Sneakers?"

"It's just for the journey down."

She snatched up her heels, hanging them loosely in one hand, and gave her father a kiss on the cheek.

"Remember to call me when you get there."

She dashed out, hollering back, "Will do. Love ya."

Outside, Sam was standing by the barn.

She dashed over, holding up her dress. "What are you doing? You ready?"

He smiled, looking down. "Converse? I like your style."

She cocked her head and gave a slight bow. "Why, thank you, kind sir," she said in her best attempt at a British accent.

Sam looked back at the barn. "Remember the first time I saw you in here dancing?"

"Yeah."

He pulled the doors to the barn open. Particles of straw fell to the ground. He turned back and took hold of her hand.

"Shall we?"

"Sam, don't you remember how well it went before?"

"Of course, but I've had a good teacher since then." He smiled at her.

She took hold of his hand. "Well, if you put it that way, then of course."

Inside it was still dark. Hailey lit one of the lanterns, illuminating a small area of the barn.

"We don't have any music, Sam."

"Don't need it. C'mon."

She could feel an electricity of expectation and strong

emotion between them as they moved into the brightest part of the light

This time Sam took the lead, one hand around her waist, the other holding her hand. She felt her breath catch as he pulled her toward him. He looked into her eyes and they began to move, repeating the pattern and steps that she had taught him countless times since he'd arrived. Again she felt an overwhelming surge of desire.

* * * * *

They had only been dancing a few minutes when they were startled by the sound of clapping.

"Bravo, bravo. I never thought you had it in you, Sam."

They turned.

"Liam?"

Liam's eyes widened with his arms outstretched. "The one and only."

Sam broke his hold on Hailey and went over giving his friend a hug.

"I thought you weren't coming."

"What? And miss my best friend's first graduation?" He emphasized the word first.

"Well, hate to break it to you, but you did. It was hours ago."

"Ah, that's just the formal hoo-har. Now the party starts."

Liam looked over Sam's shoulder and gestured with his head.

"And who is this fine lady?"

Sam turned.

"Oh, um, Liam, this is Hailey, my counselor."

Hailey stepped forward, extending her hand. Liam completely bypassed the handshake and lifted her in a big bear hug.

"Any friend of Sam's is a friend of mine."

"Liam, Liam," Sam said, pulling him away. "Give her a little distance."

"All right, all right." He laughed. Without missing a beat he continued to rattle on.

"Hey, I have a surprise for you, man. Come on."

Sam gave Hailey a disconcerted look. She returned the same and they followed him outside. As they made their way back to the front of the house, Sam could tell Liam was on uppers; his mood was always like that when he was on them. He acted like the Energizer bunny, all over the place and over the top.

"You know, I'm sorry I couldn't get down here sooner, but with the weather and all."

"It doesn't matter."

"No. I've got you sorted. I brought some of the golden liquid that you love."

"Yeah, Liam, I'm not drinking."

He laughed, looking over at Hailey and then winking at Sam. "Oh right, mum's the word. I gotcha."

"No. I'm serious."

"Yeah, whatever."

As they got closer to the house, Sam's pace slowed. His chest rose and fell faster as he squinted at the silhouette of a girl in the headlights of Liam's car. Seeing them approach, she stepped into view.

"Hey, Sam," she said in a soft-spoken voice.

Sam came to an abrupt stop.

"Kate."

She looked different than he had last seen her. Her dark wavy hair was longer, pulled back in a ponytail with one strand draping down her face. She wore light pink lipstick and a colorful dress. A flood of memories hit him like a tsunami—the good, the passionate, and finally the pain.

Liam bound around like an overly enthusiastic grown-up who hadn't grown up. He waved his arms as if conducting an orchestra and then leaned in to Sam and whispered, "You can thank me later."

Sam barely caught what he said as he couldn't take his eyes off her. She did the same but only for a moment, and then she shifted her gaze to his side where Hailey stood. Sam thought of introducing Hailey, but instead he decided not. He raised his finger to indicate to Kate that he would be a second.

He turned to Hailey. The sparkle in her eye seemed dulled.

"I wasn't expecting them to show up."

"No, it's okay."

He paused, staring at her as if formulating what to say next.

"I hate to do this, but can you give me an hour?"

She waved off his request as though it was nothing. "Sure, okay."

"I'll be back soon. And Hailey, I'm sorry about this." And with that he turned and walked over to Liam and Kate. They stared back at Hailey and then they all got in Liam's car and drove away.

* * * * *

Hailey watched the tail lights fade into tiny pinpricks as

they drove off into the night. What had just transpired? She shook her head. Had that really happened? She wasn't sure how to feel about this turn of events. She scuffed the gravel floor with her foot. What now? She decided to wander back into the barn.

She glanced at her watch. "Okay, an hour."

Taking a seat on top of one of the haystacks, she smoothed out her dress, crossed her legs, and rested her chin on her hand.

* * * * *

Inside the car, the atmosphere was thick. You could have cut it with a knife. Liam drove while Sam and Kate sat in the back. The first thing he'd noticed when he got in the car was her scent. It was the perfume she knew he loved. She'd always smelled so good. He noted that she was wearing the shoes that he'd bought her the previous Christmas.

"You look good, Sam. Healthy."

She paused, as if expecting or hoping he would give her a similar compliment back. Sam decided to avoid small talk and cut to the chase.

"Why did you come, Kate?"

She looked caught off guard by his direct manner. "I … thought it was best we talk."

Sam didn't attempt to hide what he was feeling. If his time at the Welland House had taught him anything, it was to stop holding in his emotions.

"Kind of a little late for that now, isn't it?"

"I was hoping it wasn't." She looked as if she was trying to gauge how he felt.

"Look, I know you're probably hurt by what happened."

He chuckled. "Probably?"

"Okay, bad choice of words." She glanced out the window and then back at him.

"Look, Sam, I didn't mean to hurt you."

"When did you realize that, before or after you gave your public apology?"

"Yeah, about that. I —"

Before she could explain he cut her off. "You know, Kate, cheating—that I can understand. I don't respect it, but I can understand it. But apologizing to me through the media? Not communicating for weeks on end and then showing up expecting me to just brush it all under the carpet, no hard feelings?" He paused. "I don't even want to look at you, let alone speak to you."

Sam could see Liam glancing in his mirror like an unwilling spectator. Anger welled up inside of him. "Liam, where the hell are you going?"

Liam turned in his seat. "Going to celebrate, my friend. Here, take this." He pulled a small mickey of whiskey from his inside pocket and handed it back.

"Are you both completely insane?" Sam's eyes moved from one to the other.

"Listen, just stop the car."

"C'mon, Sam, don't be a buzzkill."

Sam leaned forward and gripped Liam's shoulder. "I said stop the car."

The car pulled over to the side of the road. Sam opened the door and placed a foot out. Kate reached and touched his arm.

"Please, Sam, stay. At least let me explain."

He looked over his shoulder at her. He wasn't certain what made him step back inside and close the door. Maybe years of history, feelings he still had, or a curiosity to know why. He closed the door and they pulled away.

* * * * *

Meanwhile, back at the house, Hailey had glanced at her watch more times than she'd wanted to. It had been over an hour and a half since he'd left and she'd paced the floor so much, she could have sworn she'd created a rut in the middle of the barn.

She'd begun to think the worse. It was hard not to. Minutes away from leaving for a beautiful evening out with a guy she had fallen hard for, and who shows up? His alcohol-fueled friend and his ex—could it be any worse? Her mind had imagined every scenario possible—maybe they'd broken down, maybe he'd lost track of time, all the way through to the thought of him back in the arms of his ex or worse, slumped down in a back alley with a bottle in his hand.

Another hour, then two more passed. She could no longer entertain the mind games. Hailey looked down at her dress, feeling only disappointment. It was nearly midnight and any chance of them heading out now had fizzled. She closed the barn door behind her and made her way back up to the house. When she opened the front door, she heard her father.

"Hello?"

"It's me," Hailey replied.

He shuffled out from the living room with a puzzled expression on his face.

"Hailey? Shouldn't you be in the city by now?"

She wandered up the stairs. "I'm tired, Dad, I'll speak to you in the morning."

"Are you okay?"

Hailey didn't answer.

CHAPTER THIRTY-ONE

O n Sunday, Hailey woke later than usual. Between the mist of sleep and being fully awake she felt a deep ache inside as the previous evening's events came seeping in. She'd spent most of the night tossing and turning, keeping an ear out for footsteps in the room below. She couldn't remember exactly when she fell asleep but it had to have been in the early hours of the morning. Warm sunlight slanted directly through the blinds onto her face, adding intensity to the headache she was already beginning to feel. It throbbed behind her eye and over the left side of her head. She glanced at the clock and saw that it was already after ten. She'd never slept in that long.

She stumbled out of bed still in the evening dress that now looked rather crumpled and creased. She held the side of her head, feeling it pound with every step that she took. She slipped out of the dress and threw on some sweatpants and a fresh T-shirt. The next thought she had was—Sam.

Opening the blinds to check that his car was there, she was almost blinded by the glare of the morning. Slowly, her eyes adjusted to the light and she could see his car still parked in the exact spot that it was in the previous night.

She yawned as she made her way down to his room. She knocked at the door and after hearing no answer she poked her head inside. The bed was made, curtains were open, and there was no suitcase inside.

Making her way into the kitchen, she could see Charlie outside talking to Albert, who had his gardening gloves on. Charlie must have heard her putting the kettle on, as he came back inside.

"Hey, sleepy."

Hailey nodded, pulling out the milk.

Charlie leaned against the side.

"So, care to share what happened last night?"

Hailey poured tea into her cup. "Have you seen Sam this morning?"

"No."

Hailey spent the next few minutes filling Charlie in on what happened. When she was done Charlie simply stood there nodding for a moment, as though weighing all the facts.

"Maybe he's at one of the inns?" he suggested.

"An hour, Dad, I don't think so."

Charlie exhaled. "Well, let's not jump the gun, Hailey."

"Yeah." She poured the remainder of her tea down the sink and ruffled through some of the paperwork on the side. "Well, his time is done here, anyway."

As she walked back out, she could see Charlie looked uncomfortable, as if he wasn't sure what to say.

* * * * *

Hours later, Liam's car pulled into the driveway and Sam

got out. His clothes were rumpled and his shirt had a tear in it. Not missing a beat, he quickly waved off Liam and double-timed it into the house. Inside, Charlie was on the phone. He raised his hand, gesturing he'd be a moment.

Sam paced back and forth, looking in each of the rooms while waiting for Charlie to get off the phone. Once the call ended Charlie came out of the kitchen into the foyer and greeted Sam by gripping his arm.

"Sam, you're looking a little worse for wear."

"Yeah, it was a rough night." He touched the dry blood on the side of his lip.

Charlie studied him.

"No, I didn't drink if that's what you're wondering." He looked around. "Where's Hailey, I need to speak to her."

Charlie's eyes dropped.

Sam frowned. "Is she upstairs?" He turned towards the staircase and Charlie grabbed his arm.

"She's not up there."

Charlie pulled out an envelope from his back pocket and handed it to him.

"She wanted me to give you this."

Sam took it, studying Charlie's face. He felt a sinking feeling in his stomach.

He walked outside into the brilliant sunshine, sat down on the porch step, and opened the envelope.

Folding back the letter, he felt his stomach tighten as he began to read.

Dear Sam,

If you're reading this now, I'm sure my father has already given you the third degree, so I'll skip that. And if he hasn't, more than likely it's coming. Though don't be too hard on him, he just cares for me and what he says doesn't always come out right. I'm somewhat the same as I sit here struggling to put into words what I'm feeling right now.

I know writing a letter might seem old-fashioned in a time when we text, update our statuses, and send emails, but I find those things so impersonal. Not that this is any better but at least I get a few more characters to share what I want to say.

Sam, it's none of my business to ask you why you didn't return, and you don't need to tell me. You owe me no explanation and I'm not asking for one, so don't feel that you need to contact me to explain. It's okay.

I simply want you to know that the time that I spent with you meant everything to me. I will always remember it. Few ever get to ex-perience what we did. So if my leaving has made you doubt the way I feel, then I hope this explains. Please know that you meant more to me than any other man I've been close to. Time with you was so wonderful, intimate, and real. I had to pinch myself daily to see if it was really happening. I would be lying if I said I didn't feel anything for you, be-cause I did—I fell in love with you. I looked forward to seeing you eve-ry day. You were the one person on my mind when I fell asleep and the first when I awoke.

You might think you were the only one being healed, but your love was healing me. Your love brought me back to life again, Sam. And our conversations—they made me think anything was possible. Being with you helped me believe again.

As I write this I still feel your touch, your embrace, and your hand in mine as we walked together. I'll always remember the way you looked at me on the stairs, the way you held me as we danced, and all the laughter we shared. But most of all, I'll remember the first time we kissed. You held my attention without even trying and I would have given you my whole heart.

Everything about those times will be special to me, but now dwell-ing on them only fills me with an ache. I know you had to speak with

Kate. I know you have friends and a life that will always pull you away. And I guess last night only reminded me of that. Playing second string to someone I could never be or come close to being isn't something I want to try and live up to. But even more than that, the thought that you and I could have been together was unrealistic. For a moment I believed it was possible, but sitting alone in that barn I realized it was nothing more than a naïve fantasy. So instead I will just cherish it for what it was, a beautiful moment in time. Just know it meant everything to me.

All my love,
Hailey

Gone—she was gone.

Sam looked across the lake into the empty day. As he folded the paper in his hand the day seemed to slow down to a crawl. He felt a dull ache inside begin to build with intensity as each second passed.

"Thought you could use a coffee."

Sam twisted around to find Charlie extending a cup to him. He took it and took a large gulp. He winced as it seared his tongue and yet its pain barely compared to the sadness he now felt.

"So I guess this is where you give me heck."

"Normally I would." He glanced over at him and smiled. "But I kind of think you've already been through the mill."

They sat there for a while in silence.

"Did she say where she was going?" He glanced at Charlie.

"New York City," Charlie said.

Sam frowned. "The city? I don't follow?"

Charlie sighed. "She's returned to the Juilliard School dance program."

"Returned? I thought she'd never even been to the city."

Charlie gave him a sideways glance and raised an eyebrow.

"But the letter from the school?"

"I'm guessing you didn't fully read it."

Sam got up and went inside to find the letter he'd seen on the counter from Juilliard.

"You won't find it, she took it with her," Charlie called to him.

Coming back out, he stared at Charlie in confusion.

"So she's gone back to audition?"

He chuckled under his breath. "Sam, she didn't go to audition, she made it into the program a long while ago. She returned to continue where she left off."

"Why didn't she tell me that?"

Charlie stood up to go back inside. "You'd have to ask her that."

Before he made it inside a tow truck came up the driveway kicking up a cloud of dust behind it. Hooked onto the back was Hailey's truck. After pulling up in front of the house, Monty Farlan stepped out, a cigarette sticking out the corner of his mouth. He had a hacking cough that made you think that at any moment he was about to cough up a lung. He wiped his brow and gave a brief nod to Sam.

"Good day, Charlie."

Charlie gave a nod. "Monty."

"Where do you want the truck?"

"Can you take it around the side?"

"Sure."

Sam put his hand up. "Hold up. Weren't you able to fix it?"

"Hailey didn't ask us to."

"Why?"

"Short on cash. Probably thought it wasn't worth it. Who knows?"

"No, she loved that truck."

Monty took a few more tugs on his cigarette and then stamped it out as the remaining burning embers spread on the ground.

"Look, I don't know, I just do what the customers want."

Why didn't she tell him that she didn't have enough money for the repair? Any one of his other friends wouldn't have thought twice about asking. He knew what that truck meant to her. Sam couldn't get his head around it. A part of him wanted to drive directly to the city, to apologize and explain why he hadn't shown up. But he couldn't—not now, at least. He still had unfinished business that he needed to take care of back in LA. The thought of calling her had crossed his mind, but the letter made it clear she probably didn't want to talk. He groaned inwardly. He longed to see her again, to look into her eyes and tell her he was sorry.

Sam stuck around for a few more days. Charlie was kind enough to let him stay while he sorted out the problem that occurred the night Liam arrived. Sam figured in that time she would have phoned home to speak to Charlie, but she didn't. Several nights he thought about calling her again, but he didn't. She needed time and he needed to give her that space. At least he had plenty of time to think over what to say.

Inside the house everything reminded him of her. Her image in photo frames, a few clothes in the hamper, and the darkened barn he'd look at in the evening from his window.

In the washroom was a bottle of perfume she'd worn. He picked it up and some of its scent got on his hand. He lifted his hand to his nose and inhaled and for a second she was there beside him until he opened his eyes. Then his breath caught in his ribcage, leaving the bitter taste of regret in his mouth.

Charlie didn't say much in those final few days. It was if he knew that talking wouldn't help anything. Despite having his company, without her there the house felt empty; more specifically, Sam felt empty. At night he would lie back with his arms behind his head and gaze at the dark ceiling, wondering what she was doing. Was she lying awake too or had she put it all behind her? He reread her letter countless times in those days and thought deeply about their time together. The way she smiled, laughed, and stood beside him through his darkest moments brought a smile to his face, if only for seconds, before it was replaced with sorrow.

CHAPTER THIRTY-TWO

Eventually, Sam bid farewell to Charlie. He returned to the city and caught the first red-eye flight back to Los Angeles.

Sam had shared a house with Kate for over five years in North Hollywood. It was their home base when they weren't shooting a movie elsewhere.

Now all that was about to change.

Moving out was long overdue, but in his mind there wasn't any other option. Kate's untimely arrival in Walton and the little stunt she pulled only cemented that decision. He thought back to the events that transpired. If it hadn't been for her, he would have made it back in time and Hailey wouldn't have been gone.

He shook his head.

Even her pleading for him to give her another chance didn't cut it; he just couldn't bring himself to go through it again. He'd lost his trust, his respect for her and while it hurt badly, it was now more than that. He just couldn't see any point in trying again. Not after that and not after Hailey.

He didn't consider Kate a bad person, and in many ways he wondered if he had contributed to her actions.

It wasn't like it was uncommon in their lifestyle. His schedule was always overbooked and so was hers. It was tough to maintain a relationship with anyone who worked as much as they did. The constant traveling and little time off had definitely put a strain on the relationship, no doubt about it. He knew it was hard for anyone to understand that, except those who lived in their world.

So no, he didn't consider her a bad person, and in all honesty he still felt something for her, but it was different. Those feelings had faded even quicker once he met Hailey. In fact, everything had changed since he'd met her—in his mind, for the better. Hailey made him want to be a better person. She made him see life beyond all the crap, beyond all the materialistic bull of the circus that was his life. It was so easy to get lost in the glitz, the glamour, and the money. She reminded him of who he was before all that.

The memory faded. Sam had arranged a removal truck to pick up his belongings at around noon; until then he'd planned to make a stop by his manager's office. He knew Eric would be pleased to get an update on how his time went. And then, well, he'd head home to gather up a few main items in bags. The rest he'd lock in storage before checking into a hotel. And maybe, once he knew what work was lined up, he'd find a new pad to call home.

He shook his head and laughed to himself. *Home*—even the word was a joke. He hadn't been home in months. If anywhere felt like home it had been Walton.

Though now it didn't matter how long it would take to get settled again. He'd spent so much time living out of hotels while shooting that a few extra weeks would be fine.

And anyway, he had to return to New York to get everything cleared away with the courts since completing his time in treatment. Maybe then, if it wasn't too late ... He felt a rush of emotion at the thought.

Sam unlocked the door to the house and Duke the dog came bounding towards him. Duke was the pet they shared and if he was home it only meant one thing.

"Sam, is that you?" Kate's voice called out from the kitchen.

He'd barely made it inside when Liam and Kate appeared.

"Hey, buddy, glad to see you made it back in one piece. What a night that was."

Sam scowled at him.

"I thought you said you weren't going to be here," Sam said.

Kate shifted her weight from one foot to the other. "I didn't say I wasn't, I said I might not."

"No. You said specifically that you would be gone for the day so I could get my things."

Liam stepped in between them, lifting his hands up. "Whoa, whoa, guys. Chill."

"Whatever," Sam said. "The truck's already here, I'm just going to grab a few things."

"Sam, I think we need to talk about this more." Kate followed him as he ascended the winding staircase.

"I think you've said enough." He was already pissed that she was there, never mind Liam. What the hell was he doing there?

It seemed strange being back at the house; their bedroom instantly brought back a ton of memories. Photos of them on the beach in Cabo displayed beside the bed, exotic

gifts they'd bought while on vacation, and trinkets they had
given each other at Christmas had once brought good
memories. Now they did nothing except remind him of
what had been thrown away.

In the center was a large four-poster bed and a walk-in
closet massive enough that it could have been another entire
room. Inside the closet, he pulled down a large brown duffel bag off the top shelf and a small travel suitcase. He flung
them on the bed and began stuffing clothes into the duffel
bag. Just pack the bare essentials and then get out, he reminded himself.

Kate sat on the bed and watched him like an eagle, as if
he was going to take something that belonged to her.

"So where are you going after this? Are you going back
to her?"

Sam moved back and forth with purpose. "Who?"

"Don't play the dumb card, Sam. Give me some credit."

He chuckled. "You always did have a way of deflecting
the problem away from yourself."

"Well, I mean, you've been pointing the finger at me, but
what about yourself?"

"What I do is none of your damn business. Not anymore. And I wasn't the one screwing a director."

"Oh, so you have double standards?"

"Kate, there are no double standards here and I'm starting to sound like a broken record. How many times do I
have to tell you? The moment you decided to go behind my
back, it was over between you and me. You made that painfully obvious."

He threw in a few shirts and pants and zipped up the
duffel bag and then began filling the suitcase.

"I didn't screw him."

Sam paused, twisting back around. "Really? So what—you expect me to believe you played a game of chess after he pulled his tongue out of your mouth or are you saving the best for next month's tabloids?"

She slapped him hard across the cheek.

"Asshole."

Sam curled over, gripping his face. The sting burned like fire.

"Babe, oh God, I'm sorry." She tried reaching for him, but he pulled away.

He reached over and snapped the case together, grabbed the duffel, and left the bedroom.

"Sam, please, I promise I won't do it again, we can sort this out."

He spun around.

"Enough," he yelled. "We're done. I tried and you threw it away." He turned to walk away but then spun back. "You know, I even entertained for a moment—just for a moment—that it had all been a mistake. That the tabloids had somehow messed up. But then you show up and pull that crap in Walton."

"Please, Sam … Don't give up on me."

"What, like the way you gave up on me?" He paused, breathing heavily. Their eyes were locked and unflinching.

"Trust me, Kate, you say you don't want this now but a week, a month, or a year from now, you'll be relieved that I'm not here."

With that he turned and left.

Outside, perched on the wall, Liam was having a cigarette, watching the removal guys load up the truck. Noticing Sam, he dropped down.

"Sam, hold up a minute."

"Liam, I'm really not in the mood."

He exhaled a lungful of smoke as he spoke. "Look, I never knew she was going to act that way, I swear. Had I known I wouldn't have brought her."

Sam studied him. "It doesn't matter." He continued walking and Liam stayed in step with him.

"So—you planning on staying in LA?"

"For a week or so, then I have to go back to New York."

He nodded. "Hey, why don't I give you the keys to my pad?"

Sam smiled. "Liam, I broke up with my girlfriend, I didn't go bankrupt."

"I know. I know. It's just, I'm going to be out there in a week after I wrap up this film and it would be good to connect."

He knew connecting with Liam wasn't a good idea. Times with him usually turned into weekend-long drinking sessions. Liam wasn't the best person to have around and fresh out of rehab ... it wouldn't be smart. Truth be told, he could have used a new set of friends, people who weren't medicating themselves in one way or another, but with few people to trust in the business and having only a handful of friends, he didn't want to burn all his bridges. And besides, he'd known Liam for years. Sure, he had a way of not thinking, but he was as loyal as they came.

"Listen, maybe I'll look you up when I get there."

"Yeah, sure thing."

Chapter Thirty-Three

The remainder of the summer of 2011 passed and slowly slid into autumn. It had been a couple of months since Sam had been back in LA. The tabloids had already had their field day running another series of magazines with shots that someone had taken of him and Kate that night in Walton. He'd already traveled back to New York several times and was relieved to get out from under the weight of the court system.

On his third visit, the leaves had begun to change color, and the weather had turned cold. Despite advice from his manager he chose to do what few A-list celebs did. He rode the subway and left behind his bodyguards. Surprisingly, no one appeared to recognize him and the odd ones that did never bothered him, which seemed strange but it made a nice change.

As he traveled between Sixth Avenue and Grand Central station on his way to a lunch with a producer, the ride was everything he remembered. Getting off the overloaded train wasn't pretty—it was like being in a mosh pit as people pushed and slammed into each other.

As he made his way toward the exit he spotted a poster plastered on the underground wall advertising an event at the New York City Center. It read *Fall for Dance Festival 2011, 10 performances, 20 companies, one stage.* The underground was always full of posters and on any other day he wouldn't have given it a passing glance, but it wasn't the event that caught his eye. It was the dancers elegantly gracing the cover. Displayed in a powerful full leap were Hailey and a male dancer. His heart quickened at the sight of her. Crowds of people shouldered him as he stood frozen and completely captivated in the middle of the walkway. In his previous visits to the city he'd thought about stopping by the Juilliard School, but every time he mustered up the courage to follow through he would back out at the last minute. He wasn't sure if either of them were ready. Yet no matter how much time he put between the inevitable, he couldn't escape the feelings that he had for her.

Over lunch he listened while the producer discussed his next project and watched him shovel away a caesar salad like he hadn't eaten in a month. Producers rarely gave a rat's ass about what you thought, as long as you agreed with their vision. You could have been juggling in front of them, it wouldn't have mattered. Most of the time Sam would have been one hundred percent present, but that day he found himself simply going through the motions. He nodded in agreement, shook his head, smiled, and feigned laughter. It almost felt like second nature in his world that often seemed all too predictable. He caught the general gist of what the producer was saying, but in reality his mind wandered to other places.

Sam loved acting and he had a lot to be grateful for, but at times it felt like he was just another cog in the entertainment machine—an expendable commodity. As long as you showed up, repeated what they wanted you to say, hit your marks, and brought in the big bucks on opening weekend, the sun shined out of your backside. Deliver and you'd remain a valuable asset.

Heck, he'd known acting buddies who'd been in the business far longer than him—good actors who'd just had a run of bad luck. Those folks were rarely heard from again. They were scraping by, doing bit parts and supporting roles just to make ends meet. How long would it be before he was in their shoes? It wasn't a matter of if it would happen, but when—and then what?

Unless you had someone to come home to, it was normal to feel completely isolated and alone. Trusting people didn't come easy in this business. You never really knew who your friends were. In such a cutthroat industry, was it any wonder so many of them self-medicated to cope? And who knew, maybe next time it wouldn't be alcohol, it would be worse.

Sam often wondered what so-called normal people thought about his life. What assumptions did they make? How did it appear on the outside? What did Hailey think?

It was mid-afternoon by the time he began his journey back to his hotel. Again he saw the poster and again he stared at it. As his train pulled in behind him and the doors opened, Sam followed the mass of people stuffing themselves in like sardines, but this time he paused at the doors. Others shoved by him looking more than happy to take his spot. He wasn't sure why he hesitated to get on, he just knew that there were moments in life where it felt you were standing at a crossroads. One way took you on the same journey, gave you more of the same. It was comfortable, known, and an easy choice. The other would take you down a path of unknowns. It would stretch you and more than likely would feel uncomfortable and would be a hard choice to make. Charlie's words came drifting back to him. *Make good choices.*

The doors hissed as they closed, but this time he hadn't gotten on. As it moved off, sending up a gust of warm air, he smiled to himself. Within a few minutes Sam had changed platforms and caught the next train that would take him to Columbus Circle Station.

The Juilliard School was located in the Upper West Side. It was hard to miss, standing out like a massive ship in a docking yard raised up on wedges with the front of the building resembling the bow. Its glass windows and design were spectacular to behold. Outside, students milled around while others darted in and out of the front entrance. The school was known for producing some of the best in drama, dance, and music, and if you were one of the lucky ones to make it in, your future was meant to be one of promise and accolades.

Sam strolled through, taking everything in while approaching the front desk. Everything about the place gave off an air of prestige and excellence. Situated at the front desk were two burly security guards. Their eyes looked him over before shifting their gaze back to the monitors.

"Can I help you?"

"Yes, I'm here to see one of the students. Hailey Welland."

"Is she expecting you?"

"No, but I know her."

While one of them got on the phone, the other studied Sam. He leaned back in his chair, and a grin came over his face. "You're Sam Reid."

Sam nodded.

"God, my sister absolutely loves your movies."

Sam smiled politely, knowing where this was heading.

"Would you mind ..." He handed Sam a piece of torn paper.

Sam scribbled his name and handed it back to him. The guard looked at it, grinning widely.

"Thanks."

Meanwhile, the other had finished muttering on the phone.

"Seems she in a class right now. You'll need to come back later."

Sam nodded. "Listen, guys. I really need to see her. If I could come back I would but I'm not going to be in the area long."

The guard scratched his chin for a moment, giving some consideration to his answer.

"You have history with her?"

"You could say that."

The guard pursed his lips, as if weighing options.

"No, you're going to have to come back."

The security guard to whom he'd given the autograph tapped the other on the chest and they rolled back on their chairs. A few words were muttered between them and they rolled back.

The guard who'd made the phone call rolled his eyes. "Ten minutes. Take the second door on your right, keep going to the very end of the corridor, and take the third left. It's room five hundred and one. But remember ..."

"Ten minutes will do." Sam wasn't sure what the guard would have said but he wasn't sticking around to give him time to change his mind. Within seconds he was down the corridor and on his way to the room. Throughout the building he could hear music. As he passed different rehearsal rooms he glanced inside. Students were hard at work, busy dancing in front of large mirrors, while others were stretching. He must have stood out like a sore thumb, as several students he passed in the hallway pointed and whispered. Or maybe they just recognized him.

Counting down the door numbers, he could feel his anticipation building. His hands began to sweat as he got closer to the room. The thought of seeing her again overwhelmed him with a mixture of emotion. Despite the amount of time that he'd had to chew over what he would say, he now honestly felt at a loss for words. Would she even want to speak to him? He wouldn't blame her if she didn't give him the time of day.

He braced himself for the worst yet inwardly hoped for the best.

As he turned the final corner and saw the sign for room five hundred and one up ahead, he took a deep breath. The classes were separated from the hallways by large panes of glass, making the entire building seem larger than it was. It also made staying inconspicuous completely useless. There was still time to back out but he couldn't force himself to turn around.

As he passed by the glass that separated him from the room Hailey was in he could hear funky music reverberating throughout the hall. Inside he could see a large group of barefoot dancers in full swing, performing moves in unison. Each one moved with precision and purpose. Each one gyrated, tapped, and stepped with unbelievable speed. Spinning and jumping, their backs arched, their heads bobbed, and arms reached as they used their entire bodies as instruments of art.

Sam stood outside, scanning the groups of dancers for Hailey. Within seconds, the groups parted and at the center were two dancers moving on the floor. Through a series of choreographed moves guided by a dance instructor on the sidelines, their bodies moved with ease and technical proficiency like a painter striking the canvas. It took him only a few seconds to recognize the girl was Hailey. Her hair was pinned up, she wore dark, form-fitting dance clothes, and she was everything he remembered—beautiful, natural, and mesmerizing to watch.

The choreographer weaved through the dancers, bellowing instructions as if his words were a conductor's baton.

"Feel it, you're thinking too much."

As they both rose up and their arms opened outward like petals on a flower, the male dancer dropped down, giving Sam a clear view of Hailey. Deeply engrossed in the fluidity of her moves, Hailey leaned forward and then her gaze shifted up. Instantly their eyes met. As she continued moving he could see the shock on her face and hear the unspoken words of reproach.

Sam gave a tentative smile, but inside he knew it was wrong to show up without giving her warning. He felt frozen to the spot, unable to move as he stared at her. Still trying to keep her gaze locked on him, she made a few more steps and then slipped. The choreographer lifted his arms.

"Stop, stop. Stop the music."

The male dancer helped her back up.

She waved him off. "I'll be fine. I just need a moment."

"Take five," the choreographer said before turning back
to the rest of the group. "Okay, class, take a break and then
stretches."

Hailey hobbled over to the door and came out into the
hallway. For a second or two they simply stared at each other awkwardly, as though they both were contemplating their
next move.

"You okay?"

"I was until I saw you." She leaned against the wall and
began rubbing her ankle.

He wasn't quite sure how to take that.

"What are you doing here, Sam?"

There was an edge to her voice, which reminded him of
when he first arrived in Walton.

"I came to apologize."

She rubbed her ankle.

Sam stepped forward. "Are you sure you're okay?"

Hailey put out her arm. "I'm fine."

There was harshness to her voice. It certainly wasn't going the way he envisioned it. What a fool he was for coming, he thought.

A male student poked his head out the door, glanced at
Sam and then Hailey.

"Are you good? He's already getting pretty antsy in
there."

She didn't take her eyes off Sam when she replied,
"Yeah, I'll be there in a minute."

"I got your letter," Sam said.

"Then you know that you don't owe me an apology."

He nodded. "Where are you staying?"

She was soft-spoken in her reply. "The residence on
campus."

"Hailey," the male dancer said.

She turned her head. "I said I'll be there in a minute." This time she said it with force.

Sam stepped forward. "Hailey, I —"

"Where is she?" the choreographer bellowed, cutting Sam off.

Hailey motioned over her shoulder. "Look, Sam, I'm kind of busy. I have to go."

He nodded. She stood upright and followed the other student back in. And like that it was over. He could see a mixture of curiosity and disappointment in her expression as she went in.

Sam watched from outside as the choreographer started the music and once again the groups of dancers flowed back into their routine. He could see Hailey glancing at him from the corner of her eye. He looked away, wondering if she'd caught the gutted expression on his face. His eyes met hers one last time before he moved.

Walking away, he could feel her gaze upon him. *I knew I should have got on that train*, he chided himself, feeling like a complete fool.

CHAPTER THIRTY-FOUR

O utside in the cool autumn air he buttoned up his thick jacket, blew on his hands, and shoved them deep into his jacket. Mulling it over again, he wondered what he'd expected to happen. In his mind he imagined them picking up where they had left off. At the most he had hoped she would have been happy to see him, if only for a few seconds. At the very least he assumed she would want to hear his side of the story. If she would just hear him out he'd be able to explain, he thought.

He went back inside. One of the security guards looked up.

"Forget something?"

"Yes. Can you direct me to where the residence is?"

"Meredith Willson Residence Hall?"

"That's the only one, isn't it?"

"Yeah." He pointed in a direction. "Go in at the plaza level, third floor. You have to take the elevators but you won't be getting in there unless you're a student."

"That's fine."

Sam followed the guard's directions and a few minutes later he arrived. He took a seat inside the entrance. He spent the next hour watching the clock and seeing students come and go. He had no idea when she would be getting out or even if she would immediately head back. But he wasn't going to give up. He picked up a magazine and leaned back in one of the comfy leather chairs.

It was starting to get dark outside when another group of girls and guys came in, bags flung over their shoulders. Their clothes looked drenched, as if they'd had been through an intense workout. Sam glanced up and then continued reading, listening to the chatter of the passing students with one ear.

"Meet you in the lounge later?"

"Yes, I'll be there."

That voice he recognized. He glanced up right at the moment one of the male companions gave Hailey a kiss on the cheek. The sight of it was like a splash of cold water in his face. *She's got a boyfriend?* The guy went one way and Hailey and another girl headed for the elevators. Knowing she hadn't seen him yet, he took the opportunity while they were waiting at the elevators to slip out. He'd barely made it to the exit when someone called out.

"Hey, it's Sam Reid."

Strike me dead where I stand, Sam thought.

He kept walking, trying to pretend he hadn't heard the kid.

"Mr. Reid, hold up."

Sam's fast pace slowed to a crawl. He took a deep breath and turned around to face a bunch of wide-eyed students.

"Wow, it's really you." The guy prodded him as if checking to see if he was a mirage. Satisfied, he continued, "I'm a first-year drama student and I was wondering ..."

Here we go again.

Sam signed his autograph as more students gathered around asking questions. Over the tops of their heads he could see that they weren't the only ones who were taking notice. Hailey was staring.

* * * * *

Once the students scattered, Hailey waved off her friend and strolled over. She adjusted the bag strap on her shoulder and placed her other hand casually on her hip. Her eyebrow rose.

He shrugged and threw up his hands. "Sorry, I'm fresh out of autographs." He desperately hoped to break the awkwardness of the situation.

"You know security removes stalkers from this place every day?" Her lip curled up.

He smiled. "C'mon, at least give me a chance to explain myself."

She studied him and then turned towards the elevators. He followed her.

On the way up they glanced at each other, trading nervous smiles. As Hailey pulled at her top, he caught her looking him over from his shoes upwards.

She bit the bottom of her lip and curled a loose strand of hair behind her ear.

"I look a mess."

Acting all nonchalant he replied, "Really?"

She gave him a skeptical look.

He cringed. *That came out wrong, I wonder if she thought I meant I hadn't taken notice of her. Oh god, I'm speaking to myself.*

Quick, change the subject.

He quickly tried to fill the void with anything.

"So was that your boyfriend?"

"Who?"

"The guy. The guy who gave you a kiss."

She chuckled a little.

"What? What's so funny?"

"You."

"Well, was he?"

"Not unless he stopped batting for the other team."

"Oh." A sense of relief washed over him coupled with amusement.

She smirked as she stepped out of the elevator.

* * * * *

"Come in."

She held the door open as he stepped in. The dorm room felt a little cramped. There wasn't anything fancy about it. Some bunk beds, a desk and chair. It was simple but it gave them everything they needed.

Sam looked around while Hailey dumped her belongings inside one of the closets.

"What's your roommate like?"

"She's great, she's taking drama. So I'm sure she would talk your ear off."

On the wall was a photo of the Welland property. Sam tapped it.

"Never too far from home. Have you been back?"

"No. I'll probably go back at Christmas."

Hailey leaned against the bunk bed as Sam picked up different items on the table.

"How's your dad doing?"

"Seems fine, Maggie drops in every now and again. He has four patients booked in over the winter."

"That's good." Sam turned to face her. "Strange as it sounds, I kind of miss the place."

Hailey glanced at the floor and back at him.

"You know … I've missed you, Hailey."

She shook her head. "Don't do that."

"What?"

"That. 'I've missed you, Hailey,'" she said. "Why, Sam? I waited in that barn until midnight for you."

Sam exhaled deeply. "I know and I'm so sorry." He sighed. "But I can explain."

"No need," Hailey said.

She opened a drawer on the desk, lifted a few papers, and threw down a tabloid magazine on the desk. The front cover was a shot of him and Kate lip-locked inside one of the downtown bars of Walton.

Sam leaned back against the wall and rubbed his temples.

"I thought we had something," Hailey said.

"We did."

"Then why, Sam?"

He exhaled hard. "Look, I know the way it looks but it's misconstrued." He picked up the magazine and glanced over it. "And besides, this came out last month. You left before you would have seen this. So this can't be the reason—"

Before he could get another word out, the door flung open and in stumbled what had to be Hailey's roommate carrying a stack of clothes so high she couldn't even see where she was going.

"Hailey, what's going on downstairs, there's a stack of

photographers outside, security is trying to get them to leave but they're not budging. Anyone would think we ..."

She dumped the clothes on the floor and caught sight of Sam.

Her roommate's mouth dropped. "Oh. My. God."

"Hi," Sam said with a brief nod.

She stood frozen. "I ... I ... can come back."

Hailey stepped forward, wedging her foot to keep the door open. "No need, he was just leaving."

Sam appealed to her. "Hailey."

Hailey's roommate backed out, leaving them alone again. "Just leave," she said.

Sam stepped towards her.

"No, you've got the wrong end of the stick here."

"I want you to leave."

"Why?"

The noise in the hallway was escalating as if a fight was in full swing. Within a few seconds three photographers who had managed to break through security had made their way up. Within seconds they came into view, and upon seeing Sam beside Hailey they began taking shots. Bewildered and blinded by the flashes of cameras, Sam slammed the door shut and pressed his back against it.

"Please, Hailey."

He reached out and she pushed his arms away.

"Leave, I just want you to leave."

He studied her face. He could see the pain in her eyes as they welled up with tears.

"I don't understand, why won't you give me a chance to explain?"

"Listen to them."

The photographers were beating on the door, calling out his name.

"It's never going to change. You and me"—she shook her head—"were just from two completely different worlds."

"It's not always like this."

She shook her head.

Sam gave a final look of resignation. Hailey stepped away from the door and lowered her gaze, making it clear she didn't want to speak any further.

Sam sighed. He grasped the handle and paused.

"I never meant to hurt you." He twisted the handle and pulled it open to an onslaught of camera flashes and paparazzi trying to push their way in. He shoved his way through them and they followed him, fighting for his attention.

"Get that out of my face." Sam slapped one camera out of a photographer's hand. It dropped to the floor and smashed. He'd never done that before but then again he'd never felt such anger towards the media. There was a time he would have paid to have photographers show up and shine a light on his work as an actor. Now he resented them with every fiber of his being. They were like hungry sharks out for blood and they didn't care who they took down in the process. Diving into the elevator at the end of the hall, he turned back as the doors slid closed. Sam raised his hand to cover his eyes from the flashes. Above the heads of the photographers he caught sight of Hailey staring at him from her doorway.

CHAPTER THIRTY-FIVE

That evening, Sam made arrangements with Liam to meet him at his favorite place in the city—The Spot. It was a sultry, sophisticated joint located inside the Trump Soho Hotel. A hop, skip, and jump for Liam, being as that was where he lived when he wasn't in LA.

Sam needed to get out, get his mind off the day's events, and no other person he knew was better at that than his oldest friend. The lounge felt cramped, with a small, intimate crowd of young and old seated on a few circular, tufted leather couches. It was said you could have fit the entire place inside a subway car. Sam didn't doubt it as he squeezed his way through the guests.

Illuminating the stacked-stone walls and the tiny bar in the corner was a collection of gold-hued Chinese lanterns hanging down. A handful of people were dancing in the center in no more space than the size of a coffee table. DJ music blared over the speakers, creating an echo. The whole place was peculiar; then again, so was Liam.

Liam sat in the corner, a girl on either side of him. He

must have been telling one of his odd jokes, as the people around him had the same deer in the headlights look that Sam had whenever Liam hit the punch line.

"Sam." He turned to the others. "Everyone say hello to my good friend."

They nodded and continued drinking.

"Come, let me get you a drink. What can I get you?"

"Just a Coke," Sam said.

"What? Would you like Girl Scout cookies with that?"

"Liam, you know I'm sober now."

"How could I forget? What is it, two months now?"

"A little more."

He laughed. "I wish I had your restraint." He shouted to the barman for a Coke and a double scotch.

"So what's new?" Liam said, waiting to be served.

Sam rubbed the bridge of his nose. "I went and saw her."

"Hailey?"

Sam nodded.

"She wouldn't listen."

"That sucks," he said, passing Sam his drink. "You want me to speak to her?"

"No... thanks."

"Look, the way I see it, Sam—you've probably saved yourself a lot of heartache."

Sam looked reflective. "Maybe."

Liam downed the scotch and banged on the bar for another.

"Listen, forget her." He motioned with his head to the two long-legged ladies sipping drinks in the corner. "You know what you need? Twins. They're a bit ditzy but you can't argue with double D's my friend, am I right?"

Sam shook his head and laughed. "Liam, you never change."

"Life's too short to change, my friend." He lifted his drink. "C'mon." Liam egged him on. "C'mon, raise your glass."

Reluctantly Sam lifted his drink and together they said aloud,

"Screw the world."

In the past it had always been humorous to Sam, a way to blow off steam and give them reason to go wild. Like a gun starting a race, it would indicate the beginning of an alcohol-fueled binge that would carry on for days at a time. Yet now it only brought a deep sense of emptiness, childishness, and stupidity to the act.

Liam slammed his shot glass down and thumbed the barman.

"Another, and get something serious for my friend here. Enough with the Coke crap." He slapped Sam on the back. "Okay, back in a tick."

Sam watched him head off to the men's room. The bartender asked Sam what he wanted. Sam waved him off as he soaked in the mingled conversations and the music that was starting to give him a headache.

Five minutes later, Liam returned, his eyes all bugged out.

Sam shook his head. "Please tell me you haven't taken anything."

"Me? No. Well … just a little pick-me-up."

Sam sighed, seeing the remaining white dust around his nostrils. "God, Liam."

"Relax." He patted Sam on the shoulder and then knocked back his drink.

"C'mon, let's get out of here. You have got to see my pad."

They squeezed their way back through the crowd and out the exit. They had only made it a few feet outside when Liam stumbled.

Sam placed his hand on his shoulder and leaned Liam against the wall.

Sam furrowed his brow. "You okay?"

"Yeah." His breathing was slower. He brushed Sam off.

A few more steps and Liam collapsed to the floor in a heap. Within seconds his body began convulsing.

Sam shouted to the doorman. "Call nine-one-one." Then to Liam, "Liam. Hang in there," as Liam's eyes rolled back in his head.

"Oh God. Liam." He cradled his friend in his arms as a crowd of spectators gathered around.

"Get an ambulance," were the last words that echoed throughout the crowd.

* * * * *

When the paramedics arrived, Sam looked on in a state of shock at the entire chaotic scene, which seemed to play out in streaks of slow motion. He could see people yelling and paramedics rushing to grab equipment, but he couldn't hear a word they were saying. His eyes were fixed on Liam lying there. All the color had drained from his unconscious friend's face. Sam felt sick to his stomach as they attached cardiac monitors to Liam's chest and he saw him flatlining. An investigator on scene asked him questions about what had taken place. If it was possible to have an out-of-body experience, it seemed as if he was having one in that moment. It felt as if he was observing, answering, and moving without thought.

As the paramedics hauled Liam's body into the back and then closed the doors and sped away, Sam remained paralyzed, still looking down at a spot of blood on the concrete. Was there anything he could have done? Had he done anything? His mind was barraged with questions, guilt, and remorse. He'd seen his friend take cocaine and heroin many times and never encountered anything even close to this. Was it even real? He shook his head to see if he was dreaming.

He walked off into the night, his mind drifting from Liam and then to Hailey. At two o'clock in the morning he sat drinking coffee in a shop, gazing out into the empty night. A young couple came in, giggling. They sat in a booth, their arms entwined around each other. The young guy curled the girl's hair around the back of her ear and nuzzled her neck. After ordering, the girl whispered something into the guy's ear. He smirked and they left.

He'd felt that excitement, the simple pleasures of being with one you loved. The companionship, the secret jokes that brought tears of laughter, and the security of knowing that someone was there through the roughest times in life. Oh, how he longed for that again. To be close to a warm body, to get lost in the arms of a lover who loved him without strings attached.

God, he missed Hailey. If ever there was a time he needed her, it was now. He closed his heavy eyelids and drifted in and out of consciousness until the coffee shop owner jolted him out his slumber and told him to go home.

Outside, the cold air cut through his jacket and he hugged himself for warmth. What was he doing? What had

he become? Was he just another cog in a world that cared
more for money, entertainment, and the next hot thing?
Someone who would eventually buckle under the stress and
go the same way Liam had? Becoming nothing more than
yesterday's news? He walked past a liquor store and
stopped. An old man in his late sixties sat nearby drinking
from a bottle peeking out of a brown paper bag.

The image of Liam collapsed on the ground filled his
mind. The pressure was too much. Minutes later he came
out holding a bottle of Jack Daniel's.

In the cab ride back to his hotel, he rested his weary
head against the cold window and watched streaks of rain-
bow colors pass him as cabs and people went about their
business. In a city that never slept, he wondered how much
attention Liam's death would attract. It was odd when celebrities died. People came out of the woodwork pretending
they knew them. But where were these people when the celebrities had been alive? Within days those same people
would continue to go about their business, the news reports
would end, and the wheels of the world would keep turning.
Expendable was the only word that came to his mind.

Sam spent the next four days locked away inside his hotel with the curtains drawn. He ordered in Chinese takeout,
watched infomercials, and didn't shave. It was if all his lust
for life had been tapped out. Even walking to the bathroom
seemed like an arduous task. He never did open the bottle
of bourbon; instead, it sat on the nightstand for several
days. From time to time he'd glance at it, feeling an overwhelming urge. *It will take away the pain, no one will know,* he
thought. But every time he picked it up and was about to
crack open the top, Hailey's face came to his mind in flashes
like an angel on his shoulder. Finally he sat on the edge of

the bed, picked up his phone, and dialed her number.

"Hello?"

Sam was silent.

"Hello? Sam?"

He hung up, exhausted and overwhelmed, and the tears he'd held in broke free. He threw the bottle against the wall. It smashed into pieces, sending shards of glass all over the carpet and embedding other parts in the wall. In the room next door, he could hear pounding.

"What's going on in there?"

He grabbed his comforter and slumped onto the bed and curled the blankets around him. Over the remaining days, messages piled up on his phone until it was full, each one unanswered. Finally on the fifth day, as if awakening from a bad dream, he forced himself into the shower, shaved, and put on comfortable clean clothes. He tugged on the window covers and covered his retinas as they were struck by blinding light.

He wasn't sure what clicked inside him that day.

Maybe it was a combination of many things, though he knew it was only a matter of time before his family or manager would come knocking, and Liam wouldn't have wanted them to see him that way.

Days later, Sam attended the funeral and paid his respects. There was a small crowd mainly made up of his family members and a few close friends he'd gained over the years. The family thanked Sam for coming and asked what Liam was like the night he passed. Sam could see the anguish in their eyes as they spoke. He knew nothing he could say would ease their pain, but maybe knowing those last final minutes would bring them a sense of closure.

He saw Kate that day. Their eyes met for a fleeting moment before they both turned away. Life would never be the same again. Everything had changed. In an instant, the world he'd known felt small, insignificant, and fragile.

CHAPTER THIRTY-SIX

When the last of the golden leaves fell from the trees of New York only to be replaced by a few snowflakes drifting to the ground, Sam returned to work, hoping that in some small way, it would bring a sense of normality back to his life, and in some way it did. He'd taken a break from films and had ventured into theater, the very thing that made him catch the acting bug when he was young. It gave him a chance to hone his skills, gain a new group of friends, and rediscover life.

He hadn't had a drop of alcohol since the time he'd checked into the Welland House. He took Charlie's words to heart and faced his sobriety a day at a time. There was no denying it—it was tough. Of course there were times, usually late at night when alone, that he fought the urge to have a drink, but thankfully those days were few and far between.

On weekends he visited his father and Jules and worked on rebuilding his relationship with them. He took a deeper interest in what Jules was doing, and he never spoke about what he did when he was with them, or about Hailey, for that matter. The wounds were still fresh, but they were healing. He still wondered, though, what Hailey had said to his father, and no matter how much he fished for it, his father wouldn't say. He just had a glint in his eye whenever the subject came up.

The attention from the paparazzi had died down as a new group of actors appeared on the scene. It never ceased to amaze him what photographers did to make a quick buck or what an actor would do to grab the limelight, even if it meant flaunting their train-wreck lifestyle. Personally, he was glad to fall out of the limelight for a time and let someone else be the focus. In his downtime he spent several days catching up with friends and searching for an apartment in the Upper West Side. He was tired of living out of a hotel, and New York's seasons provided a nice change from living in the heat of LA. He'd always loved the way the trees lined the blocks like interlocking fingers. And with the snow falling, it became even more noticeable as the branches poked through the canopy of snow and twisted together.

It had been a month since Liam had been laid to rest, and since he and Hailey had spoken. Not a day went by that he didn't think of them both with a deep sense of fondness and ache. He shared the entire story with his new friends one night over dinner, and when he finished they just stared.

Before Henry, Matthew, and Brooke left that evening. Brooke turned to Sam, gave him a kiss on the cheek, and told him that as much as she loved his company, if he let Hailey slip through his fingers, he was a fool. Whoever this Hailey was, she was a gem—a keeper for sure. Hailey seemed genuine to them and at the risk of more heartache Sam had to try. He had to let her know what really happened that night. Whether she believed him was neither here nor there. That was a risk he would have to be willing to take.

That was what he loved about his new friends. They didn't hesitate in telling him what he should do. They were the type of people that he loved. Honest, straightforward, and never ones to mince words even if they hurt.

But it wasn't as easy as that.

He'd considered volunteering his time in the drama division at Juilliard in hopes that their paths would eventually cross, but trying to work out the logistics of it all seemed like one more impossibility. Then there were the times he wondered if she'd met someone else. It wasn't a long stretch to think that someone would want to date her. She was gorgeous both inside and out and quite simply the best thing that had ever happened to him. But was he the best thing for her?

Unbeknownst to Hailey, Sam had showed up every night at the *Fall for Festival* event and watched her shining performance from the balcony. After the final performance he nearly mustered enough courage to approach her and congratulate her in person. Instead, he opted to order the largest bouquet of roses and have them delivered to her dressing room, signed anonymously. Walking home that evening, he could have sworn that she saw him leaving. He wanted so badly to speak with her again but at the same time he wanted to respect her wishes. Or was that another excuse, a crutch to avoid rejection? In all honesty, he was scared of letting go and unsure how to approach her.

During the next few weeks everything in Sam's life revolved around Hailey. He wouldn't show up again unannounced but he began making small gestures, doing little things like every morning having someone deliver her favorite Guatemalan coffee to the front desk, minutes before she came down. The security guard he'd given his autograph to was a good sport. When asked who was leaving them, he'd tell Hailey he had no clue; he was doing his rounds at the time.

Another morning he had a box of twenty decorated cupcakes, each one displaying a dancer performing a different move, delivered with a note that read, *Now you've got an excuse, just say you're learning a new dance move.*

On another day he arranged for a care package to be delivered to her room, along with everything a girl could want, including a month's complete spa treatments at one of the finest places in the city.

Finally, standing in the middle of a sidewalk in Central Park late one evening in early December, as floodlights shone down on couples ice skating, the reality of it hit him like the cold weather that nipped at his ears. It sent a shiver down his spine. The thought of losing her scared him for more reasons than one. It seemed strange. Sam had always been a fighter; he'd overcome his fears and overwhelming odds to get where he had in his profession. He'd always had the courage to go boldly into auditions knowing full well that it might mean rejection. He'd faced his critics and brushed off his fair share of haters like they were annoying flies on his shoulders, and yet the thought of standing in front of her again made him feel naked and vulnerable.

Sam shivered as the wind picked up. He wrapped his scarf around his neck, wiped snow off a bench, and sat down. He stared at the bright city lights, the night sky, and the skaters. He watched as some of them fell and got back up. He saw another slip, caught at the last second. He saw a father hugging his small son, brushing off the snow and wiping away the little boy's tears. And maybe it was an epiphany he had that night, or simply him forcing the hand of destiny. But whether he fell flat on his face trying, he was determined that she wouldn't be the one that slipped through his fingers.

* * * * *

The following day, Sam awoke to the sight of a blanket of white covering the city. This was it, he thought. A rush of adrenaline flooded his brain, igniting every cell in his body. Confident and excited, he leaped out of bed to take a shower. He slipped on a loose white shirt and jeans. A quick splash of cologne, a sip of piping-hot black coffee, and he was out the door. It was a little before 7:00 a.m. and outside it was already turning into a beautiful but cold December weekend. He hurried, knowing that it wouldn't be long before the roads were congested with taxis, shuttles, and the usual tourists lost in their cars. During the short fifteen-minute drive over to Juilliard he thought of their time together before she left Walton. He remembered the words she wrote in her letter to him. *I fell in love with you.*

The revolving glass door brought him into a warm lobby at the Juilliard residential building. Seated at the desk were two young security guards he'd never seen before. He ran his hands through his hair and let out an exasperated sigh.

Here we go again.

They had their feet up on the desk and were playing a game of cards. At the sound of Sam's arrival they adjusted their ties, dropped their feet, and pretended to act professional. Sam's mind was racing and yet at the same time everything about what he was doing felt right. At the front desk he explained who he was and gave them a shortened version of how he and Hailey met and why he was there today. They stared at him blank-faced.

"C'mon, guys."

"It's against policy."

"And playing cards on the job isn't?"

One of them stood up. "Do I really have to come around there?"

Sam threw his hands up. Walking away, he heard one of them mutter behind him, "Bloody celebrities think they can do whatever the hell they like."

Crushed with disappointment, he was only a few feet from the door when he heard the elevator ding behind him. Looking over his shoulder, he saw two students stepping out. Without a single thought to the consequences of his action, he dashed and slipped in just as the elevator doors closed.

Sam exhaled, unbuttoned his jacket, straightened out his shirt in the elevator's mirrored walls, and wiped the smeared salt residue from his shoes. He watched the illuminated numbers going up. He knew he'd only have a few minutes before Starsky and Hutch at the front desk arrived to escort him off the premises. No matter what the outcome was, he had to talk to Hailey. And this time he wasn't leaving until she heard him out. It was wrong not to let her know what had happened. He wouldn't be able to live that way. Hailey needed to know, if only to give them both peace of mind. Worst-case scenario, a guy would open the door and Sam would move on, knowing that she was happy and loved by someone even if it wasn't him.

He gave her door a knock and stepped back. There was

no answer. He tapped it a few more times and listened. Eventually he heard stirring inside and feet shuffling to the door. The door swung open and Hailey's bleary-eyed roommate stood in front of him wearing a pink bathrobe and Elmo slippers. Sam wasn't sure if he should cry with laughter or with relief. She squinted and wiped at her eyes. The instant she became aware of who was standing there her eyes widened and she slammed the door.

Okay? Sam thought.

He knocked again, glancing back at the elevator. They'd be here any minute now. This time the door opened part-way and her roommate's face peered out from behind it, looking slightly embarrassed.

"Hailey's not sleeping, she's not here."

"Where can I find her?"

"She's at her father's place."

"Thanks."

He went to leave, and then turned back.

"She left last night?"

"Yes, right after the performance. By the way, nice flowers." She grinned.

He frowned. "She knew they were from me?"

"Duh, none of these airheads would do that. I'm lucky if I can get my guy to run to the store and get a carton of milk. It's like pulling teeth."

Sam laughed. "Okay, thanks."

"And Sam ..."

He looked back over his shoulder. "Yeah?"

"For what it's worth, she's never stopped loving you."

He paused, smiled, and left, feeling lighter than he had in weeks.

On the bottom floor, security hadn't even gotten out of

their seats. Too busy eating donuts and playing cards, Sam thought while grinning at them as they pointed to the door.

In his car, Sam glanced up and smiled at the sight of the Big Apple in his rearview mirror. It seemed only yesterday that he'd made that same two-hour journey to the little town of Walton. He remembered feeling annoyed, lost, and reluctant to leave. He smiled to himself at the irony of once again returning to the very place he had initially resented. This time, however, it was different. He'd never felt so happy, so certain about what he wanted. And now he couldn't get there fast enough.

CHAPTER THIRTY-SEVEN

Hailey awoke to the smell of bacon and the sound of her father grinding coffee. Snow was falling gently on the Wellands' property. With a blanket tightly wrapped around her, she partially opened the bedroom window, letting in the clear, cold, crisp December air. She closed her eyes and breathed in deeply. Even as a child she'd always loved a fresh snowfall. There was an innocence and untainted purity to it. It felt like nature's way of cleaning the slate and it made her feel like a kid again.

As she got dressed, the previous twenty-four hours hung heavily on her mind. She'd arrived in Walton a little after two a.m., and while the long drive should have left her feeling exhausted she felt surprisingly energetic. Her mind was still racing—still riding the high from the previous night's performance, she thought.

What a night that was. It was what every dancer dreamed of, the chance to perform live in New York City in front of a captivated audience. Over the past few months she'd had the opportunity several times and she'd loved every minute of it, but those paled in comparison to how well it went yesterday evening. Her mother would say there was a moment when dancing live when you could feel as if you and the audience had become one. For the first time she understood what she'd meant. It was marvelous and there was nothing that could have brought her down in that moment. That was, until she'd returned to her dressing room and saw the large bouquet of red, pink, and white roses.

She had never experienced such intense exhilaration and disappointment all at once. It hadn't been the first time he'd left flowers and each time they were more extravagant and beautiful than the previous. Yet did he know what he was doing to her every time he sent them? It was like opening an old wound. The previous weeks she'd received his gifts, they were cute, thoughtful, and funny. In all honesty she had found herself opening up to the thought of the two of them again. It would have been a lie to say that she wasn't flattered and even a little bit taken aback by his generosity and care, but then all the troubling memories would bubble to the surface. Making the wrong decision frightened her, especially when it came to matters of the heart. Maybe that was why she called her father that night. Maybe that was why he asked her to come home early.

It had been months since she'd been back in Walton but it felt good to be home, even if it was only for a short while. She needed a chance to breathe again, to step back from her busy schedule and mill around the old town. She wanted to get her hair done by Cassie and catch up on all the gossip. And the thought of a meal at Maggie's made her salivate. There was nothing like home-cooked food and Maggie was the best at it. She wanted to read a book, watch her father go ice fishing on the lake, and more than anything, think about what she was going to do after Juilliard.

"Hi, honey," Charlie said, softly hugging Hailey as she wandered into the kitchen. "It's so good to have you home."

"I've missed you," she told him.

They held each other for a while before Hailey eyed the bacon and thick homemade bread served up in the center of the table.

"I've missed Maggie's bacon too," she said.

Charlie chuckled. "That reminds me. You should drop by today, she's been pestering me for weeks as to when you were coming home."

"Sounds like Maggie."

Taking a seat, she spotted a nicely framed photo on the end table that she'd sent her father. It was of their entire class at Juilliard after a performance.

"I see you got it."

Charlie glanced over his shoulder while pouring some coffee.

"Yeah, my kid the New York dancer. It has a nice ring to it, don't you think? Your mother would have been absolutely overjoyed."

He handed her a cup and took a seat across from her. As she took the coffee she could smell the familiar aroma of Guatemalan coffee that reminded her of each morning at Juilliard.

"So, what was the reason you wanted me back so soon?" She ran her finger around the cup. "And why couldn't you tell me on the phone?"

Hailey took a sip of coffee, feeling her shoulders relax.

"What? Does there need to be a reason for a father to want his daughter to come home early?"

"Dad," she said, her eyebrows rose.

"All right, all right. But I do like having you home."

She smiled. Charlie took his time before answering.

"I couldn't exactly tell you this, I needed to show you."

Hailey gave an inquisitive expression.

"Come on."

Charlie waited while Hailey threw on her jacket and boots. The snow crunched beneath their feet, leaving behind the only tracks visible in the yard. Charlie pushed up a two by four that held together the doors to a makeshift garage they had out back.

"Give me a hand a minute." He handed Hailey a shovel and they cleared a spot in front, wide enough to swing back the doors. Inside it was dark and the smell of motor oil permeated everything. Charlie took hold of a heavy-duty tan tarp covering something in the middle of the room and threw it back. Hailey froze, her eyes widening.

"The day you left, Monty brought it by. Something you forgot to tell me, right?"

"Um, I was going to tell you," she stammered.

"Anyway, Sam was there when Monty returned it. He didn't leave that day. In fact, he didn't leave for another three more days. And trust me, it didn't look like this when it was returned. Besides what he did here, I think he left something inside the truck, I thought you might want to see."

Hailey stared at the truck as he spoke, confused but absorbing everything he said. Charlie handed her the keys, hesitated for a moment, and then returned to the house. Hailey stepped inside and slowly ran her hand over the front of the truck. Its metal was cold and smooth and not a ding or a scratch was on it. She'd seen the state it was in after the storm. The twisted metal, the hood caved in under the weight of the tree, and the window smashed. But now it was if it had never happened.

The door made the familiar creak as she opened it. She turned over the ignition and the truck roared to life. She popped the hood and took a look at the engine. It was rebuilt and purring like new. Within minutes she found herself smiling with relief.

She slid back into the truck. Its leather seats were still torn and all of her mother's items were exactly where she'd left them. Lying on the seat beside her was an envelope. As she reached down she saw the handwriting. *Sam's.* There was no doubt about it. The same handwriting she'd seen on the notes that came with the gifts and the cards inside the bouquets of roses. She gazed at the envelope in her hand for some time. Finally she took a deep breath and tore it open. Inside she found a letter.

Dear Hailey,

Where do I begin? I've been asking myself that for the last hour. Thirteen crumpled pieces of paper lying on the ground around me say I have no clue. Apologizing seems most appropriate, and yet that couldn't even come close to expressing how deeply sorry I am. I can only imagine how confused, let down and humiliated you must have felt waiting for me to return. After all that we've been through, I only wish you were here now so I could explain. So I could hold you and tell you how much I love you. How much our time together meant to me. How much you mean to me.

Hailey, you have every right to be angry, but please don't hate me. I could try to explain what happened that night but words have a strange way of being misunderstood, especially when they're not spoken in person. And that isn't what this letter is about. I will save that for when I see you again. Just know I had every intention of taking you to the city and every intention of us being together. You never gave up on me and I refuse to give up on you.

I miss you already. I miss the way you smile. I miss hearing your warm laughter and feeling your breath against my skin. There isn't a minute that goes by that doesn't feel empty without you here.

I'm sure by now you're probably wondering about the truck. Why? Well, it sure would have been easier to buy you a new one. I could have restored it by replacing all the old parts with brand new ones, and giving it a complete makeover. But somehow I guess seeing that old truck pushed to one side kind of made me think about how I felt when I came into this place. I felt worn, used, broken, and not worth saving. But someone reminded me that everyone is worth it. You didn't try to reinvent me, Hailey, or make me into something I wasn't. You simply brought me back to who I was before the damage. And for that I will forever be grateful. So the least I could do was the same for you.

I love you,
Sam

Before she had finished reading she wiped the tracks of her tears. She returned to the house a few minutes later. Still reeling from Sam's letter, she was at a loss for what to say to her father. For a while they said nothing. Eventually she slid the envelope across the table to her father and he quietly read it.

"I don't know what to do."

He gave an affirming nod and sighed.

"Did he see you in the end? I mean in New York?"

"Yes."

"And what did he say?"

She really wasn't sure she wanted to get into it, but what

harm could it do now? Over the next ten minutes she described Sam's visit to Juilliard. The gifts left for her each morning when she awoke and the bouquets of flowers inside her dressing room.

Charlie listened, scratching his chin. "Okay, back up a moment. So he explained what happened and you kicked him out?"

"Sort of…"

"You didn't give him the chance … did you?"

"I was hurting, Dad, I saw the magazine and …"

"You put two and two together and thought the worst." Charlie kneaded his forehead with his fingertips and exhaled.

Before they could finish they heard the crunching of snow as a car pulled into the driveway.

Charlie leaned back, pushed aside the curtains, and peered out.

He chuckled. "Speak of the devil."

CHAPTER THIRTY-EIGHT

With the snow covering the signs on the country roads, he'd nearly taken a wrong turn on his way through town. Had it not been for the large red barn that stood out like a billboard sign, he would have surely driven right by the old place. Upon seeing the house, Sam noted how different it looked from what he remembered. A laurel wreath with a large red ribbon was nailed to the front door and icicles hung from the porch and gutters like frozen teeth. Without the thick vegetation and greenery surrounding the house, or the overhanging trees which lined the driveway, everything looked sparse, yet still beautiful.

The first thing Sam's eyes were drawn to as he drove up the freshly plowed driveway was the frozen lake. The dock was covered in snow and all the canoes and boats had been locked away inside the white clapboard housing for the winter.

He shut off the car and sat there for a moment. He drew a deep breath and opened the door. In an instant he registered who was standing on the porch watching him. Wearing knee-high brown boots, jeans, and a long-sleeve cashmere sweater dress, she looked stunning. In her hand was a coffee mug. He stepped out of the car and closed the door behind him. For a while they stood there staring at one another.

He felt the same way he did when he'd showed up at Juilliard without giving her notice. He'd spent the better part of two hours contemplating, crafting, and perfecting what he would say, but with her standing in front of him now it was if he was experiencing amnesia. Noticing how healthy and fit she appeared, he became slightly self-conscious of how he looked. He glanced down slightly, checking to see if he was covered in crumbs from the bite he'd grabbed on the way up. Satisfied, he spoke.

"Hi, Hailey."

Her smile immediately set him at ease. "Come on in."

Inside, Hailey took his coat and hung it up. Charlie came out of the kitchen and greeted him.

"Sam. Good to see you again."

"Likewise," he said, extending his hand, but instead, receiving a hug.

"Well, I'm sure you have a lot to discuss, so I will leave you to it."

Sam nodded with a smile.

Hailey gestured into the family room. He stepped inside and breathed in the familiar scent of polished oak.

"Can I get you a drink?"

"No, I'm fine."

Hailey sat across from him, her feet pressed together. She peered over the cup as she took a sip. He studied her, searching for words. Seeing her again brought back his strong desire for her, along with the regrets.

"Sam, I can't begin to thank you enough for what you did with my mom's truck. Thank you."

He smiled. "My pleasure." He paused, then continued, "Look, Hailey, I wanted to put things straight. So much has happened I don't know where to begin." He figured it was best to skip the small talk and get straight to the reason he came.

"I, um ..." He cleared his throat. "I visited your apartment this morning."

"Oh?"

"Quite the roommate you have."

She laughed. "Yes, she is."

Sam leaned forward, his hands clasped together. "Hailey, that night." He sighed. "The night before you left, I honestly thought I would be back in an hour. Liam stopped at the Tavern, of all places. Kate wanted to explain and I wanted closure. My only mistake was losing track of time. Once I realized how late it was, they'd already had more than their fair share of drink. Liam wanted a last picture of us before we left. Kate was drunk; before I could stop her she kissed me. Liam had someone take a picture with my phone; someone else must have taken one as well. What you don't see in that tabloid is my reaction after it was taken."

Sam took his phone out of his pocket, flipped up the photo that was taken that night, and handed it to Hailey.

"Liam was cut out of the picture. That's what they're good at—twisting the truth. Welcome to my world."

"And Kate? Did they twist the truth with her?"

He glanced up. "No, she admitted it. She said it was a one-time mistake."

Sam rubbed his hand across his face.

"And you believed her?"

"No. It's over. I moved out the day I returned."

She placed her cup down. "So why didn't you return, I mean, until the morning?"

"I'm guessing you didn't read the magazine article?"

She bit the side of her lip nervously. "No."

"Surprisingly, there are some things they don't lie about. You might find the part about being arrested interesting."

Her eyebrows shot up.

Sam breathed out a sigh, lowered his gaze, and began to tell her what happened. Starting with the run-in they had with Tommy Farlan and his buddies. He recounted how Kate had noticed the animosity between Tommy and him when he came into the tavern. She tried to get a reaction out of Sam by playing a game of pool with Tommy.

"I didn't think the night could get any worse, but it did. When we went to leave, Kate wouldn't go and Tommy played right into it. One thing led to another and before I knew it, fists were flying and we'd been thrown in the back of a cruiser and taken down to the station. That's where I stayed, detained overnight until they let us out in the morning."

He paused, meeting her skeptical gaze.

He sighed. "Read the magazine. Phone the station. They'll confirm it, Hailey." He felt as if he was trying to convince a jury. "Ask your father what I looked like when I came back." He could see the wheels spinning as she digested all that he'd said. Whether she believed him or not, it felt like a large emotional boulder had been lifted off his shoulders.

"I guess I'm the one who owes you an apology?" she said.

Sam leaned forward, taking hold of her hands.

"You don't owe me anything, Hailey. You've given me so much; it would take me a lifetime to repay you. I meant every word in that letter. I love you."

Slowly she withdrew her hands from his grasp.

Sam felt something catch in his throat. "Hailey?"

"I've had a lot of time to think about us, Sam. I also meant what I said in my letter. That night, sitting in that barn, made me realize. Your life and mine are so different. You're famous and have the whole world at your feet. I'm just a girl from a blip on a map. Everywhere you go you have cameras on you. And if I'm with you, I'm part of that. I'm not sure I'm ready for that."

"What are you saying?"

"Sam, you don't need me now. What we had here was special, but to think it would last beyond here … is just us fooling ourselves. One day you will wake up and realize that I don't measure up to the glamorous women that exist in your world. There's nothing I can give you that you don't already have or could have. I'm not red carpet material, Sam. I'm just an ordinary girl and once the fantasy wears off—and it will—trust me, you'll want to move on."

For a long moment, Sam said nothing. He gazed down and then looked back at her. "Don't you think I know that? I know you have your doubts. I know you're scared. I'm scared too. I'm scared of messing up and hurting the one person I give a damn about in this world. The one person who knows me better than myself."

Sam exhaled. "But I'm willing to take that risk. Are you?"

When she didn't answer, he nodded, and then shook his head.

He got up and slowly moved to the front entrance, picked up his coat off the rack, and slid it on. He paused at the doorway and turned back to her.

"Do you remember that afternoon on the lake?"

Her eyes lifted with tears in them and she nodded.

"You said when you met the right person, your world would stop spinning and it would feel freeing and grounding all at the same time." He paused. "That's how I feel when I'm with you."

He rubbed the back of his neck, feeling it ache with tension. "So maybe ... maybe you're right. Maybe I don't need you." He lowered his gaze to the floor and paused before looking back into her eyes. "But I choose you. And I would choose you every day for the rest of my life."

Hailey scrutinized him before dropping her eyes.

He looked at her for a few moments. Then he turned the handle on the door and walked out, leaving it wide open.

* * * * *

Charlie strolled out, flinging a tea towel casually over his left shoulder. He'd been eavesdropping on the entire conversation from the kitchen. He said nothing for a moment and then drew a long breath.

"Hailey." Charlie spoke without looking at her, his gaze fixed on Sam walking to his car. "I know I joke about you ending up old and alone. And you probably won't. But if you let him walk now, I have a feeling you will regret it for the rest of your life."

She wasn't sure what to say. In the silence, she found it hard to breathe as she tried to sift through all that Sam had said. He was right—she was scared. The thought of giving her whole heart to someone who genuinely loved her and stepping into the unknown shook her to the core. A large part of her wanted to go after him. But another part was paralyzed by the thought.

The sound of car tires crunching in the snow instantly brought her back into the present moment. Without another second of hesitation she jumped to her feet and bolted for the door, leaving Charlie smiling.

The snow was beginning to fall heavily. Sam's vehicle was already halfway down the driveway. She hurried to where she might be in full view if he looked back. Waving her arms frantically, she attempted to draw his attention but it was futile; his car kept going. She kept moving through the inches of powder that now covered the ground, hoping desperately that there was a chance he might spot her. But it was useless.

"Sam," she cried out just as a gust of ice-cold needles hit her face, taking her breath. The long winding driveway was now barely visible beneath the snowdrifts. As his car disappeared around the corner she came to a stop.

Still trying to catch her breath, she closed her eyes. A fast reel of images from her time with him played in the theater of her mind. The strong wind nipped hard against her. She wrapped her arms tightly around her chest to stay warm. It had been only seconds, but it felt like forever. When she opened her eyelids, she squinted, barely able to see more than a few feet in front of her without wiping the snow from her eyes. *He was gone.*

Defeated and almost paralyzed by the cold, she turned to walk back. It was then she heard the sound of wheels spinning. Turning towards the end of the property, slowly coming into view, was Sam's car reversing.

She felt her heart leap in her chest.

A minute later, the brake lights flashed and with the car

still running, Sam stepped out. He turned and smiled.

And there, halfway down in the middle of the driveway as the snow covered them, they met each other. Hailey struggled to control her pounding heart as she looked into his face. As he held her tight, she felt the strength and warmth of his body thawing any remaining doubts. He leaned forward, his lips brushing against her ear, and in almost a whisper, he said,

"I wondered how long it would take you."

Looking up, she smiled, and then they kissed.

CHAPTER THIRTY-NINE

C harlie was right; Hailey didn't end up alone. On a warm summer day in late July, two years from the date they first met, a small group gathered in privacy beside the beautiful lake in Walton, New York.

There, Hailey Welland and Sam Reid were married beneath the same garden arbor that Hailey's parents had shared their vows under. Twisted ivy intermingled with white roses over every part of the arbor, except the lone section they'd kept from the storm. To the two families and close friends that attended that day, few would have noticed it, but Hailey and Sam did. It would forever serve as a memory of the time they first met, and symbolize that even the most damaged heart was never truly beyond repair.

It wouldn't be the only thing that guests weren't aware of that day. Despite still showing a slender figure, Hailey had discovered only a week prior to their wedding that a baby was on the way. Sam couldn't have been any more over-joyed when she told him. They made a point to keep the news of the baby a surprise until they returned from their honeymoon.

Before the ceremony, she asked her father if they could make a short stop at the cemetery. Unable to have her mother there, she wanted to take a moment to visit her gravestone. Kneeling down, her flowing white gown around her and tears streaming down her face, she leaned her forehead against the grave.

"I miss you, Mom. I wish you could have been here." She wiped at her eyes with a tissue. "I think you would have liked him." She spent the next ten minutes there, before she gathered herself together and with the help of her bridesmaid, Cassie, she readied herself.

A live string quartet played softly in the background as Charlie walked Hailey down the aisle covered in white rose petals. Sam would never forget how angelic and breathtaking she looked in her strapless long flowing dress.

In the garden that day, with the minister before them and the rows of guests behind, they shared their vows.

"Do you promise to love, honor, and cherish her in sickness and in health, in adversity and prosperity, and to be faithful and true to her so long as you both shall live?"

He stared into her eyes. He took a moment to respond as he drank in how absolutely beautiful she looked. Letting the question linger a little longer, he smiled and then answered, "I promise."

EPILOGUE

*L*ove is a strange thing to figure out. Promises are made and broken in the search for love. Some have climbed mountains, crossed rivers, and walked through valleys to be loved. Others have given up and let down those closest to them in order to feel love. And the rest? Well, they fight tooth and nail to hold on to it. And yet someone once said that you don't find love, love finds you. I guess whoever said that must have one heck of a story to tell.

So as my story comes to a close, you're probably still wondering what I told Sam's father. Trust me, it wasn't anything special. And if I'm honest, I had my doubts if it would even work. But I took the risk and made him a promise. Now I guess I should tell you what that was, but I've realized it's not the promise we make that matters. Only that we follow through. And that I can promise you, I did.

I never imagined my life would end here, in the little town of Walton, New York. But now I wouldn't have it any other way. As truth be told — it's really where my life began.

Rate and Review

If you enjoyed this book, please consider leaving a review on Amazon, Goodreads or wherever you purchased it online. Reviews from readers like you are the best recommendation a book can have.

About the Author

Jon Mills lives with his wife and two children in Ontario, Canada. He works in the advertising business helping companies sell their products and services through the written word. In his personal time, he enjoys playing piano and guitar, reading, watching movies, and traveling.

If you wish to get more information about upcoming books or you wish to get in touch with Jon, you can do so at the sites below:

Main site: http://www.jonmills.com
Twitter: http://www.twitter.com/Jon_Mills
Goodreads: http://www.goodreads.com/author/show/6526644.Jon_Mills

7517677R00195

Printed in Great Britain
by Amazon.co.uk, Ltd.,
Marston Gate.